SNOWBLIND

SNOWBLIND

STORIES OF ALPINE OBSESSION

DANIEL ARNOLD

COUNTERPOINT

BERKELEY

The Story *The Cleaning Crew*, first appeared in Issue 74 of ZYZZYVA

Library of Congress Cataloging-in-Publication Data Is Available

ISBN 978-1-61902-453-3

Cover design by Jason Snyder
Interior Design by Megan Jones Design

COUNTERPOINT
2560 Ninth Street, Suite 318
Berkeley, CA 94710
www.counterpointpress.com

Printed in the United States of America
Distributed by Publishers Group West

10 9 8 7 6 5 4 3 2 1

To Ashley and Sage

CONTENTS

THE CLEANING CREW

MENDOZA, THE AUSTRAL summer of 2005. Dry, hot December dust and soot from old cars hacking through the streets stuck to the flat-faced buildings, the trees, and the people strolling down the broad sidewalks. But not to the doors, which were polished and brightly colored and swung open on oiled hinges, looking both newer and older than the faded concrete of the street front. Paco's was no exception, and I raised my fist to knock wondering how he managed to keep his door immaculate with so many people like me coming to pound on it.

After a moment, Paco appeared and told me all his rooms were full. He looked the same, filling the vertical reach of his doorway, but not the horizontal. He and his brother could have stood there comfortably side-by-side.

"What about the roof?" I said. "I'd put my tent up on the roof."

Paco raised a shaggy eyebrow and held it there a moment. The matter needed careful thought. "Why not?" he said. "It's summertime.

Anything goes. You know? Five dollars a night. Don't use too much water. There's a queue for the *baño* every damn morning."

I piloted the seventy pounds on my back through Paco's narrow hallways, trying not to scrape the walls with the sharp edges of my load. I heard English falling down through the plaster above my head. One voice only, an avalanche of words, words, words. I passed rooms filled with things and no people, rucksacks open, jackets, sleeping bags, crampons, ice screws scattered over the beds and floor.

Everyone in the house was up on the second level, in the room stocked with third-hand couches and chairs that merged into the public kitchen and overlooked *Calle 25 de Mayo* through two large windows. Except for Paco, who was tinkering with the stove burners and could claim to be there for his own purposes, they all listened to the kid behind the voice. Paco's brother sat in a metal folding chair, and the kid—I found out later he answered to JD—sat across from him with a wobbly card table between them, though it could have been the pearly gates and an audition with Saint Peter from the way the kid talked. He wanted, what, applause? Absolution? He was trying hard, that was damn sure. A fine kid, someone's son, one presumes. Born into a generation that never shook off its bewilderment, its disbelief in the actual workings of the universe. He watched his hands, which crawled all across the tabletop, and Paco's brother stayed quiet behind the wrinkled old leather of his face. JD never swapped eyes with the rest of us, but he didn't lower his voice either, and we circled around him.

I was relieved to take the pack off my back, to be in Paco's dark, cool house, out of the city heat, to have the mountain far away and flattening to snapshots. I sat myself on the floor next to a couch occupied by an American husband-and-wife team I'd met once in Peru. He drank maté out of a gourd through a wooden straw, which disappeared into the heavy curls of his beard. She kept her hands busy sharpening the business end of an ice tool with a bastard file.

All this time, JD was sawing away, face pinched, voice stretched tight.

"It's heaven till it's hell, right? It's all make-believe until it turns to shit and you think you're going to die. You're up there with the white angels watching movie magic—like you're in a place the movies can't touch. Then the sky goes black and drops on your head. I was little-kid scared. It was that big. In real life—or flatland life, whatever—Rex was a Unitarian minister. Maybe it was a part-time gig—I fucking can't believe it myself. I didn't know him. He'd lead AA groups in the church basement, the whole ball of wax. But he was full of shit, because midweek he was pressing flesh on the rock. He should have founded Climbers Anonymous. Up there it was like he was drunk, like he was mainlining the storm.

"Rex, he had wild eyes," JD said. "He didn't look human. More like a wounded animal. The wind was in our heads. My lungs got no grip on the air. It played with us. Let us up, knocked us down. There were gaps when it went still and my brain started to clear, but then it swung back at us and you'd feel it coming. Ten seconds, five seconds—then out with the *claws*, man, and we'd be down and pinned again. I got killer-mad, was screaming at the lulls. For giving us space just enough to know how bad it was going to be.

"Rex led through the cliff band. The rocks stuck out like rotten teeth—all sharp and black. They freaked me out. I pulled on them, and they moved and spat gravel in my face. Ice covered everything, but not enough for my tools to stick. Every time I swung an axe, I got sparks jumping back, and rock splinters flying around.

"We were managing, though. That was the thing. Rex finished his lead and got enough of a break to yell, 'Come on up, girly-boy.' Something like that. 'Don't be afraid, Daddy don't spank that hard.' Stupid stuff, saying it now. The kind of thing the dickheads say at the crag. But it got me laughing, and the climbing through the teeth didn't seem as scary as it should have. The mountain was big and bad, more than we'd seen. But we weren't fools. It wasn't like that."

I thought: *Keep saying it. Maybe it'll come true.* JD was filthy. I was too. His hair hung down to his shoulders in thick, shiny mats. He had an inch of oily blond beard. His lips were split and puffy. White craters dimpled the skin around his cheekbones where the cold had done its damage, and the tip of his nose was black, though it didn't look too bad. He would probably get to keep it. But he couldn't have been twenty-three, so he still looked healthy under all that dirt and hair and frostbite. You see a forty-year-old man walk out of an extended epic, and he looks like a bus-stop bum, but JD still had a kid's flush under the wreckage of his face. Scrub him up, and he'd be a college boy. He was still wet clay.

"The snow started dumping. Spindrift came down all over us off the cliffs. *Whoosh.* At first we'd see a slide coming and hunker down. But they were nothing, like being hit with a pillow, only no pillow, just the feathers flying past.

"We tried to climb fast. Up above us, it was all grey and snow, and then black clouds came out of nowhere, just dropped right out of the grey, right on top of us. But going fast up there doesn't mean much, you know? We crawled along, too slow. I was panicking. I wanted to puke. Rex screamed at me and screamed at the weather and cursed at his feet for going so slow when we were so close. The snow was building above us—we could feel it. We could see where we needed to get to, this cluster of rocks up on a shoulder. But we couldn't move any faster. The real avalanche was coming. We knew it. The spindrift came down all the time. Both of us were covered. It found all the gaps in my clothes. I had a whole inside jacket made of snow.

"I don't know how long it took to reach the rocks. Hours is what it felt like. But maybe only twenty minutes. There wasn't a single thing up there I could trust. My mind kept running ahead of me. It would make it to the rocks, but I was stuck in the snow waiting for the avalanche. So my mind got yanked back down. Like a dog on a leash. Run, run, run, run—*pow*—yanked back to the body.

"We made it to the rocks, and the storm blew up in our face. The wind was a jet engine. It picked up chunks of ice and threw them at me hard enough to feel through all my clothes. Rocks, too. The snow came at us in curtains. I was so cold. It was in my *bones*, man. You don't understand how deep it went. I never knew which direction I'd be able to see. Sometimes in my eyes there was nothing but static. Rex would disappear even though I could reach over and poke him with my axe. Then the wind would hit again, and the snow tilted horizontal, like we were going into hyperspace, only we were lying on the ground curled up in balls waiting for space to breathe."

Who else was there? Three Eastern Europeans—probably Czechs or Slovenians from the bygone olive and brown they wore. Their faces looked carved by some sculptor with eighteen-inch biceps, one who used only long, straight chisel cuts. Formidable men, no doubt. There were four Germans who wore matching black pants and kept their glacier glasses hung round their necks, even indoors. They looked to be sucking on rocks, cultivating the scowls they'd wear to the summit or the sixth beer.

There were others there too, less recognizable to me beyond the general category: human flotsam, drawn by the mountain. The room stayed quiet except for JD's voice and the hiss and rasp of Angela's file. Maybe earlier people had made an effort to look occupied. Not now. JD never once looked around, but all eyes pointed in. He kept talking, and I sat there. Sat on my hands, so to speak, while the future loomed. I was under pressure, the lowland air frothing up inside me. I wanted to shake the kid, get him out of his shell. He had his chance. If he was going to tell his story, he'd damn well better get it right.

"We tunneled in. There was old snow under the powder, and we dug a cave. Our brains were gone. Mine anyway. The thinking parts. I guess I shouldn't talk for Rex. I've never felt more like an animal, digging into the ground on instinct. When we were done, I couldn't feel my hands or feet. It took me fifteen minutes to zip my sleeping bag. I couldn't hold the zipper in my fingers—I had to squeeze it between my hands.

"Rex was shivering bad. He kept knocking snow from the roof of the cave down on us. I told him to get in his sleeping bag, and Reverend Rex told me to shut the fuck up, he was just resting.

"No way could I light the stove. You understand? I couldn't move. My hands were still blocks. And that meant no water. Rex was no help. How was I supposed to know what was happening inside of him? I got at some chocolate—I tore open the bag with my teeth and put my whole face in—but it was concrete in my mouth. It wouldn't dissolve. I couldn't get away from the thirst. It just kept drilling at me.

"The noise never let up. The wind shook the cave all night long. I thought waves were going to come through the walls. You're sitting here, and it's ninety degrees outside, and you can't know. It was a horrible night. I fell asleep twenty, thirty times. I wish I could have knocked myself out because being unconscious was better. But then the wind would shift and blow snow through the breathing hole we'd left ourselves. I'd wake up, blind in the dark and not knowing where I was, choking on ice in my nose and mouth. It crawled into my sleeping bag. I was out of my head. I thought about termites. Ice cockroaches finding all the spaces.

"We wanted this. We were either going to get broken or remade. We'd said we were badasses. But I didn't feel badass. I was shivering so hard I couldn't see straight and burning up inside.

"Each time I woke up, I was thirstier. Preacher's hell—water all around, and my blood felt like sand. I'd check to see if my hands were alive enough to light the stove. I'd say, 'dude, get something going, get the stove, get some water.' But then coming out of my sleeping bag would have been insane. I turned on my headlamp once, and the ceiling was ten inches away from my face. Couldn't have been more. A white coffin and two half-dead climbers. I looked over, and Rex was unconscious but breathing. At some point he'd gotten half into his sleeping bag. He didn't deserve to be out like that. How could he fight back when he was beef in a meat locker? Fucking mountain. It didn't let us do what we could have done.

"We had the snow and the storm between us and the sun, so even when day finally came back around, the cave was still dark. A miserable hole. But we could see, and that was huge. I got the stove running and put Rex deeper in his sleeping bag. He couldn't use his hands, so I spooned soup into his mouth. He gave me a big plastic grin and said, 'This is it, this is what legends are made of. Give me a moment to get thawed out, and we'll get back out there.' Dude had psych even then, and where was mine? I half believed his bullshit, I always did. He was a lunatic. When I went out with him, I never had to worry about being crazy enough. But now the bullshit was real, and I was panicking, and I never knew if he knew it was real, and that made it worse.

"The wind kept blowing snow into the cave, and I wasted our fuel lighting and relighting the stove. Loose snow was all over. The walls closed in. I tried to shovel it out, but whenever I moved, I got so much snow in my sleeping bag that I gave up.

"Rex said he was amazed he could stay so warm with all the snow around, and I yelled at him to pull himself together, which was stupid because he was better off in his own world. He took a long time turning his head in his sleeping bag to look at me. 'Don't get shrill, now, kiddo,' he said.

"He blanked out then. Went somewhere else and came back. I thought he'd just shivered himself stiff. Maybe he had a seizure. I don't know.

"The fuel ran out just when the cave went dark for the second night. I never really slept. I decided we'd leave the next day no matter what. We were getting killed where we were, and I didn't know what we'd have left.

"It probably took me two hours to get us up and moving. Rex kept falling over, and he still couldn't move any of his fingers. He said it felt like bugs were crawling up his arms. I didn't look. What could I do? I shoved a piece of chocolate in his mouth and put his harness and crampons on for him and packed his gear.

"I'd hoped it would feel good to be moving. It didn't. I felt weak. Hungover. Like my brain was stuffed with cotton balls. I smelled something like formaldehyde, but I think it was just in my head. The wind blew so hard it'd throw us down, and I kept having to pick Rex up. I hardly noticed when I'd go down. My mind went somewhere else, just split from the body there and drifted. The tethers keeping me together got real loose.

"I tied Rex to me with ten feet of rope between us and pulled him along. We couldn't go down. We could barely walk, so how would we pass the hourglass, or the cliff bands? The only way I saw was going over the top and down the north side. I couldn't see anything, but I could crawl uphill. I don't know why we didn't get killed by avalanches.

"When Rex died, he just fell over into the snow and stopped moving. I screamed in his ear, shook him, punched him. Nothing. I tried to pry open his eyelids, but they were frozen shut, and I couldn't get a grip through my mittens. I don't know how long he'd been following me blind.

"It was easy to leave him. I didn't even untie the rope. I just took off my harness and left all the extra weight behind. Way too easy. Nothing felt real. Still doesn't. Not then, not now. I feel like I'm telling you all of what happened, but none of what's important. Two came, one left. My pace dropped to four breaths between each step. Even then, I had to rest after sets of thirty. I went on my hands and knees a lot because the snow was too deep and loose to stay upright.

"I got to the summit ridge and started down the north side. It wasn't snowing as hard, I think. But this freezing ice fog made the whole mountain blind. I could see even less, and my mind started making things up. It told me I'd hallucinated the ridge. I'd done nothing but turn around. I was headed back to the cave. I got totally wrapped up in the idea, but gravity pulled me down, and I kept walking. Every time I saw a rock ahead of me in the snow, I expected it to be Rex.

"Two human shapes passed me in the fog. I grabbed at them and screamed at them, but either they couldn't understand, or they were too far gone to help me. They wouldn't answer or give me any water. I followed their tracks after they disappeared, and I found the high camp of the normal route and a few tents.

"Someone took me in. They didn't want to, and they made me sleep in their tent's vestibule. Their language didn't mean anything to me, but I got that. The storm let up maybe days later—they all blurred together—and I hiked down and around the mountain to our basecamp."

JD stopped talking. No one else said anything. We waited for a last morsel. JD tapped the table with the palms of his hands. "Fuck, fuck, fuck," he said. "We were close. And the mountain never gave us a chance. You see that, right? We needed one hour. If the storm had held off one hour, we'd have been all right. Rex would have been all right. He'd be sitting here grinning at me like a jack-o'-lantern, like always. It could have given us an hour." That was it. JD looked up without tilting his head, just his eyes. His eyes were blue, and they shifted back and forth. Twenty faces, that was how many of us were in the room, looked back. The moment stretched, then the flock of us broke into smaller groups and an international babble of conversations. Paco brought JD a little glass of wine, and his brother said a few inaudible words.

I thought of going to him, I did. But there were others on the way, and I didn't know him, and I was still a creature of the mountain. Packed full of snow and shitty Andean rock.

Angela hooked her ice axe on the back of the couch and sat forward. "I don't mean to be crass," she said from our side of the room, "but his gear, do you think it's still up there with his body—"

Her husband cut her off. "For Christ's sake, Angie, it's the kid's partner. Can't you wait a day?" He turned to me and said, more softly, "Horrible, horrible. He'll have a good slideshow. I'd have put up my ten bucks. *The Tragedy of Rex.* Killable, as are we all. He got what he deserved. I wonder if anyone will miss him. You just down off the mountain?"

I told him I was, while his wife muttered to herself that booty was booty.

"How'd it go?"

"Miserable," I said. "Same storm as the kid said. Had me shitting into bags in my tent for days. Couldn't go outside. Would've ended up with a frostbite enema."

"You on your own?" he asked.

"I was going to solo the Slovene Route, but I never even got started."

"Yeah? Sounds like you should have teamed up with the kid. He didn't stay in his tent five days."

"Fuck off."

I kept my eyes on JD, waiting, thinking that someone probably would miss Rex. Most everyone's got someone. JD had a gulp of wine, put it back on the table. Two Americans who looked city-soft by contrast sat down to his right and left, and he couldn't look at them, didn't know where to put his eyes. They spoke quietly, faces milky-kind. Comforting words, sure. One put a hand on JD's shoulder. Hell, they all missed Rex now that he was dead.

"Kid must have some of the beast in him to have survived all that," I said. "He could make it up some serious routes someday."

My friend shrugged and sucked on the dregs of his maté. "Sure, but what'll his head be like after this? Sounds like he wouldn't know a fool if one up and died on him. Why should a mountain give a fool an hour?" Pleased with himself, he hiccoughed through his tea. "A fool and his hour are soon parted!" he said.

One of the Germans detached himself from the other three and walked over to the table at the center of the room. He pushed his face right into JD's and said, "You didn't put the sleeping bag on your partner?" His voice was thick, like he was talking through brown stout. "No hot drink? No help? You should not go back into the mountains."

Before JD had a chance to react, the man who'd put his hand on JD's shoulder leapt up and planted the same hand on the German's chest and gave a little shove. The German looked shocked, then shook his head and stalked off.

Angela's husband slurped his tea dregs again and spat brown leaves back into his gourd, then said: "Trust the Germans to get right to the point!" He giggled—a high sound like a dying fan belt.

But I was watching JD. I watched him watch the German get pushed back. His shoulders went up, his head tilted back, he had a sip of wine. Something unbent inside him. I wondered if anyone else even noticed.

▲

THERE WAS A party that night, a typical climber shindig. Someone's always ready to celebrate, and others have sorrows, alpine or otherwise, and at least one group of smooth, clean faces will be looking to medicate their nerves. Two Brits who had summitted via the normal route before the storm brought three cases of Andino, the local brew that came in brown liter bottles with little red-and-silver labels. Miscellaneous liquors emerged from pockets and brown bags, and Paco made available two bottles of wine with his stock benediction, "for the summertime."

All through the afternoon, JD's story continued to bother me. Maybe I thought I could have told it better, that it was wasted on him. I could find the soul of it. I wanted a go at it. While I slipped back into the comforts and claustrophobias of the house, I kept seeing the way he'd straightened up and lifted his eyes. I felt hunched by comparison.

We spilled out onto the roof at twilight, into the first pleasant temperatures for me in three weeks. On the mountain, I'd gone from heat itch to frostbite so fast my body still had complaints about the one as it warned of the other. Now I'd showered and shaved away most of my beard, which killed two razors plus most of the sharpness of a third. In the end, I had to leave a thick under-mane of coiled fur below my jaw and chin because I'd only thought to buy two razors and couldn't scrounge more than one other at the house. But my face, at least, felt light and airy. The roof was bordered on three sides by a low wall and finished with cream-colored tiles that were cracked and dusty. My tent was shoved to one corner, and from the look of things, it would be hours before the rooftop was mine.

It was nine o'clock, but down on the streets, the night had just begun, and the first evening walkers headed out for early dinner, or to enter the discotheques before a cover was charged. Strings of bare lightbulbs nailed tree-to-tree through the park blocks across from *Calle 25 de Mayo* swung back and forth on the whim of the breeze, and kids who were too young for the clubs shadowboxed dance steps in and out of the moving lights to the rhythm of the music leaking into the streets.

Paco had an old steel-housed cassette deck, and he rolled the whole system out onto the roof and perched the two speakers on opposite walls. As usual, there was a shortage of women, and Angela had an unlimited number of partners waiting to attempt a tango to her standards. Meantime I talked to her husband, each of us working on a giant Andino.

"It's no wonder so few Mendozans climb the mountain," he said. "Look at the women. Have you ever seen perfection like that? They walk around in their little skintight shirts and pants, with breasts like—god—I didn't even know breasts were supposed to look like that before I came here. I'd be afraid to touch them. I'd want a debriefing from the museum curator first, you know? You don't get climbers in paradise, man."

The Czechs sat at a square table and played cards with a Swiss trekker. They passed a communal bottle of scotch counterclockwise and periodically broke into a few lines of song based on a pattern I couldn't follow. JD had a seat along the wall looking out over the park. He hadn't shaved, and from the way his beard glistened in the half-light, it seemed unlikely he'd washed yet either. The two Brits sat next to him, squawking like a couple of birds.

The Brits were so damned happy they made me jumpy. They'd climbed their way into paradise and were making the most of it. Say what you like about beauty and brotherhood, the real reason to go up a mountain is to pile on as much tension and fear and desire as can be borne so that the other side is a blissful place to float in for a few days. That's where the Brits were. JD must have half tasted it sitting there next to them. I could have been there, too. And when you're barred at the gates, outside looking up, you get irritable—the alpinist's version of blue balls, withdrawal. There couldn't have been a pair of eyes on that rooftop that didn't look over at the Brits with envy, because the best part about going climbing is to be finished with the climb.

"You ever heard of someone dropping over dead in the snow?" I asked my friend. "I mean, walking one minute and then dead the next?"

"No." He shrugged. "But come on, what was he supposed to do, throw his partner over one shoulder and hike him up the mountain? He's not Alex Lowe."

I poked my finger into his chest. "Sure. But that's not what he said."

I finished my beer and pulled two more from the last of the three cases and took them over to JD. I opened one for myself and offered one to him, but he waved me off.

"Not for me," he said. "I don't need it. It feels good just to breathe." He had his back to the party, his feet up on the wall.

"Did you ever check his pulse?" I asked.

"What?"

"Rex. Did you ever check his pulse? I know you've thought about it since."

The Brits hastily pulled each other up out of their chairs. "Best to leave them," I heard one say. "No need for another international incident." They swung each other onto the dance floor, making mincing steps around Angela and her latest suitor.

"Get out of my face," JD said.

"Look, it's all part of the process." I took one of the Brits' chairs and slid it over so that we were sitting face-to-face. "Don't just abandon your partner up there."

"I didn't kill Rex!" he said. "It was the fucking storm. Are you crazy? We needed one more hour. That's all."

"Wasn't the storm that killed Rex," I said. "Rex killed himself. Sounds like you about killed yourself, too. The question is, did you take his pulse?"

"No."

"See, that wasn't so hard. Better, too, isn't it?"

"Fuck you." The black patch of frostbite on his nose made it look like he had a hole in his face. "I couldn't take my hands out of my gloves. I was barely standing. I checked. He was dead."

"How can you know that for sure? That's the thing. Alive or dead, you had to leave him. But you don't know which, and it's better to *know* that. We're talking about the future here. We're talking about healing."

"I'm not thinking past tonight."

Somehow I had become sidetracked. I worked to clear my head, to start over. I had lost the direction I wanted to take our talk. I tried to wrestle it back toward my original intention.

"You know what the two of us should do?" I said. "We should go back up and find Rex and build him a cairn. We'll take an extra bottle of white gas and dump the whole thing out and have a big fire. You don't want to leave him like that, just slumped over in the snow. You and I. We've got to give him a proper send-off.

"Give yourself a few days to rest and heal, then we'll do it. It'll be good. Get right back up there. The real mountain doesn't give a damn, but the mountain in your mind," I said, tapping his forehead with one finger, "will only get bigger if you let Rex fester and rot."

Then JD did something I did not see coming. I was sitting there, leaned back in my chair, with my back to that low wall that separated the roof from the street. He reached forward and grabbed my throat with one hand and pushed. He was remarkably strong—his fingers felt like stone around my neck. He pushed until my chair was tipped back over the wall and I was balanced with my top half hung out into space and my bottom half ready to come tumbling after and JD holding onto me by the neck.

"This is all climbing is," he said. "Fear before the fall. Waiting to see whether the mountain is going to drop you or not. See, we can do it right here. What do you think? Is it going to cut you loose? Are you gonna die?"

I heard approaching feet, excited voices. I stared straight back into JD's eyes, which were hard and cold and made me think of old ice that hasn't seen the sun in years. I waited for the tension in his fingers to change for better or worse. He squeezed and pulled me back from the edge and dumped me down on the rooftop.

"There, we've climbed the mountain, asshole," JD said.

Hands reached out and led JD away. Someone righted my chair, but he walked away too, and I was left alone by the wall. That was it for the party for me. I sat on one edge, by my tent, staring out at the hustle of the nighttime city, rubbing my bruises through my throatfur. Eventually the others all stumbled down to their rooms, and I was the only one.

Paco's brother came by with a broom and a trash bag. He put a hand on my shoulder. "A hard night. Happens sometimes. The liquor—it goes quickly to your head when you come down from the mountain."

I looked up, and his face seemed ancient, but his eyes were young, and his whole demeanor seemed placid and brotherly, and I couldn't imagine he'd felt a day's turmoil in his life. "It's been hard for years," I said. "It's always been hard."

▲

SIX YEARS PASSED before I saw JD again. I married a nurse
who worked at the Yosemite clinic, and I found a spot on the search-
and-rescue team for myself. We had a little cabin that came with a
refrigerator and telephone service and an electric fan on the ceiling
and a wood-burning stove. We had big trees in our yard and listened
to the sound of the waterfall at night.

On an Indian summer day in October, a tabletop-sized flake cut
loose on Zenyatta Mondatta, on the east side of El Cap, shredding
the leader's rope, and I was on body-part recovery. I hiked up along
the base toward the scene and paused on the way to talk to a climber
who was sitting at the base of the North America Wall, in the middle
of a pile of gear, smoking a joint.

"Going up?" I asked.

"No man, I had to bail out."

"You on your own?"

"I was going to solo Sea of Dreams, but I never really got started.
I've got an old rotator cuff tear, right here," he said, stretching his
arm above his head. "I could feel it, you know, getting bad. I figured
the last thing I want is for it to go out on me up there."

He was filthy from neglect and fat around the edges. His hair
was stringy, not in intentional dreads but ratty tangles. His eyes were
bloodshot, and the skin around their sockets, and covering his neck,
was thick and fleshy. His collars and hems were all stretched out. I
might not have recognized him but for his beard, which was blond

and curly and triggered memories of a rooftop shouting match in what seemed to be a past life.

The strange thing was, I couldn't be sure which oily blond beard I saw—his or mine. His present self, seated alone on the rock below the climb he'd never really started, looked more like the man upended over the Mendoza streets than the young man he'd been. And I thought: *Did we do this to you?* And I thought: *Good lord, boy, be careful who you tell your stories to. Whatever you do, don't tell them to us. You might as well ask mercy of vultures.* But maybe he should never have offered himself or his partner in the first place.

So I said, "That's the way it goes sometimes," and I cursed myself for having nothing else to say to him.

"Heard someone got the chop," he said. "You part of the cleaning crew?"

"Yes."

"Have you gotten his partner down yet?"

"He rapped down on his haul line and what was left of the lead line. We're putting him up in the SAR cabins for a few days while he gets his head together. There's always someone there who's off shift to keep him company."

JD stretched his lips into the shape of a grin. "You ought to have him up here on recovery," he said. "That'd help him figure himself out." He laughed, a harsh wheeze. "I had a partner die once. It's healthy to see at least one body in your life. Reminds you what it's all about, where the lines are drawn. We ought to celebrate that man's passing!" And he danced, a clumsy little shuffle in the midst of his tattered pile of gear, waving that acrid joint above his head.

DEAD TILL PROVEN OTHERWISE

WO AM. ANN chokes off the alarm on her watch. Her bones ache, even the sockets of her eyes. She probes her flesh, groping for her moxie. How much does she have left? Yeah, and how much will she need? Half breaths of wind rattle the fabric of her bivy sack. Ha! One vertical mile of snowy Alaskan beast below the foot-wide sleeping ledge she's chopped in the ice, and the beast is snoring. Ann unzips the hood of her bivy sack. Stars! Bright god-damn stars. And cold. Cold as a wage slave's soul. Perfect. Day three, and her weather window has held. She'll meet the sun on top of the mountain.

She pops two caffeine pills and swallows a gel. She puts her earphones in and thumbs up the sound. Tom Paine lunges at her ears like a dog barking nose-down in a hole: *Nothing more certain than death / Nothing less sure than its time*. White noise obliterates the last syllable, turns to nasty, fire-breathing music just when she's sure her eardrums will tear. Ann made this mix expressly for the small hours. The hairs prickle off her arms. Guitars peeling back her skin, that's what she wants. Metal and caffeine, the gods' own breakfast. All else is just calories. Inside her bag, Ann wrestles her plastic doubles onto her feet. Paine comes back to remind her that men *beg* for kings to rule them. No, she'll have no kings.

Ann unzips her cocoon, clips herself in short to the two ice screws keeping her leashed against gravity. She packs away her sleeping kit. Her headlamp pricks the darkness, barely wounding it. The horns of the mountain above and the mind-trapping drop below are shadows on black shadows. She steps into her crampons, her favorite part of the morning. With spikes on her feet, she can go crusading.

The cold already has its teeth in her, and she's no apple-cheeked gal. When single digits slap her in the face, the color dies out of her skin, and Ann knows she must be chalk white. She grins juicily. She should have brought some props, some plastic fangs and black eyeliner, give the mountain a scare. Deep night, laser-white stars, the gigantic black void behind and below—Ann imagines climbing into outer space. Drum blasts displace her skull bones. Heat rises through her flesh to meet the cold. The music is her armor against the void. She means someday to write out her will, which will consist of nothing but a playlist for her funeral, and that will make her happy. Ann threads the leg loops of her harness, drinks half her water, and puts her pack on her back. Her insides twitch. She feels vicious. The knife cutting open the future. She doesn't know what she'll find there, but it's bound to be different from the past if she can just make herself sharp enough.

Fuck the climbing press and their backhanded praise, the "Psycho Bitch Rises" headline most of all. She was told to relax and take it as a compliment. Fuck 'em. Does she look relaxed?

Fuck the city people hiding from death in their homes. Binding themselves to their neighbors and their neighbors' neighbors till they're left wriggling on their own webs. Secure, sure. Ann's fighting the good fight, trying to bump humanity off its inward spiral.

Fuck the whole brotherhood of the rope—they're just as bad. Dudes tied together, married by their knots and common purpose. Greybeards in Anchorage or Aspen or wherever they take themselves to rot in their own memories and dream up new certifications and associations. One way or the other, head up or down, she'll be there to remind them of their white hair and their caution.

Ann cups her mouth with her gloves and owl-screeches at the night, then takes a breath and cycles a few more times through her mantra: *DPO*. Dead till Proven Otherwise. She has the words tattooed in black under her collarbones. From the moment she touches the mountain, she *is* dead, clawing at the dirt from six feet under. She swings her right-hand tool into the ice and cleans the anchor screws with her left. If she wants to live, she'll have to prove it.

She began down at Satan's icy asshole, where she climbed gunslinger quick, as fast as she knew how, racing the sun and the devil's daily bowel movement, when he drops a white load from a serac band two thousand feet up. Then she'd been up in his lungs, where the wind blew to tear her off the mountain and the ice looked like ropes of frozen snot hanging down over ribs of black rock. And even though she now has ol' scratch by the neck, it's only if and when she tops out his horns that she'll have passed the underworld. Then she can reclaim her place in the land of the living, wherever in hell that is. DPO.

For three hundred feet, Ann climbs seventy-degree ice coated by a rotten foam of rime. Her headlamp claims forty feet of night, but she uses even less, locking in on the ice right in her face. Staring too far into the darkness is a good way to bring the sucking void to life. Which makes a fine entertainment, on flat ground, with a six for company and something to smash the bottles against. The emptiness above is the enemy, just as bad as the flesh below and harder to fight. Strung up above a mile of empty air with only a few points of steel in the mountain, Ann confines herself to the bright surfaces of things, keeps the darkness to the borderlands of her mind.

The angle ratchets out toward vertical. Warts of rock push through the ice. Ann pounds a half-inch piton to the eye, pulls the end of her rope from the loose stack at the top of her pack, threads a bight through her handle-modified GriGri, and clips the end to the piton. Her hands know how to do this frozen, pumped, and in gloves. The entire motion takes no time and less thought. Her rope is skinny as she is, looks like a spaghetti strap disappearing below her feet. She rope-solos three pitches of rock hung with glittering ice and powder snow, until the angle eases back into the seventies and she puts the rope away in her pack.

Her mechanics are brutal, ruthless. Every move carries her higher. Her thoughts don't stray. The music flails her eardrums. She hits blank rock and, minutes later, has a pendulum rigged. She swings left—instinct says so—and her headlamp digs up a rock corner plastered with snow and filled by a glittering black coal seam of old ice.

Higher, back on rotted, grainy ice with the rope stashed again in her pack, her left tool rips out of the ice. She catches herself with the right. She waits a beat, prepping for an adrenaline storm, expecting her heart rate to jack up through the top of her skull. Her pulse comes and goes, steady as a bass line, and she . . . giggles. She has ice for blood. She's inside the mountain looking out. She presses her lips, seals her thoughts, before anything else slithers out. DPO, DPO. She still has to prove up. But she can't help smiling.

The short night turns blue, then yellow. Shallow ice, about as deep as a piss on a wall, dribbles down over vertical rock leading up to the chimney that splits the last headwall. Sunlight streams by overhead. Wind rattles through her. Somewhere down below, a thunderclap of released snow reaches her through her music. *Speed*, she says to herself, imagining a two-man team fucking around with ropes and anchors and getting creamed.

She's been in a deep groove all morning. She keeps her rope in her pack, reaches up, and hooks an edge with one tool, whangs the center of a plaque of ice with the other. The climbing is delicate, kinetic, a hatchet fight with a monster. Her hand keeps twitching toward the rope, but there are no gear placements, and she has already committed. She blocks out the summit and the ground and the thought of falling.

Each move fractures her resolve, a crack here, a chip there. Her brain wanders. She wonders if she—pieces of her anyway—will make it all the way to the ground if she falls now. It looks that sheer. Maybe she'll just burn up on reentry, turn into a bloody mist. Her hands, arms, brain *scream* for the rope, but the rope means nothing without a crack for a pin or a patch of ice deep enough for a screw.

Her muscles are on fire. She forces a long reach to an eyebrow of rock and nearly blows it when her crampon skates, shooting sparks.

The eyebrow is nothing. She sees, knows, it shouldn't hold. Part of her already seems to be falling. She cuts that part away, lets it fall. She is fucking *here*, fucking *now*. Like fleeing a burning building, she forces herself under the smoke in her mind, down to the floor of thought. *Do*, she tells herself, and she locks the eyebrow off at her hip, reaches up, spears a scum of ice. *Do again.*

When the top half of Ann's brain re-hooks itself to the rest of her, she is up in the chimney. She seems to be coming out of a trance, though she remembers every move. She's never gone so deep into the reptilian bottom of her consciousness. *Another weapon.* She feels vacated and shaky. *Better not use it often.* But it's good to know what's down there.

The chimney is deep, dark. Strange children of the mountain live inside. Hanging curtains of rock creak when Ann presses her back against them. Fungoid shelves of ice crawl out from cracks. She fishes for holds under liquid powder snow.

And then she is on the summit ridge, in the sunshine. The actual summit is a fin of crusty snow that feels unstable, a trap for puffed up climbers with lowered defenses. Ann straddles it anyway, hanging one leg over the north face and the other over the south, just long enough to give the mountain the finger and blow a few kisses at the wind. The mountain looks evil, deadly, goat-ugly. It suits her perfectly. Past her right leg she can see six thousand feet down the face she has climbed. It's *hers* now. Others have come. They brought their hopes and ropes and balls. No one else has sent the motherfucker. Only her. She banshees at the blue sky and claps her hands and gets the hell off the top before the snow collapses under her butt to spite her for her hubris.

The descent is unreasonably long and drops her off far from her basecamp. Hell, the descent was a proud *ascent*. Until now. She spends the time trying to focus, trying not to daydream. Her methods, her strategy, her luck—they all *worked*. The people who looked at her and said, you need more margin, you need a partner, you need respect—they were wrong.

Ann reaches her basecamp tent on the glacier in the middle of the next night. She's completely fried but still too wired and happy to sleep. When she tries to piece together what all she did on the way down, she can only recover a sense that at times she moved too fast and at other times much too slow. Clouds blew in, right on schedule, covering the mountain and just about everything else. The wind came up. No matter. Here she is. She rolls around in the snow, cackling.

She picks up her radio. Is it too late to call her pilot? Of course it is! Does she give a shit? No! That old boy dropped her off with a lecture about how much he hated picking up dead climbers. If she has the chance to drag his ass out of bed, she'll take it. Ann flips on the machine, gets only static, throws it back into her tent, and chucks herself in after. She sleeps through the next afternoon.

She wakes starving and cooks a huge breakfast out of powdered egg, sugar, and Tabasco. The clouds have gotten organized and are sitting fifty feet overhead, spewing snow. Ann turns on the radio again. Static. She scans the channels. Nothing but static.

Next day, the snow turns to rain. Wet fog gets in her tent, her lungs, under her skin. The radio speaks nothing but white noise. She swaps batteries, but that's pointless, right? If she's getting static, then the damn thing is working. She fiddles all the knobs and gives it a few drops, wondering if some key connection has come unmarried and just needs to get wiggled back in place. She feels like a cavewoman trying to fix a toaster oven.

The weather clears. Ann steps out of her tent. The mountain looks unearthly. Impossible to think she's just been up there. She hugs herself. Hell, now it *is* impossible. The snow, the rain, the warm front. The whole face is coming apart, ice falling, avalanches pouring off ledges, white bugs and centipedes jittering all over it.

Her pilot will know she took advantage of the good window, the three days of cold and clear. Pilots know those sorts of things. When he hasn't heard from her, he'll pass by and have a look-see. Won't he? Sure, or one of his compadres. For all her grumbling and his gruffness, the pilots are a brotherhood of good guys, literal angels to the climbers. What if he's had a heart attack? One too many fried moose steaks. *Someone* knows she's out here, right? That's a stupid thought—what does it have to do with static all up and down the VHF channels?

Ann lays out every red piece of clothing she has and stamps PICK UP in twenty-foot letters. Then she cuts a chair for herself in the snow and has a seat. She watches the mountain—she can't sit through a movie, but she can stare at a mountain for hours—but now she can't focus. Her brain's in her ears, listening for that subaudible hum of a distant bushplane. The sky suddenly seems too empty, the air too quiet. Like the world has stopped turning.

She had been flying high. She has news to share! She can *taste* the lusciousness of casually dropping the bomb when one of the local hotshots asks where she's been. Sit back, let the story jump itself from Alaska to Colorado to California. She's crashed now. She'll probably blab it all out to the first pilot or wildcat miner who gives her a lift. She can feel her chi sinking down through her butt into the glacier.

Weather rolls back in. Ice. Fog. Heavy snow. Rain. The typical Southeast Alaska stew. The radio makes electric snow, the same every time. Ann amuses herself by wrapping her fingers around it and imagining a throat. Her pilot goes from overdue to long overdue. Food's running low, and the battery dies in her third mp3 player. Ann studies the map she tucked into the case with the radio. The ocean is only, what, twenty-five miles away? Someone will be on the water, fishermen. Ann's heard of guys walking the glacier. And, goddamnit, how appropriate. She climbs the whole north face alone, and now she's going to die falling into a crevasse without a dead weight on the other end of the rope to catch her. Screw it. She'll get herself out on her own. She doesn't need planes or pilots. It feels *good* to be thinking this way, taking matters into her own hands. Where they belong.

Ann bundles all her food—little enough—into her backpack. She packs her rope and harness but leaves out the pitons and other rock gear, her GriGri, her helmet, one of her ice tools. Presents. Offerings to the mountain. Three dead music tabs weigh next to nothing, but Ann can't bring herself to carry anything useless. She keeps the radio, still hoping it will come back to life and restore her to the outside world with a flicked switch—though she resents it and looks forward to ceremonially smashing the smug little one-note snake.

The next morning delivers drizzle and hanging curtains of cloud. Ann throws a snow-clod and loses sight of it before it lands. There is no point staying, but it's hard to go. She gives the pile of gear she's leaving on the glacier a kick and walks away.

Ann can't see a thing. The world is opaque, impenetrable. Behind the clouds, avalanches fall to the edge of the glacier. The noise of each slide seems solid as the falling snow. The sound tumbles down off the mountains till the air quakes. Blasts of wind punch crosswise through the clouds. Ann tries to stay psyched, to let the roaring stir her up the same way as a lunatic on the drums, but the detonations are so inhuman they make her want to crawl under a rock and take shelter. Beyond the curtains hung round the mountains, who knows what might be happening? Anything.

On the clear day, when she watched the north face come apart, did she see any planes at all? Passenger planes? Jets? Should she have? Ann can't remember if flight corridors pass over this corner of the Alaska panhandle and didn't bother noticing planes until now, when she wonders if there are any left in the sky at all.

She keeps to the middle of the glacier, steering by the concussions of sound as much as anything. She's below the firn line, and crevasses are scarce, but Ann feels sure one has her name on it, so she keeps her eyes in a vice trying to find it through the white-on-white of the clouds and snow.

Whenever Ann goes into the mountains, she always half expects she'll return to a changed world. Shakeups, revolutions, they happen. So when she does emerge to see the same people doing the same things, it surprises her every time, even though she knows better.

Now something has happened. Ann can't trust the loose-wire-in-the-radio theory. The sky has emptied out. *Yeah? When's the last time you saw more than ten feet overhead?* All right, explain the radio. She chases her tail round and round. If all the world's pilots have been put to some other use, what does that mean for her?

For fuck's sake, Ann tells herself. *Volcanic ash in the jet stream. Malware at the FAA. The Apocalypse is only a song.* But it's hard to stay focused and believe in benign causes when megatons of snow keep banging down all around her. Damned hard to keep faith with stability while moving through avalanche country.

Ann pushes down the glacier, blind to everything beyond the snow under her feet but pretty sure the Pacific Ocean is somewhere that way. Hours and miles pass. Presumably. Seeing nothing but whitish grey scale, Ann's eyes invent shapes, people, creatures uncurling from the clouds. It's a fucking primeval mist, from before the separation of land or darkness. Nothing fixed, everything malleable. Her watch tells her she's put in a full day, but she keeps going an extra hour because she's driving herself crazy on the hoof, and when she stops she knows it will only get worse.

She's been soaked by the day. When Ann gets into her tent and sleeping bag, every surface clings damply, and the wet sucks the heat from her. She hadn't expected rockstar treatment, but goddamnit, abandonment and a survival trudge through a marine fog seem a damn poor reward for her climb.

Ann tries the radio again—given the miles she picked up, she ought to be easily in range even of fishing boats. Static. She pitches the infernal thing into the corner of the tent—and knocks down a rain of condensation drops, which splash all over her. She howls into her fist, afraid to take her frustration fully off its leash, afraid she might begin to crack. She pulls her sleeping bag over her head, tries to turn rage into clean, dry therms, and wills herself to fall asleep.

There's one good thing about the night: it's brief. The sun dips over the pole and comes back like a yoyo on a string. At least Ann assumes that's what turns the wet murk from black to white. She hasn't actually seen the sun in how many days? Ann is up again before she's really slept, which hardly matters since she's had nothing to do but sleep since she got off the mountain.

The air in the morning is so heavy with water that just passing through it cuts loose rivulets. Ann can see fat grey nothing. But staying put would be succumbing. The weather could still blow up, go from bad to nasty. Her food will only hold out so long. A rescue will never find her here. Fuck that thought. No rescue is coming.

Ann slogs down the glacier through the blind wet. The mountains have declined. Ann can tell because they've gone silent. No inhuman roars, no spooky crosswinds blasting through the fog. Ann drifts left and right. When twenty feet of cliffed-up ice loom out of the grey, it might be a twenty-one-foot-high pimple or the toe of a mountain at the edge of the glacier for all she can tell. Ann has one corner of her much-too-wide-scaled map and the needle of her eight-dollar compass to guide her.

Ann thinks back to 9/11, when all the climbers sat around toasting America and joking about the bad luck of waiting for a pickup while every plane in the country was grounded. Is that what's happened? A world war, a jihad? Or a slipped circuit in her radio.

With nothing to see, her mind wanders its own corridors, rattling doors and throwing rocks through windows. She wonders if there will be dead people on television when she emerges—assuming she does, assuming TVs are doing better than her radio. Anyway, there are always dead people on TV. She wonders if anyone will still be around to care about the north face. Will she? If the whole knotty-rotten stump of the American century had split open, will she still climb futuristic alpine routes? Hitchhike on fishing boats and do overland approaches to obscurities no one wastes a damn on anymore? Stick out her neck with no one to tell it to afterward? *Call yourself a soloist. You'll climb mountains alone, but you get back, and you need applause.*

Her watch numbers the passage of another day and extra hour. She flops up her tent, gritting her teeth against the damp fabric and what waits inside. In theory, she's made miles toward the ocean, but this camp twins her last. She leaves her compass in her pocket even as she sets camp up, not because it will tell her anything new now that she has stopped moving. Keeping it close calms the voice in her that says she has no idea where she is and has spent the day backing and forthing over the same ground, ending where she started. The rain turns to snow, then back to rain.

In Salt Lake, where she overwintered last season, twenty-five miles was a long training run, four hours if she didn't try to bust her ass. How slow can she be going now? The ocean must be close. Even on snow, with a pack, weaving like a drunk, she's still dropping miles. Has to be.

Inside her tent, Ann examines her feet, like a pathologist fingering a drowned corpse. The relentless wet went down into her boots. All day long, her feet swam with the fishes. The flesh is white, bloated, waxy. She pinches one big toe hard enough to crease it and feels nothing. She dries her feet as best she can and shoves them into her dank sleeping bag. *It's a race between trench foot and frostbite. A footrace. Ha. Fucking joke's on me.*

Her food bag has crumbs in it. Ann can live on air and NoDoz, but it doesn't come easy without music. She would *kill* for some sound that puts nails through her face, wakes her up. She might kill just to do it, separate dark from light. Better than unending grey. God, what a bitch. She hasn't seen a live thing for a month. Now she's fantasizing about twisting the neck of the first rock sparrow that flies by. She slips an inch below the surface, nodding off into twitchy half sleep.

Ann wakes to rain and static. "Screw it," she says out loud, finding her voice rusty and thin as a reed. "Today, the ocean." She shoves herself willfully into the downpour. Saltwater, salt air. She tastes each damp inhale, searching for the sea.

The rain hisses against the snow. Ann draws the hood of her jacket tight around her face. The world comes to her though a tunnel. The clouds bleed all over her. Even the candy red of her jacket looks grey. Wet noises surround her—the atmospheric pissing seems to be coming from left and right and straight up out of the snow.

No, those sounds *are* coming from the snow. Ann hears a hum, a roar, then she stops at a trench cut through the surface of the glacier by a boiling-fast whitewater creek. The water mesmerizes her. It looks muscular enough to rip off a leg. Ann fantasizes about a kayak, calculates the slim possibility of not getting pulverized by the current.

She tracks along the edge of the creek, till another vein of melt joins the first and strands her on the inside of a V. The two join and double and punch a hole through the surface, howling into the bowels of the glacier. It would almost be worth it, a hell of an exciting ride.

Ann turns upstream along the second creek. The rain drills down. Froth and fresh chunks of ice float past. *Son of a bitch*. It dawns on Ann that she is walking through the middle of a glacial flashflood. One minute, the rain falls and just disappears, and the next thing you know, the line gets crossed, the water heaves back out of the ground, takes over, and the whole world comes apart at the seams. Happens just like that, no warning.

Ann finds a low snow bridge over the torrent. Now that she's looking, she's sure she can see the creek level rising. The water rips handfuls off the sides and bottom of the bridge. Ann cat-foots over before the current tears the whole thing away, forcing calm, not hurrying, because, damn it, she is still in the mountains, *her* mountains, and she refuses to get pushed around.

Ann takes out her compass and points herself back southwest, the orientation of the glacier on her map. Every few minutes, she checks the needle again. Another creek slices in from the side and cuts her off again. Ann follows its edge, not too close, to where it drains down into its own round suck hole. Past the drain, the freshly wet track of the creek continues. Ann boulders down into the trough, sticking her front points into hard, freezer-tray ice. The ice is polished, milky-blue. The suck hole must have just opened, a trapdoor under the creek that popped and diverted the whole shebang into some subsurface vein. Ann climbs out the other side.

DPO, DPO. It's still in effect. There are trapdoors all around her. In fact, she's more dead now than she ever has been on a mountain. She has split from the outside world, dropped down a suck hole herself, siphoned off to fuck knows where. Nobody knows where she is, least of all Ann. And moreover, it's not at all clear that Ann will recognize the world when—*if*, adds her inner demon, twisting the nail—she returns.

There are no visible features, nothing to sight her compass on. She glances at it every few steps, trying to keep the needle steady in her mind.

She made a deal with herself that morning: No more speculating about the outside. It changes nothing. She chose to walk out. Until she hits saltwater, nothing else matters. But it's impossible—the scenarios belch out unasked for from the corners of her mind. She has no distraction, nothing to look at but the snow under her boots and the clouds in her face.

Earthquake. Alaska could unhook a monster. And the sky would be full of planes and radio talk. War. (With . . . China? Arabia? Some nuclearized -stan no one has heard of?) Solar flare. What is she, an astrophysicist? Just stop it. What does she know, really? But that maddening static, those empty skies. Something isn't *right*. She feels space all around her, no signals in or out.

She hears another creek and searches for it in the fog. It's loud, close. She looks left, she looks right. Nothing but snow. The sound comes from all around. Not all around. Below. The snow collapses under her boots. She's quick; god, her reflexes are sharp. She swings her axe far from the sound, sticks it in good snow just as the ice water grabs her feet and tries to yank her boots off. Her body recoils, jackknifing up out of the creek. She thrutches and rolls away from the water and unstable snow—and glances downstream in time to see her eight-dollar plastic compass, which she'd held in one glove, floating away under the ice.

It's still raining, she's shivering, she has to get up, has to reduce her profile, get her rain gear pointed in the right direction—which is good because she has a strong impulse to lie in the snow till global warming lowers her back to solid ground. She's not soaked. *You dropped your compass.* Her left foot got a strong, cold splash, but what is she going to do, stop and light a fire? Her shell pants and plastic boots repelled the rest. *Dropped your goddamn fucking compass!* This Boy Scout bullshit is going to kill her. Ann gets up, feeling very tired.

She looks around. It's hopeless. Clouds, clouds, snow. West is where? Ann tries to visualize her angle to the creek when she last checked her compass. She tries to pry open the clouds, as if a landmark or compass rose might appear through force of concentration. Nothing. She puts the water sound to her right and starts walking.

Fuck it. She'll walk a line. It might not be precisely right, but if she follows it straight, it will lead her somewhere. Anywhere will do. She'll walk to Wrangell or fucking Vancouver if she has to. Who's going to stop her? She'll walk right down the glacier's throat.

A crack oozing slush crosses her line, and she jumps it. She end-runs around a jumble of blocks and fissures, an old scar in the snow. Rain slops down. Another creek—a big one, some branches must have accumulated—swings in from the left, and Ann tracks it a quarter mile to a shelled-out snow bridge that shifts and pops under her weight.

Her line fades. She curves around a soft patch of snow, imagining a sinkhole to hell. The degrees of uncertainty multiply. *Pathetic*, she thinks, pushing forward because it seems slightly less pointless than standing still. *Might as well shut your eyes. Take your chances the next water you fall in will be salt.* The clouds press low and bleed and bleed. *Like a whale artery in the sky. Beast won't die.* There's nothing but the rain to walk toward.

Her watch marks the end of the day. Ann doesn't bother adding an extra hour. She puts up her tent, fighting the snow's invitation to sit and let her shaking muscles play themselves out.

Inside the tent, Ann swallows her last gel and eats all the scraps out of the bottom of the food bag. It's necessary. Her body needs the fuel. It's also another line crossed. No more food.

The calories and shelter pacify her muscles. Ann feels a little less like simply drifting away. She pokes at her feet. They look decayed and smell like a graveyard. Black edges four toenails on her left foot, which took the creek splash. She loosens a strip of white skin off her arch and cuts it away so it won't tear and rub the next day.

Ann slides into her sleeping bag and falls asleep like a dropped stone.

She comes to in the middle of the night. Something waked her. A noise. The *absence* of noise. It's not raining. She throws off her sleeping bag and pulls on her jacket, then her boots, done gingerly because her feet are dead flesh and live nerves. She unzips her tent and steps out into the snow.

Stars. Not a full sky of them. Clouds still jam the horizons. *Stars.* Bright and hard. Motionless. Nothing else. No planes, no satellites. Empty space and frozen stars.

Ann turns a slow circle, looking up, searching the sky—for anything, a blinking wing light, a sign of the times. The stars stare back. She's dazed, on the verge of falling up into space.

She gets hot angry with herself. The emptiness shouldn't matter. It hasn't ever mattered before; it doesn't matter now.

There are signs up there. Practical signs. Ann's no whizz with the constellations, but whichever way the stars are wheeling is west, minus some whadyacallit, tilt or declination. That's logical enough. The horizons are choked off, so she can't use them to judge motion. She grabs one ice tool, raises the shaft over her head, makes herself as stiff and straight as possible, memorizes the patterns of star clusters around the spike of her axe. Then she gets back into her sleeping bag because the wind and cold are nosing around her like wolves.

Ann checks her watch, sets her alarm. She tries not to think; she tries not to sleep. She does some of both. The stars seem to be in the tent with her. They come right through the roof. She imagines reaching the ocean and finding . . . nothing. And if she lives, if she can catch fish or whatever? What then? In the Stone Age, the mountains were full of trolls. You don't risk getting killed in the mountains when you're eating roots and berries just to keep ahead of death anyway. *Right now, I'd eat dirt. Handfuls.* Suicidal alpinism, symptom of a decadent culture with a protein surplus. Fight the softness, show the rest of the tribe what soul-fat slobs they've become.

Half an hour passes. Ann's alarm jerks her into the present. She ducks out of her tent, plants her feet in the exact steps she used before, raises her ice tool over her head. The stars have moved. Just a giant clock spinning west, nothing more to them. *Keep on saying it, Ann.* She brings her arm down in the direction they've turned and kicks a twenty-foot arrow in the snow pointing that way. Then she gets back into her sleeping bag and drops away again.

Ann resurfaces into grey daylight. It's not raining, but the clouds are low as ever. The arrow she stamped in the snow is there. She half expected to find no sign of it. It makes a right angle with her melted-out tracks leading up to the tent from the day before. At least it doesn't point back the way she came. Ann feels hunched with cold. The temperature has dropped, or her body is shutting down. *Both.*

She walks into the fog, and it wraps itself round her. Her eyes crave and wander. Ann remembers hearing that sharks need to stay in motion or they die. Something about their gills and asphyxiation. Ann feels driven before the same lash. Hungry, jagged, adrift and unable to stop.

Snowflakes shake out of the dirty cotton overhead. Little buggers look fat enough to eat. Ann imagines running around with her mouth open and her tongue out in a blizzard of barbecue drippings. She licks them off her glove. Cold ice. *Damn.* The flakes pour down in lazy, windless spirals. Ann retreats deep behind her eyes, away from the snow and the lines tracing themselves through the air right in front of her face. She nearly runs into a copse of twenty stunted alders.

Trees. *Trees.* Ann's eyes all but pop out of their sockets in their eagerness. Awareness rushes to the surface. She may yet come back from the dead, a thought Ann hasn't entertained since she exited shit creek without her compass. The trees stand isolated. There are rocks under the new snow, and withered old snow-ice shows through gaps. Could be a glacial edge. Could be a skin of rock and soil riding the back of the glacier. One way or the other, Ann has located the land of the living.

The snow keeps dumping, and Ann keeps walking, past rocks, shells of wind-carved ice, a rubble ridge that has to be a moraine. Alders come out of the ground. The land is changing, tidewater approaching.

Ann hits a chain-link wall of alders. There is rock and snow underfoot, snow in the air. No chance of walking forward. The trees are knit tight. Left or right? She can see about forty feet in either direction. Ann chooses right—it beats standing there deciding. She follows the wall of growth to where it turns ragged and the rocks end at the edge of glacial ice. Back on the glacier again? Ann struggles to put the jigsaw cuts of the map together in her mind—she has about six pieces out of five hundred, and none of them fit with the others. It isn't just the map; her mind's also full of gaps. The cold has its wedges in her. Hunger digs into her brain.

Ann stays in the fringe of the alder pack, unwilling to let the trees out of her sight. There she flounders. Loose rocks somersault under the snow. Gaps in the alders suck her in, then pinch off and force her back out. Her instinct for direction scatters like de-flocked birds. She's close, she's sure of it. But the fatigue, the drowning panic, return. She can feel the suck of a downward spiral. She detaches herself from the trees, gets back out on open ice. For ten minutes she walks, seeing nothing but skydiving snowflakes six inches in front of her eyes. The alders reappear. This time on her right. The same trees or new? Ann tries to scream. What comes out is hoarse and pathetic. Where is the goddamn ocean? It's only the biggest thing on earth.

Ann zeros in on a brown boulder that appears ahead through the snowfall. She knows she hasn't seen it before. She'll turn it into a landmark, trace out a map with search patterns and a center. She needs a system, that's all. Twenty feet away, the rock shrugs and swings a huge dished-out moon face Ann's way.

Two things Ann hates: Avalanches. Bears. Big, dumb, unpredictable, uncontrollable. Randomness given mass and teeth.

The bear lifts its head. Its eyes are small, black, unbelievably far apart. *It's fucking huge.* Ann doesn't move, couldn't move. She's locked down. She has often sensed that a mountain has its teeth in her. Now the feeling hits her as physical pain, as if the bear has already crunched her. The bear stands up on its hind legs, sticks its nose in the air. Ann imagines airborne traces of her sweat, her fear, her exhaustion, going down that big brown snout. The bear is so close she sees the bristles in its lips. Mentally, Ann gives herself the finger, kisses herself goodbye. Two bounds, and the bear will be at her. It's going to be over in less than a second. At least the bear won't get much satisfaction out of her skinny ass. Ann stands straight, prepares to let the bear crash down on her like a wave.

The bear drops. Turns. Ambles away.

Thoughts flash by Ann in a series, going off like firecrackers on a string.

Turn. Run.

Bear knows where it is. You don't.

Bears look for food. Nothing to eat where you came from.

Don't you fucking do this!

Ann races after the bear.

Its big brown haunch is still just visible through the blizzard. Ann chases it through the flying snow. The bear's tracks are deep, but new snow fills them fast, and Ann knows she isn't seeing well or thinking clearly. When Ann loses sight of the bear, even for a moment, an edge-of-the-world terror seizes her. The bear will cross its own trail, vanish in the woods, blink back out of existence, and she'll be left alone again. And when she has the bear in sight, all she can think of is it swinging around a second time, freezing her with its moon face, knocking her down with a paw like a spiked club, and digging into her guts.

The bear is as alien as a meteorite, half a ton of muscle and unknowable intention. It sniffs the wind. Swipes the snow. Ann watches it flip a hundred-pound stone as casually as a kid turning over a rock. It gallops fifty yards, then stalks along with its nose down. Ann follows, fast or slow, through bunkers of brush and over moraines, straining to keep that furry hind end just in view and no closer. At a hundred feet, the bear is still too near. Ann's legs twitch like a rabbit's, trying to turn her away and send her into flight. Each time Ann catches a side view—of hooked claws, a shoulder built like a steam piston—the horror movie looping behind her eyes shows the bear coming all the way around and lunging through the storm, leading with its teeth. The bear enters dark woods with snow underfoot and soil under the snow.

It occurs to Ann that this might be all that's left of the world for her. She'll reach the ocean, and it will be salty. She'll follow the bears and stars until she starves or something kills her. Just because she asked them doesn't mean her questions will be answered.

She follows the bear through the woods, between trees and outbursts of devil's club. The snow drops between the trunks, white on black, a feathery carpet-bombing. Ann drifts closer to the bear. She is starving, tired, numb—and what difference does ten feet make? The bear knows she's here. It will cut short this parade when it damn well pleases. But if Ann loses the bear, she will be on the dark side of the moon. The trail of scents and signs they've followed is so convoluted Ann barely knows her left from her right anymore.

Ann gives in to tunnel vision, gives up any pretense of paying attention to the warp of the land or the composition of the forest. Her hood is cinched tight; the bear is in front of her. It is goddamn ironic, is what it is. For how many years she has slapped aside every effort to hook her up with a partner, and now, at the end, she is a donkey on a string behind a side of bear-flesh that would on an average day eat her, or just kill her for mucking around in its tracks.

Fallen logs on the forest floor look like bodies under the snow. Buried deeper, their outlines soften, until Ann runs them over and frags the soft curves. The bear bulls through the drifts. And sure, if Ann were as Stone Age as the mountains, maybe she'd take the bear for her totem. Pray to it, ask favors. But her world is all probabilities and lottery wheels. And she sees her number spinning down to zero. The big void lurks behind the numbers. From the mountains, Ann has watched it draw close and recede, her personal black hole.

Sneaky bastard, to catch her like this. The bear rips open a rotten log and sniffs its insides. Ann is almost tired enough to welcome that treatment. Freezing to death might be more peaceful, but it will give her a long damn time to think.

The bear shambles into a run. Ann follows, her legs clumsy and spazzing. The woods quit at an invisible line, and Ann pops out into space, bewildered. The land slopes down. Above, a low, flat ceiling of cloud spews snow. Below, a second expanse of grey cloud is speckled white. No, not cloud, water. Ocean. A tidal flat. A bay held in by two brown arms of land. Filled with boats. Motherfucking *boats*.

NO PLACE FOR VAGABONDS

J AY'S SUBARU RATTLED through a labyrinth of streetlight-slicked asphalt and into the bowels of LAX. Chase Vox had come back from Pakistan, and Jay was his welcoming committee. In his car in Los Angeles, Jay felt close to the days when horse carts and automobiles had bickered over the roads. Sleek, hungry machines roared angrily past him and the other stragglers. Jay was allied with the fat white men with bald tires and bald heads driving rusted El Caminos and the workers in broken-backed pickups laden with ladders, pipes, shovels—all moving at one speed while blurs of paint and dollars hurtled by. Jay found Chase squatting by the arrivals curb on a boulder-sized duffel, looking like an island apart from the other passengers milling around. A wild tangle of black hair blew off his head in a permanent wind. In the pink and green lights of the airport, his face was nineteenth-century gaunt. Jay knew the look. Chase could have just stumbled back to basecamp after two weeks pinned up high. But usually in the time it took a fellow to get to an international airport, he had put on weight and washed the grease out of his hair. Chase looked like the mountain was still just over his shoulder.

Jay stopped his car and jumped out. They embraced, then they each grabbed one handle of the duffle and swung it into the back of the Subaru, which bucked and settled lower. They took their seats, and Jay eased back into the river of cars washing through the airport.

Chase's expedition had not gone well, that was clear enough. He seemed ready to fend off words like fists. Jay could imagine Chase's seatmate on the plane leaning way out into the aisle, pushed away by the psychic tide. But Jay didn't mind it himself. The man could take as much time as he needed.

"The mountain was a shitstorm," Chase said, at last. "I'll tell you about it. Just let me get used to talking again."

"Sure," Jay said. "What's next, now that you're back?"

Chase said nothing. The car groaned up onto the freeway. Jay began to think he might not answer at all.

"Guess I'll go to Joshua Tree," Chase said, and Jay concluded that Chase had actually been pondering the question, as if he hadn't thought about it before. "Look for a guide job," he continued. "Probably lie on top of a rock for a few days. Play the lizard. I left some boxes of my things under a rock out on Queen Mountain. It was cheaper than storage."

"Is your bus out there, too?" Years ago, Chase had acquired a yellow school bus, one of the short ones. He cut a hole in the roof and installed a four-legged, potbellied iron stove and chimney. He pulled out the rows of seats and built a bed frame from scrap wood salvaged out of a derelict house south of Olancha. It was easy to tell if Chase was about—around the mountains, there was only one decommissioned school bus sporting a chimney. On a storm day, you could knock on his door and come in and sit on old bench seats turned in toward the stove and listen to the rain on the roof, and he'd make coffee and tell stories.

"I sold it for my plane ticket," Chase said.

Jay whistled. The freeway rattled below them. Lights sped by.

"I know," Chase said. "What could I do? I heard from a friend that Bill Coleman was trying to find me. So I borrowed his phone and called. 'Come to the Karakorum,' he said. That's Bill. No questions. He doesn't ask them." Chase's voice dropped and rasped in imitation: "'Come to the Karakorum.' 'Come lead this pitch.' 'Come here, boy.' He liked to be at the center of things. 'Attend me now,'—he said that—'Attend me now, I've been up here before.' A member of his expedition had dropped out. Can't imagine why. Didn't think about it at the time. The permit was paid, high-altitude gear already bought. They were leaving in three weeks. I'd only need a plane ticket and my own things."

Jay waited for more, but Chase's tongue had jerked awake and then lapsed again. It was good to have him in the car, a moody, bristly presence whom Jay could understand. Jay was uncomfortable around the violent optimism that made people build freeways and own fine automobiles. He exited the 405 and bumped along patched pavement six lanes wide, Inglewood Avenue, 190th. The roads matched the cars. Shiny asphalt laid down right by potholed lanes, as if they'd run out. Maybe they had. Sometimes Jay imagined the weight of concrete pushing all of Los Angeles down, cracking the ground, causing earthquakes. He glanced over at Chase, who was staring out the window.

"Just think," Jay said. "A hundred years ago, none of this existed. It was practically a Mexican pueblo. How did you meet Bill Coleman?"

"In Alaska. Denali basecamp. I'd just gotten off the Cassin. Bill seemed impressed with that. At least he wanted to make a lot of noise about it. He grabbed my shoulder and pulled me around to all these people he knew. Like I was his prodigy even though we'd only just met. I was half dead, and Bill kept pulling me through the snow from tent to tent." Chase paused. "So what the hell are you doing in LA? I mean, I'm grateful and all. I'd be sleeping in the airport without you."

"Back in school," Jay said. "We started to think we'd want a family with all the trimmings. Didn't seem right to raise kids in the Subaru." Jay pulled the car around a corner and parked on a street walled with flat-faced apartment buildings. They left the car and the duffel. The walls were thin, and the Subaru's years had given distinction to its sound. Carrie came to the door.

"Where have you been?" she said to Chase. "I saw you once at the Druid Stones. Jay used to talk about you. But then you vanished." She gave him a hug. "You reek," she said, pleasantly. "Welcome home."

Chase came in, gulped a beer, looked overwhelmed despite Carrie's best efforts to ease him. He was happy, that much was clear. He'd wrap an arm around Jay, or Carrie, or both of them at once— the apartment was so small, they were usually both in reach. Then he'd let them go, wash his hands in the bathroom sink, unlock and relock the front door, pull books off the bedroom case and leave them unopened on the table. "I went to the snow," Chase said. "Rainier then Canada then Alaska. I was looking for big ice mountains. Mixed climbs that would blow my mind. So I kept moving north. I missed California, but it's hard to leave Alaska. Impossible, actually. If it storms in the Sierras, you just drive down into the desert. You can practically coast in neutral. But when it's bad in Alaska, in winter, dark, cold, forty below, what can you do? The Alcan Highway is buried, and I didn't have the money to put my bus on a ferry. I ran out of wood once and spent three days in a blizzard under all the sleeping bags and blankets I had. There were icicles two feet long hanging down *inside* Big Yellow. And then summer would come back, and the mountains were incredible, and it never got dark. So I couldn't leave then either."

Jay and Carrie had a round table about the size of a deluxe pizza in the middle of their apartment. Carrie laid out plates and forks. "Here," Carrie said to Chase. "Sit." She took Chase's hand and guided him to a chair. He sat, and she pressed down on his shoulders as if trying to plant him. She was small, but he was smaller yet, five two to her five three. Watching them, Jay felt pressed up against the ceiling. They were like the moon and the night; Carrie blond, pale, her hair in a wreath around her oval face, rising above Chase with her hands on his shoulders. Here was something Jay couldn't see too well out his window anymore—the moon and the night—and it made him happy to see the two of them like that. Carrie grinned back at him. Chase was still talking. His tongue had recovered.

▲

IT WAS APRIL when I talked to Bill. I was in Talkeetna waiting
for the snowpack to stabilize. If I could meet them in Islamabad on
May 10, I was in. Of course I said yes. The only thing I have is no
attachments. It would have been a betrayal not to go. And I wanted
to go, you understand? We've got stone on this continent, but they've
got *mountains*. What did I care that I didn't know anyone on the
team—didn't know anyone in Asia? Bill had been there before. It
almost felt good selling Big Yellow. Snip. The last attachment. I knew
a guy in Banning, a welder I'd met in Joshua Tree, who had always
wanted her. It took me nine days to drive there, and it didn't matter
because I was staring at the Himalayas the whole time. I showed up
at the airport with the duffle and three thousand dollars in cash, and
the woman behind the Emirates Air counter looked at me like I had
syphilis.

Probably she thought I was running drugs. You know pot grows
wild there? You're walking up some valley staring at the river or the
mountains, and then you realize you're in a crowd of five-fingered
hands waving back at you. The bus drivers smoke it. Their tires are
three inches from the edge of the Indus Gorge—no guardrails and
straight down—and they're up front hacking and giggling and rocking out to Hindustani disco pop.

The team had rooms near the bazaar in Rawalpindi. I was the
last one to get there. It was 102 and raining. It's obscene for it to be
that hot and raining. I felt like I had been taken out of the icebox
and thrown in a lobster pot. Most of the city supplies had already

been bought. I was jet-lagged and stir-crazy. Nine days in Big Yellow. Three days in Banning with the welder and his greasy car buddies. Two days in airplanes and airports. Rawalpindi spun me around like a kid on a merry-go-round. I had gone from white to green to orange to brown. Brown faces staring at me, imploring me, ignoring me. I felt like a ghost. Some people laughed at me, some begged me, some looked right through me and refused to see anything there at all.

There were eight of us, all Americans. Five were out gawking and getting the last of the gasoline for the stoves. The other two were in a teahouse attached to the hotel, seated side by side, drinking out of china cups as if the British had never left. When they saw me, they barely moved, just waved me over. Frank and Hubert—a lawyer and a doctor—good men to have on a third-world expedition, I guess. I learned later that their offices shared a building in Minnesota, which meant that they could eat the cold, and salted pig feet, for breakfast. Both balding, but whip-cut and tough, the way forty-year-olds get when they don't quit, skin stuffed with rocks. I had felt jagged, edgy, a little bit mean and dangerous, taking my first steps through the Wild East toward the world's baddest mountains. Looking at those two took the air out of me.

"Bill tells us you did well on the Cassin Ridge," Frank said. He was the lawyer. "How long did it take you?"

"One push," I told them, maybe too proudly. "Thirty-six hours."

Hubert shook his head—wait—it was more like a quiver, an inch to the left, an inch to the right.

"It's different here," Frank said. "Slowly, slowly. People are always racing around, losing their heads. They get infected by the people and the mountains." But what if I wanted to get infected? "I like to think that each extraneous motion adds a drop of fluid to the brain"—that's him, still going, he talked real slow, like he was charming a snake—"the cerebral edema, you know. It's not scientific, but I find it useful."

"You look tense," Hubert whispered. He had a moustache like two squirrel tails stapled to his lip. He spoke so softly I had to lean in to hear him. Even then I felt like I was trying to read his lips. "Sit down. Have tea."

I found out they had the best résumés of any of us. Broad Peak. Ama Dablam. Annapurna. Still, we were all B- and C-listers. None of us with sponsors or big names, except for Bill, and him only because of his money. None of us had done anything important that hadn't been done before. So our reasons for climbing the mountain were strictly personal, and that, at least, seemed right to me at the time.

Bill came back with the other four and convened a meeting. "Come here," he said, "gather round." As if he were trail boss, or maybe Moses—maybe he thought he was the burning bush, for all I know. He had methods. He had principles. Now that we were all together, he could get on with the business of extolling them. Have you ever seen Bill? He's got this wavy hair that comes down low in the back, like he's the wild man in the executive suit. His eyes open a little too wide. I don't know whether he does that on purpose, but it gives you the feeling he's seeing something you can't. When he gets going, the veins stand out in his neck. He's a big broad-shouldered dude. I bet high-heeled women and corporate soldiers get all fluttery around him.

What was he saying? It was inspiring. It was invigorating. We were his lieutenants, his comrades. He had built the expedition like a machine, and each of us was a part with a job to do. He expected us to work hard, keep our heads down, do our part for the greater glory. The machine depended on each of us, and we depended on the machine. It was bizarre. Like Lenin lecturing in the boardroom. We were being collectivized by a capitalist. We were being sent to war. Once I had the gist of it, I stopped listening and watched the other faces. Frank and Hubert—that's the lawyer and the doctor—looked attentive. Kind of like buzzards. They could have been watching theater with maybe the hope of a meal afterward. Three of the four I hadn't met looked freakily rapt. They were receiving a message. Strong, shining faces ready for the campaign. March on, soldiers! The last of the four was also looking around, and we caught each other's eye and shared a moment.

Everyone else called him Stump because of his build—short, wide, and strong—but he introduced himself to me as Gregor, so I called him that. Later on, I asked him how it was that we were climbing in the middle of a corporate team-building exercise. One of the others, Alan, was a stockbroker! Another one—Luther—liked to talk about "bagging" the mountain as if he were going to stuff it and put it on his wall. Where were the bearded vagabonds? I had read the books. I knew who was responsible for setting the Himalayan standard. Hairy vegetarians and bleak, foul-mouthed Brits, and none of them had retirement accounts.

"You tell me," Gregor said, "how an unsponsored hippie gets to the Himalaya today. Who pays the permit fee?" When he talked, he rumbled. His voice came up out of his chest. "Where's-ah-money-come-from?" Like that—no real spaces between words. He told me that if I was hoping for bearded desperadoes and poets, I should have tried hitchhiking on an expedition from the Czech Republic or Slovenia, not America. So what in the hell happened to us? I mean, we started the counterculture, right? Didn't Yosemite in the sixties mean anything? Gregor blamed Reagan. I don't know, maybe. The point is that yours truly was going to be climbing with rich men who thought that Charles Fucking Darwin had sanctified the corporate hierarchy from the bow of the *Beagle* and anointed the CEO as the right and proper expression of man's highest potential fulfilled.

And Bill didn't help any. He barely noticed me. Maybe I was shorter than he remembered. A slap on the back and nothing more. He didn't even bother to go round the group with names. Which left me in the awkward position of introducing myself. As in: "Hey, I'm Chase. I'll be climbing K2 with you. What's your name?" I just don't think Bill thought of small gestures like that. He was too busy running his expedition machine up the Baltoro Glacier in his mind. Alan from Seattle, Nick from Denver, Luther, who did something with natural gas, from Wyoming—those were the other three.

We spent the rest of the day packing gear into bags, and the next morning, we loaded onto a bus bound for Skardu. A bus is a different kind of beast there. If you were to take an old Bedford flatbed truck, put it at the bottom of a lake for a year, bring it up, clean it off, paint it with rainbow sherbet, and plaster it all over with butterflies and epic poetry, you'd have a start. But then you'd still need to weld the double-decker platform onto the back, where the eight of us wedged in with all our gear plus two old women in head-to-toe black, hauling baskets of trussed chickens. We never did figure out who they were or what they were doing on a bus that Bill had supposedly hired just for the team.

Our liaison officer showed up an hour late. He had a daypack, a hard-sided rolling suitcase, a pith helmet, and a swagger stick. When he walked up to the bus, he thwacked it with his stick—I'm not sure whether he was testing its structural integrity or hoping to change it into a Mercedes—and said: "Now we will show the mountains what we are made of, no?"

The heat was alive back there. The sky looked like wet wool, and that's what the air felt like—hot, damp, and rotten. Smothering. It was the Magical Mystery Tour meets the Joads—eleven people and seven chickens packed into a tin box perched on top of a psychedelic bus bumping and grinding through Rawalpindi. Donkey carts held up traffic. Old men with long white beards on bicycles dodged in and out of the gridlock. Entire families with their groceries held on to fifty-cc Swingline motorbikes—dad up front, mom hanging off the back, kids on the handlebars. Some tour busses filled with freaked-out-looking white people lumbered toward Islamabad. Everyone else honked and jockeyed and waved their hands around. It was all a negotiation, like haggling over an apricot at the bazaar. No one seemed to care that they could get where they were going faster if they just got out and walked. I felt feverish. The mid-morning call to prayer echoed out of the mosques. The women in black chattered back and forth and laughed and poked each other's knees through their burkas. They had comfortable seats. The liaison officer sat across from them with his legs crossed and his arms out and a big grin. He had huge, bright white teeth. He had a comfortable seat. Where had they gotten so much space? I was balled up in a corner like dirty laundry. Bill kept looking around and giving us all the thumbs-up. Gregor had told me that if I was smart, I'd stay up all night the night before. Now I knew why. He was snoring on top of the ropes duffle.

We were on the bus thirty hours. When we got to Skardu, I wasn't even sure I'd be able to walk. For thirty hours, I had been breathing road dust, pot reek, diesel fumes, ripe sweat. Even though it was still damp and hot, the air up there tasted so good. It was like being resuscitated. I stumbled around, just remembering how to breathe. The LO, whose name was Shafiq, but who we all called Captain, *ambled* next to me.

"Mister Chase," he said. "Are you not very small?" I admitted that I was undersized. "But should you not be a large strapping man like Mister Bill in order to climb mountains?" I told him that Bill would make a bigger target when the mountain started throwing things at us. He chortled, and just for a moment, the buffoon look vanished off his face and he said, "Mister Bill makes a very fine target for a mountain, does he not?" Then it was like he caught himself, and his eyes went dumb and happy again, and he twirled his ridiculous stick and walked away whistling.

Skardu isn't Boulder, but it could be Moab. Restaurants. Gear shops. Guide companies. Tour groups. We had journeyed into deepest northern Pakistan, but it was the least foreign place I'd seen yet. It looked like it should be foreign—up on the hills above town, there were homes that were basically dugouts closed up with sticks—but town was filled with white people and badly translated Urdu in a bunch of European languages. Eight Norwegian women with short shorts, ponytails, and sunglasses propped on their heads sat in a teahouse on the center street. A German expedition headed the same way as us was making a lot of noise and not very much progress packing porter-loads. An American expedition to Masherbrum was just leaving. Four French snowboarders were planning a first descent on Broad Peak. Some scruffy Poles sat on the ground against a wall smoking cigarettes, and I thought of what Gregor had said and wanted to go join them. But I still wanted to play my part, too, I guess, so I didn't. There were Spaniards walking around arm-in-arm singing soccer anthems—I think that's what they were singing. Big raindrops came down in bunches. There was concrete along the main road, but everything behind was dirt, and then the foothills jumped up into the clouds.

Everything on the main road looked hasty. People and buildings. Unfinished concrete. Jury-rigged electrical wires strung roof-to-roof, hanging down in the street. Back from the road, time ran backward. Go one block, and you stepped back a century. Two blocks, two centuries. Much further, and you lost a thousand years.

With all the foreigners around, there were guys lined up to sell stuff to us—expedition pimps, basically, which is what we called them. Food, porters, gear, vodka, hash. There were porters milling around—hundreds of them, and there still weren't enough. Bill planned on using a hundred and forty porters just for our expedition, and there was no way we were going to find that many in Skardu with all the other expeditions there too.

Nick took out the Pelican laptop case and got to work updating the expedition blog by satellite. Bill ruffled his hair, watched over his shoulder, dictated. He was pleased. "One hundred and eighty-two hits since yesterday," he announced, which was our cue to clap. Here was a man who owned a goddamn empire, but he was slumming for a couple hundred bored armchair mountaineers to read about his expedition and wait for the mountain to start killing people. Here was one of his principles at work: "The only thing that matters is that it's happening right *now*." That's Bill. He was always performing, and there was more than one audience. He could be vicious, too. Sometimes he got slit-eyed and furious, and I never knew whether he was playing that or not.

Gregor and I, with Captain Shafiq, had the job of buying porter rations. Hundreds of pounds of dahl, ghee, rice. And six goats. That was important, Frank told me, for morale. What the hell did I know about choosing goats? If expedition morale was going to ride on my goats, I'd have preferred a more experienced goatherd. I had a pouch around my neck uncomfortably stuffed with rupees. Captain told me not to worry. "They will try to trick you, cheat you, bully you, and swindle you," he said, in his cheerful singsong. "But they will not mug you." I asked him why not. I mean, wouldn't you? Pale infidels show up in your valley with sweaty wads of money—more money than you'll earn in a lifetime—and they've got machines and gear that might as well be from Mars. And for what? To walk past you and try not to die on mountains. But they could just as easily try not to die on mountains in Skardu. So, Captain, why not? "Mister Chase," he said, "poverty does not turn men into animals. Meanness and meaninglessness are what make animals." And the goofy bastard was right. And I still might have snatched the money.

Negotiations began on a dirt floor in a wood hut with china teacups. Half an hour later, Gregor was snorting like a bull with his hands rolled up into enormous fists, Captain was screaming, eyes bulging, sweat pouring down his face, and the dahl man was crying and invoking Allah, which was the only word I could understand the whole time. In another half hour, we signed a receipt with all the pomp and mutual congratulations of a new-made Palestinian peace treaty. And then we joked back and forth and drank more tea on the ground. When we left, I asked the Captain how we had done. "Who can say?" he said. "It is not your money or my money or his food."

We spent the night in the K2 Hotel, and the next morning, an aging squad of Land Rovers was ready to take us and our expanding pyramid of supplies to the end of the road—Askole. The road couldn't have been more than two inches wider than the Land Rovers—cliff on one side, air on the other. All dirt and crumbling edges. Then we stopped again and rounded up more porters and more supplies. Feeding an expedition is like some sort of nightmare paradox. For each porter, you need another porter to carry food for the first porter and a third porter to carry food for the second.

I was so antsy, those days. I wanted to *move*. In California, in Canada, Alaska, everything you do moves you closer to the mountain. You can feel yourself pulling closer. But I had been sitting in buses and haggling over goats with bags of money tied around my neck. And all of that was an experience, but none of it felt like mountaineering. I hadn't even been for a run since Banning, let alone done any climbing. And I could see how the others were dealing with the time—Bill with his commands, read each morning to us from a list he'd made the night before, Frank and Hubert with their mantras and tea, Alan with his big talk and Norwegian girlfriends, Gregor with sleep—the man was amazing, he could sleep eighteen hours a day if nothing was going on. But what did I have to fall back on? All I knew was the climbing itself. I wasn't any good at not climbing.

What I'm trying to say is that I was hardly in my right mind when this big tan Oregonian named Wind came walking up to me in Askole. He'd picked his name himself, he told me proudly, and grown into it. No last name. He had a fuzzy blond beard and fuzzy blond dreads coiling off his head like snakes. He wasn't one for inter-personal barriers—he'd wrap an arm around you just to say "good morning." His clothes were kaleidoscopic. Like a Pakistani bus. Impossible to tell where the old cloth ended and the patches began. But the stitches were all neat and small. He talked high and quavery, and it sounded all wrong, like size-seven shoes on a six-foot guy. Maybe he was twenty-five, maybe older, I was never sure.

I asked him where he was from. "I started out as a little newt in Camas," he said. "I've been crawling along ever since." A newt? What? "Dude, you know, a newt? The lizards that like creeks? They look like fetuses." No, I told him, they don't. "Sure do," he said. "Black eyes like glass. Half-webbed fingers. Kind of wrinkled and smooth at the same time. Take another look." I asked him where all he had been. Up in the hills, he told me. Praying with the monks. What for? He wasn't sure. He hadn't gotten that far. "Those guys are pretty seriously quiet, you know." For someone so hard all over—he was a stone tower—his mouth was weirdly wide. It flapped. There was something rubbery about his lips, something gross. Loose lips for making loose thoughts, I told myself. So what was he doing now? "Waiting for you," he said. But not for me specifically. He was waiting until there were enough people moving up the trail toward the mountains. He didn't have a permit, and he needed cover.

Captain came up to me later and asked me who the man with the dreadlocks in his hair was. I told him he was with the American team going to Masherbrum. Captain suggested that he did not look much like a mountain climber. I allowed that the fellow was unique. "I like you, Mister Chase," he said. "Please do not put me in a difficult position." Trouble was, I liked him too. In fact, I liked him better than I liked Wind. But he was a captain or a major or whatever in the Pakistani *army*. His job was to watch us. To make we sure we didn't take pictures of bridges or climb mountains outside our permit or pass messages to India, I guess. And Wind was—what? The pure wanderer. A miracle. He made me feel rooted, attached to my baggage and my position in Bill's machine. What made him so goddamned free? He didn't seem to be struggling at all! I was mesmerized by him. Like suddenly seeing a wooly mammoth.

The next morning, we were supposed to begin walking up the Braldu Valley. Eight climbers, the Captain, and 141 porters. It took us three hours just to get started. All we had to do was give each porter a load, a pair of sunglasses, and shoes. You put a hundred Americans together, and a line just magically appears. We do it unconsciously, without even talking. But a hundred Pakistanis look and sound like three hundred. A scrum of hands and voices, shouts, laughter, grasping fingers. It was a mob. I thought a riot was on, though I didn't know what for, but in between translating Bill's hollering, Captain assured me it was quite normal.

The valley started out brown and a little green, but huge. Mound over mound of brown river-cut hills, bigger than our mountains. The water looked like dirty silver. Massive and fast. God, we were small in that place. We weren't supposed to carry anything—we were supposed to be saving ourselves for the real work ahead. But it made me uncomfortable to have half-naked locals doubled over with my gear while I strutted around with a daypack and a camera. I wasn't used to anyone doing anything for me in the mountains. I didn't much like it. I wasn't there to be waited on. I live in the basement—by choice, I know—but I didn't know how to behave around someone living below me. When's the last time I even ate at a restaurant? I don't get served. But it didn't bother the others. Frank would've happily let the porters untie his shoes for him in the evening. He was just a half-century late for that treatment. I caught him mumbling "coolies" to himself one day on the trail, trying the sound out in different ways, rolling it around his mouth like he was tasting the word. He shrugged, grinned at me, said that he belonged in a simpler time.

He made my skin crawl, not really so much because he was volunteering his services as a plantation owner, which just seemed outlandish, but because he assumed the white guys were all friends. I wasn't feeling friendly. I asked him how far back he'd want to go. He thought about it for a moment, treated it as a serious question.

"Nineteen twenty-three," he said. "Imperialism falling apart, sure. That only seems fair. But I'd prefer to call a coolie a coolie and not pretend otherwise. After the first World War, but with good years to go before the second. A year before Mallory and Irvine died on Everest. The mountains still all brand-new. That would have been the time to be in the Himalaya."

And I was implicated in this. Wasn't I using the locals the same as him? Sure, shower them with paper currency, Tylenol, antibiotics. If the pills don't work, they can wipe with the paper. Did that change the fact that we were driving them like glorified donkeys?

We were a small country. The rich and powerful doing bizarre stuff at the top while the workers labored at the bottom. And it worked, just like in real life. The porters never said: Screw this, what a waste, I could feed my family for three months with what I've got on my back. They wouldn't even have had to riot. They could have just walked home. What could we have done to stop them? And our little republic of America wasn't alone. Germany was on the move that day, too, and we caught up with Italy the next day. So it was complete chaos. A few dozen white people all speaking different languages trying to herd hundreds of brown people down a trail six inches wide and five hundred feet above a river like a roaring freight train.

My fever spiked somewhere along here, and I started shitting green goo. Hubert tutted over me, fed me pills, scolded me for exerting myself so pointlessly. I stumbled along during the day because I didn't want to be left and because I was certain that somewhere up ahead was a mountain that I had come around the world to climb. Wind stuck with me in those days. He helped me along when I was in a bad way. Kept me steady when the path was crumbling right into the Braldu Gorge. "Careful there, chief," he'd say, and he'd keep his hand on my shoulder. Tucked me in at night when I was half out of my mind with fever dreams. Kept me drinking water and eating rice, which was the one thing that seemed to stay in me. I was grateful, but it was also embarrassing. Here I was, the mighty mountaineer, come to duke it out with the most dangerous mountain in the Himalayas. And I could barely stay on the trail on the approach. And there was Wind, looking like a lumberjack dressed as a court jester, with no plan or experience—he'd just decided it would be cool to see the mountains. And he was the one taking care of me.

Of the bad nights, I only remember things in snatches. We roasted one of the goats, and Bill cut it up, giving the porters each a sliver of meat. Bill waved this giant knife around and bellowed enthusiastically and asked each porter what cut he'd like, even though they couldn't understand him and he didn't care anyway. There was a huge fire—flames ten feet high, shadows, glowing faces, singing and dancing. Gregor stomped out some kind of Russian jig that made the porters wild. Even Luther and Alan got up and pranced around. Wind was sitting shoulder to shoulder with the porters eating goat. I don't know how he got his hands on a portion. I don't think he knew more than six words of Urdu, but it didn't seem to be a problem. Somehow he was still joking with the porters, slapping them on the knees and getting the same in return. But he never forgot himself, either. He always had twenty yards' separation from Bill and the Captain. During the dancing, Captain charged him from the other side of the bonfire, like some kind of flanking maneuver, winding up his stick like he was going to impale Wind, but Wind rolled backward into the dark and disappeared while the porters cheered.

There was trash everywhere from past expeditions. Maybe some of them didn't care, but most, I think, were just too desperate to get away to pay attention to their garbage. Anyway, Wind had been scavenging. He found a shredded backpack that he fixed up the same way as his pants. Piece by piece, he accumulated clothes as we moved higher and the temperature dropped. A mouse-bit sock here, a dirty sweater there, a strip of Gore-Tex that he sewed on to a shirt to start a jacket. He had stiff competition—the locals were the ultimate recyclers, and the expedition junkyards were like a Goodwill to them. But he was ingenious, and the sand was always shifting and exposing new leavings. One scrap at a time, he added insulation. After all, what did he really need? He drank the river water—which was basically liquid silt—straight without getting sick. I guess he had been hanging out long enough in the valleys that his guts ate the local bugs like candy. He schmoozed food from the porters who looked on him as some kind of mascot or fallen white demon or something. Maybe he stole a pinch of rice or sugar here and there—there were enough expedition kitchens, it couldn't have been noticed. What more did he need? The ground was free. The air was free.

My fever burned itself out, and I shat myself clean through. I was light as a feather. Weak, but floaty, like my bowels had shed lead. That day, we reached the Baltoro, and I could see the mountains. Great Trango Tower. Nameless Tower. Muztagh. They were beautiful. Like, I wanted to cry they looked so good. I don't know much about music—my mom used to play the piano in the house when I was growing up, but it didn't rub off on me. But sometimes I hear a sound that's pure and deep and it swells up big, fills all of Big Yellow and keeps going, and kind of makes me ache. And I'll have to turn off the radio to let the sound roll around in my head because I want it to last a while. Those mountains are like that—beautiful and scary big, uncontainable, and I had to stand there a moment and let them echo through my brain.

Alan came up to me while I was staring at Trango Tower. "You're feeling better, man, that's good," he said. He stood next to me, chin up, tan, square jaw stuck out, blond hair just the right amount disheveled. Christ, what am I saying? What did I care that he looked like Captain California? "Trango, huh?" he said. "Epic. You know what that makes me feel like?" He cupped his pecker in his hands and worked his hips. "Here, I'll show you," he said. He made a big show of whipping out his digital point-and-shoot, then held the screen over his crotch. He turned the camera on and zoomed the lens all the way out. He cracked up then, like that was the funniest thing. "Bro, it's epic out here," he said, and he slapped me on the shoulder and walked away hooting.

Wind walked with me for a while up the glacier. His pants were irregular. One leg was patched with threadbare wool, or maybe rotten burlap, I wasn't sure, but it looked like leopard-spotted camel. The other was covered in wisps of purple and green fleece. He had found a good sun shirt missing a sleeve and a stripe out of the back, and he fashioned the missing bits from duct tape and strips of a torched tent. He was still bulking up his winter coat. He was a great shaggy hulk of a guy, and he hardly knew what to do with all that strength. Earlier, I had watched him catch a rock that was bouncing down the gorge toward a porter. He just stuck out one paw and cradled this flying granite basketball. And then he looked kind of sheepish and uncomfortable while the porters made a lot of noise and he held this big rock in one hand. He took a few steps with it and then flipped it into the river.

That first day on the glacier, the ice was mostly covered in moraine rubble with paths through it from all the passing feet. A lot of the porters were still barefoot. They'd sold the shoes we'd given them in Askole. We'd sent about a quarter of the porters back already because their loads had been eaten. I asked Wind how far up the glacier he planned to go. He asked me how far it went. About fifty miles, I told him. He thought for a moment and told me that that sounded far enough. I asked him if he had even thought about his destination before the moment I'd asked. He laughed at me, rubbery lips flapping. "You mean physically or metaphysically?" he said. "Are you fooling around in the cosmic punnery?" I told him I wasn't. I just wanted to know, when he woke up in the morning, did he think about where he was headed or did he just walk?

That made him get all serious. "No difference, man. The whole point is to *move*."

Which was weird, right? Because the whole time, I had been wanting to move, too. But I wanted to move *toward* something—the summit—and Wind just wanted to *move*. I wanted the destination, and he wanted the action itself—a pure desire for the world to turn under his feet. And it had gotten him to the same place I had gotten to. Here we both were. Only he had no baggage. No obligations to Bill's list. No army of porters carrying his belongings. No obligations to the mountain up ahead or the hubris in his own mind. Of course, the porters *were* carrying him, just like they were carrying me. I was the class above the workers, and he was the class below them. If it had been 1923 and the mountains empty, he would have been stuck on the outside unless he press-ganged his own coolies or found a way to live on the river water alone. Which made me consider my life stateside, which only works because there are farmers growing cheap food and people paying taxes to maintain the roads. Course, it's no different for Alan. Jerking off in the stock market doesn't produce anything but his own juices. It's not like he's making anything but money.

Wind told me that he didn't think Bill cared for him. I asked him what gave him that idea. "He reminds me of my dad," he said. "He pays attention to all the wrong things."

I didn't really see the connection: "You think he doesn't like you because he reminds you of your dad?"

"Sure. I totally offend his sense of order."

I suggested that maybe it was because Captain Shafiq wanted Wind thrown out of the Karakorum but couldn't get his hands on him and kept threatening our permit instead. "I know!" he said. "It's like war games with him! He makes me feel like I'm some kind of international criminal." I reminded him that he *was* an international criminal. I'm not even sure he had a passport. I don't know where he would have kept it. His pants—at least the pants I first saw him in—didn't have pockets. He'd named himself well. He passed right through the cracks in the walls. But what I said seemed to make him unhappy. Bill wasn't the only one paying attention to the wrong stuff. What difference could him being here possibly make to Captain Shafiq? What difference did he make at all? All he wanted was to roam around some. So maybe he should have joined Frank in 1923 after all.

The mountains crowded around the open strip of glacier. Too many to count. Pick one at random and stick it down in California, and climbers would come running from all over the hemisphere. But over there, it might not even have a name. They *erupted* out of the glacier. Rock and ice spikes shot straight up from below. We were colorful little lice crawling all over the glacier, shitting and scattering trash, and the summits watched us from ten thousand feet above, cold, sharp points that made me feel soft and vulnerable like shish kebab meat.

Luther asked me about Wind the next day, and what could I say? That he was an elemental gas that should be left to blow around in peace? That he was going to get us all kicked out of the Karakorum? Luther and I ended up walking together for a few hours. I'd hardly talked to him yet. He was pole-thin, always frowning, bones sticking out of his cheeks, but he seemed more serious than unhappy. Dark eyes—hard to tell the pupil apart from the rest. He hardly ever laughed at other people's jokes—like, he wouldn't have even bothered to notice Alan's antics, and Alan knew that, so the two got along just fine. But every once in a while, this huge Cheshire grin would split his face, usually when no one else was laughing, when he had discovered some private irony in what was going on. Sometimes the first sign that you'd said something funny was Luther's moon-grin staring back at you.

Luther called Wind a "fleabag hobo"—as in, "whatcha know about that fleabag hobo?" The mountain, K2, our mountain, had come into view dead ahead. We had been walking through a place that felt musical and unreal, but K2 was where the music stopped. Its shape was too abstract. It was its own abstraction. All straight lines and menace. Unrelenting. What did I know about Wind? What did I care? I'd finally seen the mountain. I'd finally seen something that scared me scalp to toe. Something so huge and implacable that I had trouble looking at it. It filled me up, made it hard to breathe—it was getting harder to breathe anyway. The advantages were all on its side. This is what I'd come for. I didn't care about anything else. I told Luther that Wind was just a guy wandering through.

"Yeah?" Luther said to me. "You two seemed kind of tight. I figured you'd known him from somewhere before." I told him that I didn't know him at all. But I repeated what Wind had said about Bill reminding him of his dad. Luther agreed. He thought Bill was a titan. He misunderstood Wind's meaning completely. He said he thought Bill should run for president. He said that was why he climbed with Bill whenever he could. With him, he felt safer; he thought the odds of getting home went up. My dad wasn't around too much when I grew up. Maybe that's why I didn't know how to act around Bill.

Luther asked me if I had eaten any of the goat the other night, but I had been too sick. It turned out that when Luther wasn't climbing mountains or pulling natural gas out of the ground in Wyoming, he traveled around shooting things and eating them. He'd eaten grizzly in Alaska, python in Brazil, waterbuck, hippo, in Tanzania. "Now, your roo—I mean your wild roo—has got a real strong flavor," he told me. "It's not for everyone. Too wild." And I'm thinking, wild roo? Is there any other kind? Do they have herds of them somewhere?

"It kicks," he said, "in your mouth. Taste follows form—ain't that cool?" I asked him whether, if he had the chance, he would eat human. I mean, there are places it still happens. If you were there and it was dead already, wouldn't you be curious?

Anyway, Luther grinned at me. "The long pig," he said. "Sometimes it's called that. Hard to say till it's on your plate, but I guess I would. People get consumed all kinds of ways." The guys he employed—they knew and he knew that roughnecking was taking years off their lives. He thought he might as well do the consuming when the body was dead rather than alive. "Probably worse getting killed than getting eaten," he said. I told him I'd keep that in mind if we got pinned up high. He said not to worry, I was too small to mess with. And then—how could we help it?—we spent a half hour under those toothy mountains speculating about which member of the team would be tastiest—we chose Nick—and how he could be best prepared in a high-altitude tent with a single-burner stove.

Basecamp was a city complete with neighborhoods, block parties, crime. There was the Italian village, the French Quarter, the Serbian ghetto, a gated community of thousand-dollar Japanese mansions up on a step in the moraine. Everyone was there, and we were all converging on the same route. It was a bleak, cold place. No shelter. The mountain staring down all the time. Big black ridgelines cutting through the ice. An enormous, ugly icefall crawled toward us, crevasses open wide. We were running around in a slow-motion scene from a monster movie, the mountain coming at us.

We sent the last of the porters—except for a guy named Dho, who would cook and watch basecamp for us—home with their rupees and cigarettes. They dumped their loads in a big pile that would become our camp, then raced down laughing and shouting, glad to get away. Part of me wanted to join them, but another part reveled in it, watching them. I'd gotten to a place that normal people ran away from, but I was staying.

We hardly had a choice spot. All of those were already taken. What was left was shit and sharp rocks. Toilet paper blowing around and fungating out from under stones. Bill was pissed. There were more climbers than he had expected, and some were already established to Camp 2. And more were on the way. Captain assured him that several teams were coming up the Braldu, and maybe more coming over from the Chinese side, even as we unpacked our loads in the shit fields.

Bill took it out on Wind. He finally caught up to him in the Italian camp, where Wind was pantomiming to a couple of insulted-looking guys with dark faces and hair who seemed totally uninterested in trying to understand what this crazy American caveman was saying. It was a train wreck. Wind had his back to us and was trying to make himself understood. He kept gesturing at the mountain. Bill came up behind him. I could have yelled something. It would have been easy. All he had to do was turn around. But I didn't. Captain was standing right next to me, eyes glowing. And what was he to me, anyway? Bill grabbed him by the dreads with one hand and threw a half nelson around his shoulder with the other and dragged him back. The Italians slapped each other's shoulders and laughed. Wind could have fought back—he was just as big as Bill and probably broader. But he just flopped around and pedaled his feet while Bill yanked him around and presented him to Captain like a recovered prisoner.

The Captain puffed up to twice his size. I thought he was going to burst buttons and blood vessels. He harangued and spat and switched Wind's legs with his stick. Half of Wind's hair was in Bill's fist, and the other half was in his face, and he twisted around when the stick hit him but did nothing to get loose. Bill grinned huge, veins popping in his neck and forearms. I was sick. From the ugliness of it and the rest of us standing around spectating while the Italians called their buddies over to watch. And also from a feeling that Wind wasn't afraid enough of this place, and he should be. Eventually Captain began to run out of steam, and I think we all wanted to know what was going to happen then. What was he going to do? Call in air support to deport a fleabag hobo? Handcuff him to his own wrist and wait for some corporal to hike up and retrieve him? Turn right around and march him back down the glacier? He grabbed Wind by the collar, hauled him to the edge of camp—which looked ridiculous, like a golden Lab collaring a rottweiler—then put his foot against the seat of Wind's pants and kicked hard, as if he could punt him all the way back to Askole. Wind tumbled down through the snow-covered moraine rocks. Bill and the Captain stood side by side and watched as Wind picked himself up and walked away down toward Concordia. They watched him ten, fifteen minutes, till he disappeared.

There was something a little spooky about how the first storm came up then. The mountain had suffered us to look at it all day, and maybe looking back, it didn't like what it saw. The moment Wind was out of sight, the real wind came up—like Bill had traded one for the other—and black clouds started foaming up out of the clear sky. The Italians vanished into their tents. First we had hail, then snow, falling practically sideways. We ran around throwing tents up, moving rocks, scraping shit away and only unearthing more, getting tarps over the food and the gear.

Bill was manic, wild. He was laughing and throwing rocks around to make tent platforms but not bothering to look where the rocks were going. It wasn't safe to go anywhere near him. The snow collected in his hair until he was wooly with it. He didn't need gloves— later I saw him barehand gear at twenty-three thousand feet without flinching and no frostbite.

By the time we were all inside, we were soaking wet and stuff was strewn all over in random tents and piles under tarps. None of us knew where anything was. I was in a tent with Gregor. He told me a story about an expedition to Nanda Devi where they spent the first eight days in the tents arguing about Bruce Springsteen lyrics while a monster storm dropped nine feet of snow on them. They didn't even see the mountain during the first month they were there. And then he went to sleep. I lay there on my back staring at the roof of the tent, which was rocking and popping in the storm. I had my own sleeping bag, but a bag of someone else's clothes was shoved down by my feet, and a wad of soggy down suits fought me for space. I felt wrung out. The altitude was making me fuzzy in the head, and being sick had sucked something out of me. I'm used to feeling sharp, you know, jagged, ready to bite down on the mountain and not let go. But I just felt weak and unplugged. It was no good, the state I was in. And I hadn't even done anything yet.

The storms hit us on and off for the next two weeks. You could practically watch the pressure ridges come and go. We'd get thirty-six hours of heavy weather and then twelve or twenty-four hours of clear. We'd try to work in the gaps, but someone was always getting caught and pitching into a tent half frozen in the middle of a white-out. Sometimes visibility was so bad it was hard to make out which tents were which. You'd get yourself in and try to bring yourself back to life and check and see if your toes were all there and then notice that the colors inside were all pink and green and the paperbacks in Italian. And sometimes you'd just stay, then, because they were probably somewhere else on the mountain and it was raging outside. Which was all well and good until you got back to your own tent and found that the chocolate-chip cookies had been cleaned out by some unknown foreign national. Luther kept petitioning the Captain for the right to carry a gun, said the mountain was infested with bandits.

I spent most of those first two weeks shuttling loads to our advanced basecamp and up to Camp 1. From ABC to Camp 1 was the worst kind of work. A vertical scree field covered in melting slush from the storms. Rocks falling down all the time, either from people moving around above or the mountain tossing stuff down. Impossible to move fast with sixty pounds of food, gas, ropes, hardware on your back. The whole time waiting for a rock to choose you for its bull's-eye. Camp 1 was pretty safe from avalanche, but it was exposed and was our first taste of big wind up high, up on a narrow shoulder with big drops on both sides, tents sunk down in the snow. The middle was already crowded, so the two tents we put there were perched right on the edge.

Gregor and I worked as a pair. He was a beast. He could haul ten pounds more than me and still leave me behind. But Bill knew that, and just before we'd get going, he'd say, "Hey, Stump, can you take this rope, too?" Or this last stove and fuel bottle. Or Nick's down pants because he's up there and forgot them. And what could Gregor say? No? I'm not that strong? I need to pace myself? That wasn't in his personality. So he'd end up with eighty pounds on his back, and by the end of the day, he'd be beat or struggling through the beginning of the next storm.

I didn't like getting caught in storms, and I was a miserable donkey. I started leaving things out of my pack. I'd "forget" a bag of soup packets or a fuel bottle—hide them away somewhere they wouldn't be noticed. I felt like such an asshole when Gregor would come stumbling into the tent an hour after me. I'd make him dinner, keep the stove going for water. But I wasn't dumb. Bill gave us our jobs. At first we were all ferrying stuff to Camp 1. Then he and Nick, then Frank and Luther, pushed us higher while Gregor and I kept hauling loads. Pretty soon, it'd be my turn at the front, and I wasn't going to get there spent. I wanted to be ready.

It was a circus up there. People going up, people going down, people going back and forth between the camps. Getting in each other's way and knocking rocks on each other. Half the time, I couldn't understand anyone around me. We were all attached to this mountain together, and we couldn't even talk to each other. And every other day, the weather would explode, and we'd all go underground in one tent hole or another dug by someone we might not even have known. And the next day, we'd be back on the surface, crawling all over each other and the mountain.

Everything I'd done in Alaska had been about speed. Get yourself acclimatized, catch your weather window, and *go*. Tag the summit, descend, no stopping. Up and done in thirty, forty hours. This was something totally different, and all of my instincts resisted the grind. But it was *different* there—Frank had told me that. You can't just step into the ring and be the warrior the way you can with a hard pitch in Yosemite or a mixed route in the Rockies. The mountain was too big and high for that. It felt alien, like something thrown from a star.

Weird stuff started happening. The Italians went to war with the Serbs over a pair of ascenders that went missing. There were so many people up on the mountain at any given time—headed up, headed down, carrying loads, fixing more rope. It was impossible to tell who was who. But there was a feeling that there were more people than there should have been. You'd tally up the people you'd seen in a day and the number never quite made sense. And bodies started coming up out of the glacier. You know, people die up there, and who's going to carry them out? Most of the bodies end up getting put down crevasses. But now bodies were coming back out. You'd see a new dark spot way away somewhere, and sure enough, it would turn out to be an ejected corpse. And it was disturbing, sure, but we were all pushing hard on half oxygen and there was only so much we could think about. The Germans had held onto some high-altitude porters—the local version of Sherpas—and those guys were telling Yeti stories. Said they'd seen something shaggy in a storm and found tracks and fur.

My turn finally came. Luther and Frank had gotten us to Camp 2. Gregor had gone down with pain under his kneecap. I told him he'd be fine in a day, be right back up, and I put an arm around him, but he only shrugged at me—those big shoulders of his rolled me right off—and I couldn't tell where he was pointing his disappointment. What could I say? I'd only known the guy a month. He wasn't my brother. Hubert helped him down to basecamp and tended to him. Luther and Frank were on their way down, too, and Alan and Nick were at basecamp already, so Bill and I took the front. "Ready, boy?" he said, and I just gave him the finger, which wasn't very meaningful since I had on mittens.

Luther and Frank had fixed ropes most of the way from Camp 1 to Camp 2. But then, so had the Germans, the Serbs, the Japanese, everyone who was up there. And it seemed that every expedition for the past thirty years had left its ropes in place, bleached white cords all tangled together. "Look at this rat-work," Bill said, like he was personally offended. "Someone's going to die in this—don't let it be you." As if that was going to really screw up his efforts, here, if he had to disentangle my corpse from the cobwebs of expeditions passed.

It was ugly, no doubt. I could hardly even see House's Chimney behind the ropes matted in front if it. We're at twenty-one thousand feet, nothing but razor lines all around, rock and ice. Past your crampons, you could look straight down four thousand feet of the South Face to the Godwin Austen Glacier. But up on the ridge, we were bushwhacking through vines—it was a jungle. One of those ropes was ours, but which one? And what did it matter? The anchors were all mixed up together anyway, nests of pitons and slings, some new, some old, the Germans' and the Japanese's interconnected with ours because there were only so many places to put them. And we all had different ideas about how cozy we were. The Italians would jump on the first rope they saw: new, old, theirs, ours, it didn't seem to matter to them. The Germans were hyper-possessive and would scream at anyone who even looked at theirs. The Serbs were practically inviting people onto their ropes, but we figured out that they wanted to use ours in return. Theirs looked like something you'd find on a sunken ship.

Bill and I took a day to move up to Camp 2 with a little extra food and gas. An Italian with a shredded nose—a falling brick of ice and the wrong moment to look up, as best I could understand—was being photographed grinning and bloody by his partners, and we passed them. We were caterpillars on the fixed lines, bobbing up and down on our ascenders. And everywhere below us was white and black with a little ice-blue. But up close it was the nylon web we'd made, with us caterpillaring up our strand of it, chunks of rock and ice banging down, a medium blizzard cranking away, the wind shaking the web, and Serbians coming up behind us and Japanese sliding down past us. We'd greet them and ask for news, and they must have known exactly what we were saying (Because what else would we be saying?), and they'd reply as if it were the most normal conversation in the world except they were panting for breath (just like us) and speaking Japanese.

Above Camp 2 was the Black Pyramid, and that's where the real climbing began. Steep black rock, curtains of ice pouring out between fracture planes. I don't know how hard the climbing would have been at eleven thousand feet in Canada, but up there, I got pumped just unclipping gear from my harness. Testy, friable gneiss that flaked off under my axe tips. Ice like stone—something about the wind and the altitude and the alien star-ness of the mountain turned the ice into granite, and my tools dulled fast.

Bill and I led in blocks. I'd take two pitches, and he'd take two pitches, and that's generally all we'd get done in a day. I began to see what Luther had said about Bill. When he climbed, he was brutal—he imposed his will on the stone in his face. It wasn't necessarily pretty to watch. He was an engine. He was relentless, just like the mountain. Legs pistoning, arms swinging. And he had a way of calling me up to account. He'd tell me to do something, and I'd jump to it and lose track of whether I was wanting to climb well to climb the mountain or to not disappoint Bill.

The junk and people started to thin out, but in places, past teams had left cables with aluminum ladder rungs clipped to blank sections. Hauling them up that high must have cost more than what they saved. Anyway, they were incredibly scary. They bounced against the rock and creaked, and I had no way to know what they were attached to at the top. But I'm light, right? And they were way faster than climbing for real. So I just tried to think pixie dust thoughts—which was pretty easy because I felt stoned by hypoxia anyway.

We never really stopped. We were moving so slow we couldn't afford to. One of us was almost always in motion. But at one belay ledge, we ate a little food together and had some water. It was dead calm, which felt unreal. Bill was shining. He was in his place. He was seven feet tall. He looked out west and said, "See where the land goes brown?" We could just see the color change on the horizon. "That's for the sheep." He was a god, and he was welcoming me into his domain.

We got passed by a couple of Chinese. They had simply snuck onto the German ropes and were fixing their own at each new anchor. Bill roared at them. I'm not sure he even bothered making words—maybe he figured they wouldn't understand him anyway—but the meaning to the sound was something like: Dirty dogs, you're cheating, and the summit won't recognize you. The Chinese said hello and good afternoon in impeccable songbird English and went right on ahead. If they understood Bill at all, they must have been perplexed because we were using the ladders same as everyone and if we got to something really hard we'd use another team's fixed lines for twenty or thirty feet, too. It was impossible not to. Who's going to risk broken bones at seven thousand meters when there's a rope dangling five feet to your right? It turned out that we were all pragmatists; the Chinese were just taking pragmatism to its obvious extreme.

It took us three days to fix lines to Camp 3. Each morning we'd get up, spend an hour making water and an hour struggling into our boots, gaiters, jackets, gloves, and crampons. My vision would swim just bending over to put on a boot. That was the worst part of the day. By the time we were out and moving, I didn't feel so clumsy or stupid anymore, and the climbing woke me fully up, not jittery, just wide awake. I was feeling good. The mountain couldn't touch me: wind, blizzards, falling rocks, none of it got through below my skin. Inside I was warm and sharp. And Nick and Alan were stocking Camp 2 each day from Camp 1, so we'd get back, and there

would be a new kind of soup or candy bar waiting for us, and sometimes they'd even leave us water so we could spend less time bowed
down around the stove. I was no one's donkey. I was high above the
brown land and the brown souls. I'd been promoted—I was white-
collar now.

"Damn right," Bill said when I finished out the last hard lead
before Camp 3. "I'm making you dinner tonight." Which he did with
great ceremony, even though the preparations involved putting a
soup packet in a bowl and it was his turn anyway. He said he had big
plans for me. He wanted me to join his Makalu expedition in a year.

Once we had the ropes to Camp 3, it was Nick and Alan's turn at
the front. Bill and I planned to drop down to basecamp for a day to
get some oxygen back into our bodies. Bill headed down first thing
and left me to melt water for Nick and Alan. It took all morning,
but I didn't mind because it meant taking my time and not worry-
ing about the minutes I was fumbling away. The stove was as sleepy
as I was, and the ice I wanted to melt barely budged. I stared at the
flame in a totally enjoyable stupor waiting for the ice to give up and
wondering how to distinguish high-altitude lethargy from carbon
monoxide poisoning.

When I had milked out a couple of lukewarm bottles and stashed
them in a sleeping bag, I called it good and headed down. A trickle
of people were on their way up to Camp 2, up fixed lines alternating with well-tracked snow, but I was in my own bubble and didn't
even try to talk. I passed maybe seven or eight people in ones and
twos. Another guy came up ahead of me in the snow. He was tall, in
a red jacket and black pants, badly scratched glacier glasses, black

balaclava—no skin showing, not that any of us were showing any skin we wanted to keep. He was *lumpy* under his outer layers, and something opened up in my mind, like I had understood all along but just hadn't bothered to look. The snow was steep enough that when we pulled up in front of each other, we were face-to-face. I reached out and pulled down the mask of his balaclava and found a blond beard and pair of loose, rubbery lips grinning back at me.

"Chase, my man," he said.

He was happy to have someone to talk to, happy to be able to share his little joke. He had been going up and down the mountain with us all along; there *had* been an extra climber up there after all. I asked him about the bodies. "Fishing," he said, but then he stopped and looked uneasy, like he didn't know whether I'd find that funny. He needed boots. I didn't know whether to laugh or scream. "Shouldn't have left them out," he said. "They were hard to get at, and I didn't know what else I'd need." He perked up. "Got my jacket that way, too. I haven't really stolen very much."

I didn't care that much about the bodies. I mean, what good were they doing anyone down a crevasse? It really was pretty funny. But what was his *plan*? I wanted to know how far he was going to take this. Did he know where he was? He might as well have been in Islamabad or San Diego. "Never knew mountain climbing was such a cinch." That's what he said. "Once you got the clamps on the ropes, there's nothing to it." Everything he did he just copied. He didn't understand anything.

I didn't have an answer for him. One part of me wanted to turn right around and follow him up the mountain, and the other wanted to kick him back to Askole myself. He'd cut off all his hair so it wouldn't show. Which explained the yeti fur, too. I asked him whether Bill and the Captain had hurt him. He laughed—remember, it was more like a whinny coming out of him, a balloon squeaking. He said that was just some theater. He'd gotten tired of being watched all the time. I wanted to topple him backward out of the steps. I had felt bad for him! I could see his body tumbling down off the ridge and going airborne off the South Face—and that's what he should have been imagining, too, because I never stopped seeing that happen to myself the entire time I was up there. I noticed that his harness—another item he'd stripped off a corpse, I presumed—was on all wrong. I bent down and rethreaded his leg loops. He stood there at attention like I was doing him up for school.

"Thanks, bud," he said. "Gotta go—more guys coming." He crushed me with one arm and then pushed past. Just another Gore-Tex lump lurching up the mountain on the steps we'd all kicked in the snow.

He couldn't be gotten rid of. Bill and the mountain were relentless, but so was he. How could you push back against him? He slipped through your fingers without you even knowing he'd done it. The mountain didn't touch him. He was taking boots off the bodies the mountain had made and then going right back up to where the mountain had made them! If the mountain couldn't drive him off, how could the rest of us be expected to? He had said that some Italians shouted at him at Camp 1, once, but he couldn't understand them, so he just ignored them. And what were they going to do? Throw him off the mountain? Haul him down themselves? We could barely drag our own bodies up and down—none of us were going to pull him down, too.

I descended—I was dazed. I was dumbstruck by Wind. Somehow, he was bigger than any of the rest of us. He was nobler, truer to the fuck-all roots of alpinism. In his own way, he was the only purist among us. He wasn't constrained by anything but the desire to go up high and see the world. Which is what climbing mountains should be all about, right? But I had made my place in Bill's machine, and I wasn't ready to give that up. So I couldn't follow Wind, and I didn't want to. He was a rubber-lipped hippie, and he made me queasy: the sight of him, the *fact* of him. I was opposed to him. I had to be. The higher he got up the mountain, the cheaper my efforts looked. He didn't know anything about what he was doing, and I was supposed to be a badass. But I also knew that maybe he had more of the genuine spirit than the rest of us.

So I was in a foul mood when I got back to basecamp. Gregor came out and met me a half hour outside camp. His knee was improving; he wanted to hear all about the climbing on the Black Pyramid. He brought me hot curried rice and dahl, and I had been living on powdered soup for ten days, so it tasted amazing. And I tried not to be too much of a bastard to him because lord knows he of all people didn't deserve it, but I was in a dark place. I felt alienated in the basecamp hubbub. I was like a newbie to a big city, who's more isolated because of all the people than he would be on his own—I'd never felt alone on a mountain, but I'd never had to share one with so many people. And that just made me feel worse because Wind was up there thriving on feeling alone, and I was luxuriating in my own basecamp with my cook and big tents and partners, feeling more than a little psychotic.

The oxygen went to Bill's head. He baited Luther into a push-up contest, right there in the snow, no gloves. They went at it face-to-face, and each time Bill came up, he had something to say: "Toy," "Limp dick," "Flower," "If you stop now, I'll have you hauling to Camp 1 for another week." When he won, he jumped up, clapped his hands, turned his back on Luther, who was flat-out in the snow, tipped his head back, and hooted—at us? At the mountain? How should I know? Luther tried to laugh it off, but he looked shaky and had to go warm up his hands in one of the tents.

Bill was happy. He was making speeches. "I've seen the mountain. She'll kill the weak. So get to your weakness first, and kill it before she does." He was frothing over. "This is living. Brothers fighting a monster. We'll have ballads pissed out about us." Ballads! That's what he wanted. But maybe he's done it—bought himself a starving poet who can urinate in cursive. He wrapped an arm around my neck. "You boys are making me proud. Best team I've had."

But I think he was an only child, just like me. I don't think he knew what it meant to be a brother. I watched the Serbs drinking together around a metal cassette deck, *Dark Side of the Moon* coming out sounding stretched and tinny, speaking more with their eyes and hands than their mouths. They made me feel like a kid. They looked old in the eyes. And amused. Like they knew that the mountain was made of dirt, and they were made of dirt, and the relative positions of the big dirt clod and the little dirt clods mattered less than nothing, and the fact that they were here at all was part of a colossal joke planted in the human mind. Best to play along and not take the joke too much to heart. They looked tribal. We didn't look anything like them. We were making so much noise! We were a nation of only children. Bill started talking about a summit bid. If Nick and Alan got up to Camp 4 and carved out a platform and left a tent, and if we started working our way back up the camps after a rest day, ferrying up a bit more food and fuel, we could be ready in five or six days.

All six of us left basecamp. Gregor and Hubert went to advanced basecamp, and Frank, Bill, Luther, and I continued to Camp 1. Two of us would have our shot at the summit, with the other two in reserve, and then it would be the reserve pair's chance. Bill didn't put names to the pairs, so we were left to wonder. Frank found this amusing, I think. He kept humming the stare-down tune from *The Good, the Bad and the Ugly*. I asked him if he had our roles assigned. He told me to look around, we were all ugly, which was right enough— shaggy, sun-scorched, zinc-smeared beast-men, all of us. Frank didn't seem at all affected by the actual question of who would be in the first summit team. Which left me and Luther to twist in the wind together. And it was blowing hard up there, though the sun was out.

The summit had become more than ordinarily important to me. I had gone so far from where I had begun. Half the planet just to climb dirt a few thousand *feet* higher than what we've got at home. Dirt swarming with monomaniacs all standing on top of pyramids of human flesh and garbage. Monomaniacs just like me. I was having trouble laughing at the joke. I looked around for Wind, and sometimes I thought I saw him, but I was never sure and never got close.

I'm sure Luther wanted the top badly, too, in his own way, though he was still talking about it as if it were a boar's head for his living room. To me, the summit had begun to feel like a pardon in the sky. Because if I didn't get the top, what would I have? No boar's head. No living room. Just me and my own head.

Back up to Camp 1, back up to Camp 2, we had two tents at each, so the four of us moved together. Nick and Alan passed us going down. They had been to Camp 4 and left a tent there and had thought about the summit but were too gassed. There was only one tent at Camp 3, so Bill had to speak his mind. He sent Luther and Frank back down to relay up another load of food and gas. Luther took the decision manfully, I guess you'd say—I mean dumb silent. What did I want from him? Rebellion? I guess I did. I wanted *someone* to rebel. He hugged me and said he'd look for my tracks on top. Frank punched his shoulder and said, "Come on, foot soldier, we've got work to do."

Camp 3 was like living in the mountain's lungs. The wind was moving all the time. It felt like a permanent avalanche without the snow. Even in the tent I was holding on, waiting for the wind to pick us up and flick us away. We could hardly talk at all during the day, but in the tent, Bill went over and over a list of the people he thought were most likely to die: the Italian with the earring, the German woman with the pointed chin, the Japanese guy with the rising-sun patch on his jacket. One was too slow, one was too sloppy, or too technically weak on ice, or too cheerful. "Did you see that toy Italian? If I were the mountain, I'd give him a little shove and see if he'd hold me then." He offered me a bet: we'd each choose five climbers, and the one who had the most die off his list would win. He was acting carnivorous. His beard had gone bushy, and his mouth was a pit flashing teeth that kept opening and closing, like he was chewing instead of speaking. Maybe he'd woken up with a hangover from his cheerfulness. I told him that the only thing I could bet with was my plane ticket home. He offered that I could include myself on my own list.

We called up basecamp on the radio and got the forecast from Captain. It was unclear. The edge of a front was sitting on us. If it moved a few miles one way, we'd be in the sun. A few miles the other, and we'd be in a stewpot of bad air. Bill broke the connection and asked me what I thought. I wasn't expecting the question. For a moment, there was nothing to listen to except for the wind while he waited for me to answer. I was so used to him commanding, it took me a moment to form an opinion. And then I had to think, was he testing me? What answer did he want? Because here was my chance to get a finger on the wheel, but for all I knew, he was just measuring me and it wouldn't matter. I told him I wasn't overly attached. "Oh ho!" he said. "You're a dangerous man." That felt good, hearing him say that. I was proud. I remember wondering if there were people making bets about us, too, and that also felt good.

So the next morning, early, we started for Camp 4. There were a few fixed lines, but mostly old and pointless. Nick and Alan hadn't left any. The snow felt big and hollow. I don't know how I knew it, sound or sense or what, but we were on a drum skin; nothing anchored the layer we were climbing to the mountain. The point was that if something came off, it was going to be so big that ropes weren't going to matter. The whole shoulder would collapse, and the sky would fill with falling snow and climbers.

Clouds swallowed us. The sun disappeared, the sky, the other mountains. It was all the same, the snow and the clouds. My mind drifted far. I went traveling in and out of time. I'd check back in on the present and remember that I should have been piss-terrified by the void I *knew* was somewhere under my feet, but instead I just drifted off again.

It started to snow. A few flakes. Nothing bad. Then a few more, shaking down pretty as Christmas. Then demons filled the sky. Howling, shrieking. All those pretty flakes turned into angry white bees. I was deep asleep at the wheel, my mind fully separated from my body, and then I was back all at once. Before too long, Bill and I were standing next to each other. We couldn't really see or hear, we were screaming over the wind, and we were pointing downward.

There wasn't any other decision to make. The storm broke out into a raging whiteout. Everything shook in the wind. The snow, the air. Me, too. It was an earthquake up there. And even still, each step I took down, I thought, no, no, no. This is my shot. Got to go up. Can't go down. But then I thought, okay, no one else is going up today either. We're not spent. Bill wants the top, too. We'll get back to the tent, we'll reload, we'll be ready for the next window. Just got to get to the tent, warm up, eat, sleep—get ready to go again.

With gravity pulling us, we were three times faster going down, even in the storm. Which was good, because the snow shredded me. A river of frozen, broken glass, that's what it seemed like. I got so cold I felt like I'd been turned inside out.

The camp was wrecked. Tents exploded by the wind. Tents collapsed by fleeing climbers so they wouldn't get exploded by the wind. But ours was standing, and we piled in. That first moment of shelter was incredible, even with the tent straining and popping. But after two seconds of mindless relief, I realized there were three of us there. Wind was in our tent. Not the wind—you see?—Wind. He was sprawled across our sleeping bags in his own greasy bag, stripped down to some corpse's stained long johns, munching on a Kit Kat I'd squirreled away for a post-summit celebration.

"Oops," he said. "Looks like it'll be a crowd tonight."

I lost it. I grabbed him. Which didn't do much because he was close to two of me. But then Bill joined me, and Wind was half pinned inside his bag even though he was flailing and struggling. I unzipped the tent with one hand, and the storm blasted in, and we rolled him out the door into the snow and threw all his Frankenstein gear after him.

For a moment, all I could do was get in my sleeping bag. We'd let in so much weather that the tent was full of snow and I was shaking with cold. I balled up inside my bag and clenched until the shivering stopped.

Outside the storm was raging. Inside Bill was raging. But I wasn't anything but cold. I'd murdered the man. You understand? You don't throw someone into a storm like that in his underwear and expect him to live. And which man had I killed? Not Alan. Not Bill.

Bill went on all night long. Most of it. I faded in and out. Some of what I thought I heard was maybe nightmare. The howling. At the storm, at Wind, at me, I don't know.

In the morning, the storm had dropped. Inside the tent, I packed up my gear. Bill told me that if I left, I was done. He still wanted to go for the top. I packed up and left.

I checked some of the collapsed tents looking for Wind or his body. In the daylight, I didn't feel any better about myself. I had bloody hands, red and fresh. Couldn't wipe them off. I didn't expect to find Wind, and I didn't. He'd gone over the edge after all. Body in pieces down on the glacier.

I worked down the fixed ropes, spoke to no one, just clipped anchors and rappelled. I grabbed as much food as I could find out of our advanced basecamp, then took a long detour on the glacier to avoid basecamp altogether. I cut myself off from all of them.

Wind's last minutes looped through my brain. A mammoth on his knees out in the blizzard without his fur. Hands like bricks straining to pull on his insulation. Eyes frozen. The edge of the ridge *right there* because that had been the only place left to put our tent. The wind stealing back the clothes he'd made, tugging them right up to the edge like baited hooks, and him chasing them around half blind.

For two days, I was a shell. A body walking around without a soul. Being alone settled me. My *I* crept back in. It didn't do anything about the guilt, but I felt like me again. I walked each morning and sat each afternoon. I watched the mountains. I'd find a rock surfing the back of the glacier and just sit and stare. White snow, grey mountains. No color. An infinite corridor of mountains like doorways. What will you see behind this door? Another reflection of yourself, stripped to your bones. I sat and tried to reacquaint myself with myself. The wind shook me down. The glacier inched me downhill. India crashed into Asia and pushed the mountains higher. I kept my mouth shut and my tongue paralyzed, afraid something important would leak out.

I put myself back in the tent. Tried to call back up what I'd felt when I went for Wind. Because, right, we all could have slept a night in there. People have crammed more bodies than that in a two-man tent and climbed the next day. But he was *trespassing*. It was my turf—*mine*. The mountain, the tent, all of it. It was East and West, Bloods and Crips. So, mirror, mirror on the wall, if he was my opposite, what did that mean for me?

Wind had said he'd been up in the hills around Askole, sitting with monks. I didn't have anywhere else to go. I couldn't fathom Islamabad, let alone Los Angeles, and I figured I could at least count on monks not to ask me questions.

After a few days looking, I found a couple dugout hovels where some toothless old men sat facing the opposite side of the Braldu Gorge. Wind's monks were like his mountaineers: strictly C-listers. They had clay bowls and hairy blankets and expedition turds: plastic bottles, T-shirts, empty Pringles cans. Maybe it was a monastery, but it could just as easily have been the local retirement home. The leathery old coots pointed and laughed at me, and I took that as a sign I could stay.

I sat for a while, days, I mean. Time seemed broken off behind me. And the future didn't come, even though the earth was turning. So I woke and slept up there in my holding cell, hoping for someone or something to hand me my sentence. Wind's monks farted and scratched and waited. I resolved to quit climbing. I'd opened that door and gone all the way through. Heart and soul. And I'd accomplished, what? Killed a man and an ideal.

Of course I hadn't. That was just another delusion of grandeur. Wind came walking up to the hovels one afternoon, eating the ground with his gigantic strides. I got another "Chase, my man" and a hug that pressed my face into his ribs. He exchanged some kind of coded bow with the monks. Where he'd learned that, I don't know. They gripped his shoulders and rubbed his head and made clucking noises in the backs of their throats.

He'd burrowed. Into the snow. Grabbed his gear, burritoed himself in an exploded tent, and wormed down below the surface. He'd read about huskies sleeping buried in Alaska—he figured it was like that. "Kinda cold at first," he said. "But once I got my shirts on and the snow covered me up, I was all right." He had some black around his fingernails, no big deal. He didn't blame me for anything. "Kinda hairy up there," he chuckled at me, whinnying his pony laugh. Like I'd pranked him and gone just a little overboard.

I wasn't sure the simple fact that he was unkillable cleared me of much, but he was alive, and the relief was like a popped cork. By walking up the hill, he rolled a great big damn rock off me. I could get on with my life, devote myself to stock brokering or drilling natural gas or whatever.

Wind had kept a breathing hole clear by poking at it all night long as the snow piled up. In the morning when I left, he saw me through a long white tube. He said he was happy as a clam in the mud. He thought about popping up and surprising me, but even he knew that was a bad idea, with Bill right there in the tent. An hour later, Bill descended, and Wind had the tents to himself.

It took him some time to dig free, because his gopher hole was well and truly buried. Then he borrowed our tent again—"no problem, it was empty," he said, like I hadn't been there—and rubbed himself warm and dry. And then? He broke off. He got shifty. Uncomfortable. Eyes wandering, that infantile smile crawling over his rubber lips. At first I thought he was having some kind of tic. Then it flashed on me. He hadn't gone down. That's why he'd stopped telling me. He'd gone *up*. How far? Damn it, how high did you go? He rocked back like I'd hit him. I must have been a sight. I was so sure I didn't want to hear his answer that I didn't ask again.

I couldn't get away from it. I wanted to throw him into the storm all over again. I was right back to where I'd been. If I'd stayed, I might have gone after him with a rock. He was too much for me. I all but ran away. From him or myself or fucking Asia, I don't know. Los Angeles suddenly seemed sane. I feel like I failed the test. I'm the hillbilly who gets visited by an alien but spends the whole night hiding behind his pitchfork.

▲

THE NEXT MORNING, Jay drove Chase out into the desert. They talked about solo circuits in Joshua Tree and autumn ice climbs in the Sierra.

"You don't sound like you're done climbing," Jay said.

"Nah. Like I said. I'm back to where I started."

"Sounds dangerous."

"I'll be fine."

"You headed back to the Himalayas?" Jay asked.

"No. No way. Weren't you listening?"

"I was listening."

"Okay then. No."

"Right."

The road narrowed. The concrete peeled back layer by layer. Jay felt the same buoyant *pop* he always experienced when Los Angeles receded in the west, as if he'd come up for air. The Mojave jesters, the Joshua trees, crowded the roadside. Jay drove them higher, up to the pyramids of monzonite, heaped skeletons of the past weathering to sand, returning to the ground. The rock was orange and so was the heat coming off the ground.

The road curved between the rocks. The Joshua trees pressed close. Chase pointed to a dirt road that split off toward Queen Mountain, and Jay nosed the Subaru along the twin ruts.

"Want to stay and climb a few days?" Chase asked.

"Nope," Jay said. "Carrie. School. Work."

"Want to boulder just this morning?"

"No. But we get out here a few times a month. Though I don't know how we'll find you. Particularly without Big Yellow."

"I'll be around. Look for me."

Chase told Jay to stop at a bend where the road swung near Queen Mountain's farthest outlying cliffs. They got out and swung the duffel off the road into the sand. They shook hands. Jay got back behind the wheel and turned the car around. When he had himself pointed west, Chase waved once. The car rolled back toward the ocean and the city, and Jay watched in the mirror as Chase left the road and disappeared into the Joshuas and stones.

THE SKIN OF THE WORLD

|

DARKNESS AND COLD come early in December. It was not much past five o'clock, but David and Ian had already cocooned themselves in their sleeping bags. They sat upright, side by side, on a ledge a few feet wide and a dozen feet long. Between and above them, the ropes and hardware were stacked, racked, and tidied for the night—though the result looked more Gorgon-ish than tidy, with coils of rope and cruel-looking metal geegaws dangling from slings. They had their backs against the stone, their legs in the bags hung over the edge. A thousand feet down, the green-black pines rocked back and forth in the wind like waves on dark water, shadows in the blackness above the snow that buried their trunks and lowest branches.

"I think I've found a mountain for us," David said.

"Is it beautiful?" Ian asked.

That was just like Ian. Not "how high?" or "how hard?" He would never admit to wanting to know the gross measurements of a mountain. David rubbed his hands together, trying to rub out the cold from inside his bag. "Like nothing I've seen before," he said. "Honestly." He studied his mental image of the mountain, which was never far from the surface these days. "It has cheekbones. Like Sophia Loren."

"And where does Lady Loren live?" Ian asked.

"In China. Near the old border with Tibet. It's called Yunshan."

"Yunshan," Ian repeated. "I've never heard of her. What does the name mean?"

"Yunshan?" David said. "I don't know."

The moon lifted itself up out of Tenaya Canyon, flooding the valley with light, turning the snow to glass and the granite to silver. It was the Yosemite Valley below their ledge, which meant there were signs of the other world down there: headlights, even tacked Christmas lights, on cars being driven to the little outposts of commercial cheer within the park. Seeing those lights, imagining the heavy windows of the lodges shielding fires and compressed voices— the merry bunching of humanity against the cold—only increased the distance David felt between himself and the ground. He felt pressed up against the rim of the world.

"It looks hard," David said.

"Sure it does," Ian said. "You wouldn't be taking us to China otherwise."

That was the risk of climbing with Ian. He didn't say no. Which didn't mean he was fearless. He'd whimper and shake his way up a scary lead just like anyone else. But he would agree to a big climb without even bothering to say yes, and that worried David sometimes. By the time he made a suggestion, it was a reality, with no chance to step back and laugh it off. Already, sitting there in the cold on their ledge on another climb, he could feel them inching toward the Kunlun Range. He didn't even know how to get there, really, or where the money would come from, or what lengths of red tape the Chinese would wrap around their mountain. Still, he felt the first stirrings of gravity pulling them toward Yunshan. So there was the risk, and the payoff, too. David would dream big, and Ian would shrug as if it were the most natural suggestion in the world. The wheels would turn, carrying them to the Alps or Peru or Alaska, and then David would climb outside of himself, beyond the limits he imagined, pushed on by Ian's refusal to confess any notion of the lunacy of their project. But Yunshan was the biggest dream yet, and David had half hoped he would get some kind of new reaction from his partner.

The cold was looking for him through his layers. David could feel it brush his skin and then retreat, waiting for his blood to slow. He was wrapped up in every scrap of clothing he'd brought, plus his harness and the rope, which ran up out the neck of his bag to their anchor so that he wouldn't roll off their ledge. As far as he could tell, he would not be taking off his harness or even a single layer for another three days—and that assumed no blizzard was tracking down from the north to ambush them first. The cold dug deep, even for December. They had waited until a river of arctic air swung down off the Bering Sea, icing the entire West. This had been another of David's ideas, to try to make a Yosemite winter feel like a Himalayan summer. They were evaluating their fitness to handle hard climbing in the cold. Ian said they were prospecting their souls.

David had left his tether too tight. He slipped one hand out to loosen the clove hitch tying him to the anchor. To get to the anchor, he had to reach through the snakes of rope and also through the charms and juju beads Ian had hung there when they set up for the night: a string of feathers, a chain of amber teardrops, two old coins with center-holes, and John, Ian's shrunken head. David had never quite gotten over his revulsion of the head—the wrinkled skin-leather, the grotesque features, the history it represented. Ian had explained that he was misdirecting death, which made little sense to David, since the thing looked very much like death. Anyway, it hardly mattered. They were hauling six gallons of water—enough for the two of them for five cold days—so Ian's talismans weren't exactly holding them back. The feathers were something new. David finished fiddling with his rope and snatched his hand back into his bag and retightened its hood. "Ian," David said. "What's with all the feathers?"

"I'll tell you," Ian said. "A month ago—a Thursday—I walked out to my car, and there were two white birds on the hood, staring back at me. Not pigeons, not gulls, I don't know what they were. But they stared at me till I put the key in the door, and then they were gone. I drove up 140 and slept by the river. The next morning, I walked up to Arch Rock, and when I got there, two climbers decked right in front of me. Two white birds. Two dead climbers."

"What?" David said. "What happened? Why didn't you tell me?"

"Leader had just started the last pitch of Lesser Evil. He fell and ripped the anchor. Gone just like that. Bloody mess. You were doing that concrete job, and I didn't see you for a couple weeks. Besides, I hate telling you stuff like this. You're such a skeptic."

David tried to clear his mind of sarcasm lest anything about albino sparrows wriggle off his tongue. He knew he could be a bastard, and Ian had watched people die, so it didn't seem to be the time. "What did you do?" he asked.

"Not much to do," Ian said. "I poked around at the bodies a few minutes." (David was always caught by Ian's frankness. He, too, would have stayed to poke at the bodies—he had never seen what granite teeth would do to human flesh, though he had imagined it often enough. But would he have admitted to it so casually? He wasn't sure.) "Then I walked back down and called search and rescue. I spent the rest of the weekend soloing, looking for nests."

Of course. Only Ian would watch two climbers land in front of him like that then go on a soloing, feather-collecting, spree. And then wait a month to mention it.

"You all right?" David asked.

"Yeah, all right," Ian said. "It wasn't me that fell—though it felt like it at first watching them come down."

"Did you ever find out who they were?"

"I asked around," Ian said. "A couple of guys from Georgia no one had ever seen before. Makes me wonder how word will get back home for them. Who's going to track down their wives, girlfriends, moms, or whatever?"

"You could make that your work. Saint Ian of the fallen climber. It'd suit you."

"No way. I'd creep them out. Can you imagine me showing up at your door? Better leave that to guys with crew cuts and uniforms."

David waited for Ian to say something more. In truth, he wanted Ian to say something about the mountain in China. Dead climbers and feathers were surprisingly uncomfortable subjects once the basic facts had been covered. What could David say? What a tragedy? What do you suppose those birds were up to? Did you see their livers? And here, David had proposed that they climb a mostly unknown mountain on the other side of the planet, and all his partner wanted to know was what the name of the mountain meant! David had things to say on that subject: this many thousand feet of rock, so many pitches of ice, stacked overhangs at half height, the choice between twin ropes or a ten-millimeter lead line. He knew, in part, his reason for wanting to talk through these details. He was afraid of Yunshan, maybe even terrified of it. The mountain dwelt on a plane they hadn't touched before. Talking about the tools they would use and the sections they would climb would help still his mind. But Ian wasn't biting. Apparently he wasn't ready for that sort of business yet.

"How did Yunshan find you?" Ian asked, at last.

"Who says *I* didn't find *it*?" David said.

"Don't be vain," Ian said. "The mountain comes for you when you need it. I guess Yunshan wants to show you something."

"Have you been going to church again? You sound like a priest."

Ian laughed, a braying sound that came out in short, wheezy barks. "Not often enough," he said. "You should try it. I'll take you sometime. All those old Semites had their revelations on mountaintops. It's inspiring stuff. So, where did Yunshan find you?"

"UC library."

"Ah—secular church."

The hood of David's sleeping bag, cinched around his face, kept him from looking over to Ian when they spoke. Anyway, what would he see if he could? A nylon mummy draped over the stone, hardly a person. So he spoke out into the silvery night, and Ian's voice, his hoarse rasp, came to him from out of the air. "In pictures in an old copy of the *Alpine Journal*," David continued. They were from a photo reconnaissance from the 1920s, after the World War and before Chiang Kai-shek shut down south China, a time when there were still blank spaces on maps even as airplanes filled in the sky. The author— an Englishman with a fitting name, Mosshole, something like that— had wandered through the Kunlun, goggling and taking pictures and being imperious and British. He got tossed out by the new guard, and visitors were no longer welcome. And then Mao shut the borders, and that part of the world went dark for decades. "The pictures of Yunshan are incredible," David said. "The mountain comes right up out of its glacier—a thousand feet of rock, then mixed climbing and a band of ice, another thousand feet of rock, and then the overhangs, more ice dripping down, snow, spires on top. Solid-looking granite." David paused a moment to see if any response would return to him out of the night. "Ian? Mountains are made of rock, you know."

Ian's fetishism of the mountains did not sit easily in David's mind. He didn't care for stories of the hidden world when the surface of the real world was so intricate and alive.

Up and down the valley, the granite glowed, and David felt himself becoming mesmerized by the moon. He closed his eyes, popped them back open again. It was much too early to drift off. He flexed his hands, which were raw from tussling with the granite. Already they were cracked, bleeding, coated black with aluminum oxide. His fingertips felt plastic in the cold. He wondered if he would be able to feel the difference between fingers punished numb and fingers losing feeling from frostbite. He imagined the grief he would get from other climbers if he frostbit himself in California.

The moon floated higher. David tried to stay awake. Going to sleep now would mean waking up at three in the morning with nothing to do but lie there and wait for dawn. Ian told a story, set in the desert. David lost track of whether it was in Australia after the year Ian had worked on a sheep farm or in New Mexico where he had been looking for mushrooms after a big spring rain. The land was all red and orange and flat except for the cliffs, which came up at perfect right angles. Distances were impossible to guess. A lean, hard, brown-skinned man with long black hair had wandered by and asked Ian whether he had seen his dog. They had ended up spending two days together driving dirt roads looking for a mutt the same color as the desert. The man had known just where to go at the hottest part of the day to see a mirage that looked like a tidal wave rolling off an inland sea. And then it was three in the morning, and David was awake and cold through and begging the dawn to hurry west.

▲

FOUR MONTHS PASSED. They celebrated the purchase of their plane tickets at a beer-and-whisky dive with a peanut-shell floor. Ian wore his snakeskin boots with the heads left on—mouths open—at the toes. He jumped up on the table and stomped out a jig. David pounded the table with his bottle, keeping his hand moving fast to avoid getting kick-bit. Ian tilted his head back and howled at the ceiling. The barman, roused at last, lifted his jiggly chin an inch off his massive chest. "Get *out* now," he said, "'fore I break heads."

Ian collapsed back into his seat. "I found out what Yunshan means," he said, when he caught his breath.

"Oh?" David had forgotten all about that question.

"The mountain on the cloud," Ian said. "How about that?"

▲

THE FINAL WEEK stateside was a roar in David's ears and a confusion of images with gaps in between he didn't know how to fill. He made lists: Four gallons of kerosene. Fifteen pounds each of rice and flour. Fifty-four carabiners. Six cases of Baby Ruths. Two lead ropes, two tents, two spoons, two 100-count bottles of multi-vitamin pills transferred to plastic bags to save on weight and bulk. Twenty-four pitons. Two sets of cams. Eighteen ice screws. There were revisions, additions, subtractions, a file folder an inch thick of different versions and permutations. Ian had no patience for this papering of the mountain. "Start pasting this to your walls," he'd say, "and I'll call the asylum. They'll come and take away your pen and put your hands to better use."

Then there were the duffle bags and the airports and the noise and press of people. Hours (days?) rattling around a railcar. A market for the rice and flour, where David understood nothing and Ian vomited in the dirt behind a stall after eating a bird on a stick, much to the amusement of two boys, who watched him unabashedly. A diesel truck farting black smoke bounced them over dirt roads up through foothills covered in orchards. A smiling woman gave them a bag of pears and waved them along wordlessly. The wheel ruts ended, and Ian found a man with a donkey cart who agreed to take them further, and they could feel the land swelling up, puckering toward hills and then mountains.

Then, suddenly, there they were, at the toe of the glacier, and David's mind felt present, and moving in real time, for the first time in weeks, though he also felt drained and hungover. They had a mound of gear two days away, back by the river where the cart had dumped them, but here they were, with a smaller mound at the snow line.

"We're in deep now," Ian said. He was sprawled on the ground, head propped on a ripped and bursting duffel. "You're the only one I know who can bury me this deep."

David blinked against the high-altitude sun. Far off in the distance, he could see the upper wedge of the mountain. It split the sky, an isosceles of black rock and gleaming ice, a hatchet head turned up to attack the blue.

"If we were in Nepal," Ian continued, lying on his back at the place where the earth ended and the snow began, high above the last bare-boned wintersweet, "we'd be drinking chai from a thermos and

snapping photos of Sherpas toting our stuff. Here we'll haul baggage
for a week just to set up basecamp."

In fact, it took twelve days. They divided their supplies into sixty-
pound loads and ran relays, first from the end of the donkey track
to the snow, then up the glacier, inching toward the wall of peaks
where the side of the mountain tore up out of the snow. Now the ink
abstractions of David's lists had coalesced into pounds and ounces,
and the two men toiled under their loads.

Up on the glacier, they could not help seeing Yunshan. In person,
their lady mountain wore no come-hither look. Her face was elegant
and severe. The rock, steep and smooth, overhung at her cheek hollows. A fine network of fragile-looking ice runnels veiled her chin
and jaw in lace, then ran together high on her head in a crown stud-
ded with snowy towers. In fact, it was best not to look straight at the
mountain, at least not yet. Better to stare at the saw-toothed chains
of subsidiary peaks sprawling to the north and south and let Yunshan
lurk on the periphery.

On the snow, the sun was an enemy, turning the surface to knee-
deep mush, weakening the skin over the glacier's complicated insides.
Two hours into the very first carry, David felt the snow slump
beneath his feet as the outer layer collapsed. The crevasse pulled him
down slowly, the snow sticking together even as it moved. He had
time to escape, to pitch forward toward the stable pack. He even had
time to imagine the fall waiting for him below: bouncing at the end
of the rope that attached him to Ian, his sack pulling him backward
and upside down, then hours spent down in the snow hole mess-
ing around with frozen prusiks and fighting to emerge through the

bombs of snow sloughing off the sides. And still it was hard to move. He seemed mired in syrup, ballasted in place by the weight on his back. He lurched ahead and stuck his ice axe into the slush just as the snow beneath his feet fell completely away. For a moment he thought he would slide down anyway, but his axe found a firm layer and held. He crawled away from the crack, panting and pushing.

"All right?" Ian said.

"Hell . . . man . . ." David pulled for breath. "Let's go wallow through a swamp instead. We'll get nowhere like this."

So they worked at night instead. On clear nights, an eastern moon lit the snow. When the moon declined, the mountain's shadow engulfed them and shrank the world to the ten yards of light produced by a headlamp. During this period of moonset, they struggled through a black-on-black world with ruined depth perception. Mountain shapes reared up out of the dark, and David would be sure they had veered off their track and were cutting crosswise toward the chain of peaks. But then the mountain would become a hill, then a ridge, then a crest that would take ten steps to top. David would tell himself again to stop looking so far ahead and to keep his eyes within his cone of light, that outside of the light-cone, there were only tricks. The shapes in the gloom ahead, and to the left and right, were only there to distract and confuse. When the moon finally abandoned Asia, the mountain shadow dissipated, and the stars, hot pricks of light hung absurdly low, retook the sky. They switched their headlamps back off even though the starlight didn't really do much to drive the night off the glacier. Batteries weighed just under an ounce a piece, and they had only eighteen of them.

Meanwhile, the glacier churned down the valley. Middle sections, where the flow was strongest, slid away from the mountain a foot an hour. Creaks and groans chafed the night air and the nerves of the two climbers; sounds like trees—a whole forest—having their limbs torn off, the sounds of great tonnages of ice rubbing each other and the rock below.

‖

THE SKY WAS blue, the mountain vertical, the air cold enough to keep the ice firm, but warm enough that David could still feel all of his toes. They were in the middle-mountain, now, where top and bottom seemed equidistant and equally inaccessible. Down below, through a vertical half mile, he could just make out the yellow half sphere of their basecamp tent, but it looked two-dimensional, like a grain of sand on the floor. Not much to hide under. Up, they could not even see the summit, blocked as it was by Yunshan's tangled crown. *No point looking at either*, David told himself, *they'll just drive you nuts.*

A flight of griffon vultures—seven of them—spiraled on a fast updraft headed up toward their belay. The griffons were the only large live things they had seen since moving onto the glacier. David watched them and wondered what it was they ate, but maybe they were only using the mountain winds to gain altitude before drifting out over the plains. Still, he could hardly believe they could fly so high. They were enormous birds, wings outstretched and arched over their heads, which hung down off coils of neck. They seemed to eye David in return as they drifted by, with eyes made of black glass, frank and curious. *Back off*, he thought, *I'm not dinner yet*. A few hundred feet higher, two of them riding the column of air in opposite directions collided. They righted themselves after some squawking and scrabbling, and a shower of black feathers drifted down past the belay.

It was David's lead, and Ian handed him their anemic rack of gear. The specific items clipped to the nylon sling were the result of an intense two days of negotiation. These had been their rest days, a chance to inventory basecamp and readjust to the sunlit world. They spent most of the time staring at the mountain, trying to make some sense out of it, trying to imagine what might be up there.

"The third runnel, just below her right cheek, you think that's consolidated?"

"Looks like cotton candy crap to me. Has it sloughed at all today? In the fourth runnel, two hundred feet up and over, we'd have a sleeping ledge."

"There? We'll be sleeping upright. I think that's a shadow tricking you."

It was nothing but steep. There would be few places to stand, let alone sleep. The sole exception was a recessed area lodged into her snowy forehead like a third eye. It might offer something like ground to walk and stand on, some relief from the unrelenting vertical.

"The lighter we go, the faster we go," Ian muttered from behind their spotting scope in the afternoon of their second Sunday. "The faster we go, the less we need. If we were just inhuman enough, we'd start up and never stop and be on top fifty hours later. We're not ready for that. Damn! Too anchored. Too in touch with our suffering." He was seated on one of a collection of rocks in the snow—mountain debris surfing the back of the glacier. He tossed the scope to David. "Five days," he said. "We can do it in five days if we keep the packs under thirty pounds. Six if we get pinned by a storm."

"With packs like that, we'll starve," David said.

"We don't need food for the storm day. Just fuel."

"We'll be ghosts by the end of it."

"We'll float up the mountain. We're in the land of the mind. Monks fast for weeks in these mountains. We can do that. You know we can both lose a few. We're skinny, but we're not Ethiopians."

The plan taking form was no plan at all. They'd abandon their aluminum and nylon advantage for a tool kit of promises: strength, luck, speed. But to climb in one lightning stroke. No tedious hauling or unspooling of fixed ropes. No slow grind of mind and body against mountain stretched out over weeks. This was beautiful.

"We can shed some gear weight, too," David said, at last. They would depend on speed, and speed was a function of weight. Every ounce would count. "It's all snow and ice up there. We won't need as many pitons."

"You realize," Ian said, "we'll be heroes if we pull this off."

Now, attached to the mountain by a few bits of nylon and chromoly, David took the rack of gear from Ian, stared straight up at the undercurve of the lady's cheek, and wished for every one of the nine pitons and eight cams left at basecamp. The mountainside bulged out beyond vertical, sheltering the cliff bands below and leaving them bare. The day was ending, the sky blueing toward purple. Above the overhangs hovered Ian's promised sleeping ledge and the potential for rest. But steep, complicated overlaps of rock blocked the way, and David couldn't yet see a route through.

"Talk to me while I'm up there," David said.

"Careful what you ask. I've been thinking about bones," Ian said.

"Keep it to yourself, then."

David climbed past the belay, where Ian had anchored himself to the top of an ice runnel with two screws. The ice immediately thinned to a glass curtain, and David swung his axes trying to think like a surgeon, but feeling like he was the one under the knife. He felt the surface vibrate with each move, had no idea what kept it from disintegrating into falling shards. The runnel ended in a translucent point glued to black diorite, and David dry tooled away from the ice, scratching at the mountain's bare hide with his axes, crampons sparking and scraping against the rock. Whiffs of dynamite hung in the air, the exhale of rock crushed by steel points. He teetered on the barest contact between metal and stone.

Ian was rattling on about something. Cathedrals. Ossuaries. Prophets on mountaintops. Tibetan lamas.

David reached a little groove that would take a piton, but not one of the ones he carried. He fumbled in a cam, but it was so absurdly upside down and flared that he took it back out. He searched for other options. He looked down between his crampons and saw Ian's face notched there, staring back up at him as through a bombsight. If he fell, Ian would have nowhere to go.

Ian didn't look away, and David felt goaded on by his partner's wide-open eyes. If Ian wasn't going to turn away, how could David?

The rope hung down from David's waist, uninterrupted, sixty, then seventy feet. *So?* he thought. *I won't let go.*

David reached the overlaps, where the rock bulged out above him like an inverted staircase. He pounded a piton into a rotten crack, but from the way the rock flexed, he knew that it would rip out if he fell. He clipped his rope to it anyway. The analytical part of his mind was receding; its warnings, barely heard echoes. His blood was up, and it felt good to clip his rope to the pin, like carrying a lottery ticket in his back pocket. Ian was screaming at him now.

David reached up and out and hooked the tip of one axe pick into a cavity between two of the steps. He leaned back, and the pick crunched against the rock, but held. He moved higher out under the staircase. Gravity, like a second rope tied to his waist, pulled him backward and down. The blood surged to his arms now, and the pump clock began to tick. Tick-tock, his swollen veins strangled his forearms, and he could feel his fingers relaxing around the axe shafts. Just above, the bulge flattened, and above that hung Ian's ledges, safety, a place to rest. But he couldn't see any of that, only the rock right in his face, the final edge of the curve. There must be something up there, but he could not see it. Could he believe in it without some visual assurance that he could get from here to there? He looked back at that one rotten piton, the only thing separating him from a fall that would surely rip their anchor and send their tethered bodies down to the glacier. There might still be time to reverse what he had already climbed, to retreat and rethink their route.

"Do it!" Ian yelled. "Beast it!"

His mind asked for time, but his hand, guided by his blood, reached out one axe and locked it onto the lip at the farthest end of the bulge. He pulled against his higher axe and reached blindly up with the other, and then his feet cut loose from their holds, and his legs swung out away from the mountain, and for a moment he was connected to the mountain by a single point, an inch of steel on rock, and his feet were swinging out away, and all he had left was his right hand. As the upper mountain rolled into view, he saw that the rock above was covered in holds, neat horizontal rails. He pulled hard—he could always trust his right hand for that—and his second axe locked into one of those perfect slots, and he hauled himself up. (*What if the rock had been blank?* But he pushed that thought out of his mind.)

He climbed the easy ground above with exaggerated care, his muscles trembling from fatigue and adrenaline. There were ledges, a terrace of them, though none were very wide or long, and they'd have another night spent sleeping sitting up. He placed two pitons and a cam, clipped himself to this anchor, and sat down with his back to the mountain. He let his mind drift on euphoric waters, happy to be alive, happy to have fought hard and won. A few moments passed like this before the image of Ian, still hanging in his harness anchored to the ice down below, pressed hard enough into his reverie to bring him back to the present and pull up the rope and then shout down to his partner that the anchor was set and he could climb.

Ian arrived at the ledges panting and cursing, the tight rope from above eliminating only the psychological trauma of the pitch. He flopped down next to David, who tied off his section of the rope to the anchor and then took him off belay.

"Buddy," Ian said. "Fantastic. Ridiculous. Psychotic bastard. I thought you were going to kill us both."

"Really?"

"Sure, I thought you were going to come off. We'd both have been yelling into the breeze then. For sure."

"But you told me to go for it."

"Well, sure. It looked like you were headed up anyway. I thought I might as well keep things positive. Yelling at you was better than sitting there and quietly crapping myself."

David's adrenaline buzz was on the wane, the chemical triumph dropping out of his bloodstream. He still felt good, but the center had fallen away from his feeling of victory. The summit appeared no closer. He had allowed his hands to climb that pitch ungoverned, and now he worried about the degree to which he had become beholden to luck. Ian's attitude bothered him. He had thought that his partner was cheering him on. And he noticed, for the first time, how cold the air had become, how few minutes of day remained.

"Hand me your sack," David said. The stove lived in Ian's pack. "I'll get the snow melting. The cold is coming."

"Good. Thanks. Here." Ian handed it over and leaned his head back against the rock. "Don't get me wrong. It was a beautiful lead. That's what we're here for." David stood up—there was just room enough for that—and put his heels at the edge of the drop so that he could prop the pack against the spot where he had been sitting. He undid the buckles and loosened the drawcord. "Wait!" Ian said, and he jumped up so that they had to jostle each other for space. "I'll take care of it. I'm recovered. Give it to me."

It was too late. David had already opened the inner compartment.

"What the hell is that?" David said, staring down into the bag.

"Come on. He always comes. You know that."

David stuck his hand down into Ian's pack. "Not up here, man. Not when every bit counts. Your sick souvenir weighs two days' fuel."

"You didn't see me slowing us down. Don't touch John. I'm telling you, fucker, keep your fingers off."

David pulled the shrunken head—he had never been able to call it John—out by the hair. It was the size of a baseball, brown skinned, the nose left disproportionately large and snout-like, the eyes and lips sewn shut. It dangled at the end of a foot of straight black hair, now brittle with age.

"Put him back," Ian said. "Put him back! He's been with me at the top of every mountain. He'll go to the top of this one too."

The head bobbled in the wind, the dark skin-leather looking altogether foreign against the rock and ice. David thought of Ian working in the Guinean gold mines, trading with the natives, his broken Walkman for this head. Then he thought of wind scouring rock. "We don't need it," David said. "What's it doing for us? You shouldn't have brought it up here. Not if you wanted to keep it." He held his arm out away from the mountain and opened his hand. It seemed to hang there for a moment, while the mountain itself rushed upward, but the illusion could only sustain itself for a fraction of a second, and then the head was rocketing downward. David watched it tumble with the stomach-sickening lurch that he felt whenever he watched the fall of a dropped object from up high. It was too easy to transpose himself and the head, to feel the wind whistling in his own ears. But soon it diminished and vanished, and all he could see were the places where the head struck the mountainside and knocked free little puffs of snow and falling rock.

Next to him, Ian was leaned as far back in his harness as his rope tether to the anchor would allow, face turned down toward the drop. Slowly, he pulled himself upright, and David watched the gathering storm of rage ascend through his partner's shoulders and mouth and eyes. Ian sucked in air, and David concluded that his own time had slowed, because this inward half of Ian's breath seemed to go on and on, as if Ian would draw all the air off the mountain. David had a momentary vision of them brawling right there on that tiny stance, tied to the same anchor with nowhere to go. When at last Ian pushed all of that air back out, the sound was pure toothy anger, and David faced him silently with his head up and his shoulders high because he figured that this was a moment like facing a bluff-charging bear, when one needed to show force of will. So he let Ian's growl wash over him without flinching, and Ian sat back down, took back his pack, and said, "Dumb fucking bastard, why do you have to be so serious all the time?"

Necessity kept them moving. Certain things had to be done. The stove had to be lit and passed back and forth, sleeping niches had to be cleared, the sleeping bags and pads had to be taken out and arranged. Speaking was not necessary, and silence settled on them with the cold. In turn, they melted snow for their water bottles and for dinner. David ate his single-packet ration of chicken soup and watched Ian do the same. David's stomach rumbled, but he was not yet hungry enough to curse his pack's emptiness. The lack of weight was still too clearly a blessing, though it was disturbing to think of how little equipment and provisions they had to shield themselves from the mountain.

When Ian finished his soup, he spoke again. "You're an asshole, but I don't care that much about that." The flat evenness of Ian's voice came as a surprise. "What's pathetic is that you still don't know how to handle your own mind. You're strong as a roided chimp, but all that muscle is run by a five-year-old's soul."

It was too much. David felt overfed on Ian's voodoo, but he ended up laughing instead of yelling. "Man, you carry a *severed head* with you when you go climbing. And you call me the five-year-old? We're this close to dying up here, and you brought your head. You should never have brought it up here. It's got no place here. We could have each had a Baby Ruth for dessert instead."

Ian was quiet for a long moment, and David wondered if he had gone mute again, or if he was just silently sharpening his axe to plant in David's forehead. But then Ian let loose a snort and a snigger, then a full-blown gale of laughter. "The man wants candy!" Ian shrieked. "The man wants candy. We're in the land of the mind, and the man wants candy!"

Now they were both laughing and whooping and hollering, for no reason that David could think of except that it felt good. Eventually their noise died, and the silence pressed back down along with the night. David buried himself in his sleeping bag, wedging himself in amongst the rocks as best he could, half curled, half seated. Somehow they had resolved nothing. He tightened the hood of his sleeping bag around his rope umbilicus to the anchor. He was exhausted enough that he figured he would get some sleep before his hunger and the sharp stones he was leaned against woke him. The laughter had been good, but the silence afterward had fallen crushingly. The next day, they would make for Yunshan's third eye, and hopefully there they could pitch their tent and get a little more rest. As he sank toward sleep, he thought of John flying down the mountain and felt some guilt for what he had done to Ian. But he also felt clean, as if he had dropped ten pounds, and he knew that if he had let that ugly bit of magic stay with them, it would have festered in his mind and pulled hard against him. Now, though he felt wrung out by the day, he was light, and he drifted away.

|||

AT LAST THE black turned into grey, and David knew that morning had arrived. Sometime after midnight, the cold had fully infiltrated the loft of his sleeping bag, and he had been trapped in a shivering half sleep since then. So it was a relief to commit to wakefulness, even though he hardly felt rested and the day looked grim. No sun would light this dawn. Black clouds ripened in the sky, their lowest shreds and vapors close enough to hit with a thrown stone. It would snow, there could be no doubt—the only question was when and how much.

The thought of a blizzard hitting their tiny ledges sent David's mind to work, but his hands were slow to follow, stiff and cold-hooked as they were. He unzipped his sleeping bag enough to reach out one arm and fumble for the stove. The small manipulations of the stove parts: the plastic pump, the ridged wheel, the cigarette lighter, took an age, and David felt ridiculous to be stationary and fiddling when the snow might start dropping at any moment.

Ian stirred inside his down cocoon and said, "It's an evil-looking day, ain't it, buddy? A good day. It's what I expected. We're going to get what we deserve."

David was relieved to hear his partner's voice, and he laughed too loud and long in response. "Come on out of that bag, voodoo man. I'll have water ready soon. We should hurry."

"Today is going to skin us alive," Ian said. "I hope you're ready to have your soul exposed."

"My soul is spotless," David said, purposefully trying to load his voice with sarcasm, hoping it might come across as an acknowledgement or apology.

"Sure," Ian said. "Spotless like an alligator."

Taking care that nothing slipped through wooden fingers slowed them further, and an hour passed before they were ready to climb. Periodically, Ian would turn out away from the mountain and say, "Hold on, just hold on a damn minute," or, "We're not ready. Come back later. Pushy old witch." The clouds congealed into a single bloated mass the color of lead, and stray flakes of snow floated by, though it was impossible to tell whether they had fallen from the sky or been blown off the mountain by the escalating wind. The temperature showed no sign of rising after its overnight drop.

When they began at last, they found tedious, dangerous climbing through unconsolidated powder. There was rock (or was it ice?)

down there, somewhere, below their feet. But a two-foot layer of fine, loose snow covered the solid surface, and when they brushed it away, more would slough into place. So they felt along blindly, with eyes wide open but unable to see the layer that mattered, using axe-spikes and crampons to search out holds under the powder. David could imagine the holds well enough, mental images of brittle ice sticking loose rocks together. With each upward step, he waited for the crunch and lurch that would signal the fall's first moments, then acceleration and the clatter of stones.

But it was better to be climbing than waiting at the anchor with nothing to do but watch the darkening sky and Ian's struggles to keep them attached to the mountain, or to look inward and feel the invasion of the cold as his blood retreated toward his core. In the later morning, the snow began in earnest. Ian, already a formless shape under his red unisuit and helmet and scraggly blond beard, became blotted out behind the falling snow. By the time he reached the two-hundred-foot limit of their rope, David could hardly see him at all.

When David rejoined Ian at the next anchor, he tried to be enthusiastic and positive. "That was a good lead," he said. "Spooky loose rock. Nice work."

"Cut it out," Ian said. "You're using your baby brain. You've been acting like that all goddamn morning."

David felt lame and slow for being called out. "Fine," he said. "Your gear was crap, and you took a year to turn the roof above the groove."

"That's better," Ian said. "Now you're talking like the mountain. Better grow up fast. I can feel the knife under my skin already."

David couldn't tell whether Ian meant his words lightheartedly or otherwise. The wind snatched away intonation and whole sentences, and Ian's face was masked behind numb lips and the tightly drawn hood of his jacket. David felt like they were being dragged over rocks. They were coping all right, he thought, trading words that were mild enough to still be friendly but sharp enough to offer some release, but then one of them would say something that jabbed too hard, and they'd be back to spitting glass at each other.

"Just give me the rack," he muttered into the wind, "and go fuck yourself."

"Quick now, little beaver," Ian said. "Cut your teeth."

The storm revved up until it seemed like the jet stream washed directly over Yunshan. Pockets of turbulence struck at them, heavy fingers of air that seemed to want to pluck them right off the mountain. David hunkered down, gasping for breath, commanding the fragile holds to stay attached for a few more seconds and bear a few more pounds. He flailed and hacked at the mountain, and sometimes he imagined it was Ian, but other times he looked down and a gap in the blizzard showed how carefully Ian tended his rope, and he felt, again, the corded assurance that bound them—and sometimes, when the wind seemed to drive bits of ice right through his brain, he thought nothing at all.

Imperceptibly, at first, the angle decreased. But then David found that he was crawling as much as climbing. He plowed ahead through the snow on his knees, in order to stay low, in order to give the wind as little leverage as possible. He lost feeling in his hands, but he could still move his fingers and hold onto his ice axe.

The mid-afternoon was as grey and murky as their starlit nights down on the glacier. The ground leveled out to the point that they could stand and walk unroped in the wind lulls. They did not explore the boundaries of this area but dropped their packs and immediately began to dig down toward the hope of a stable layer to which they could anchor the tent. The wind blew sharp points of ice into every open seam of their clothing, and soon they each wore undershirts of slush. They worked feverishly, at first, so that the snowfall would not undo what had already been dug, but then Ian stopped and stood up.

"What's that?" Ian said.

"What do you mean?" They had to shout at each other nose-to-nose in order to be heard through hats and hoods and above the avalanche of wind noise.

"That sound," Ian said.

"It's the wind!"

"No. Listen. Over there." Ian abandoned their partially constructed platform and staggered off into the gale. The outline of his body fuzzed out, as if the reception were fading away on an old television, and David hardly knew whether to follow his partner and risk losing their spot entirely to the blizzard, or to stay and lose his partner. But then, as he strained his eyes through the static dropping out of the sky, he saw that Ian had stopped and was waving at him with one bent arm. David followed, ready to hogtie Ian and drag him back.

"What the hell are—" but then David stopped as he pulled even with Ian.

There was a man on his back in the snow. His nose was charcoal black. White frost-craters dimpled his cheeks. Ice cased his thick dark beard. His mouth was open and, David realized after a moment, from between his cracked and blistered lips came a sound which David's brain had been filing away as wind noise but now clearly separated into a scream.

They grabbed the man under the armpits and dragged him back to their packs. As they lifted him out of the snow—his lower half had been buried by a drift—they caught sight of shreds of nylon and pack cloth. Ian swiped at the snow with one foot, but he turned up nothing more than wreckage and fragments: bent tubes that could have been tent poles, a stiff, frozen ball that could have been a jacket or a sweater, red slices of tent fabric. All worthless.

With the man lying by their packs, they attacked the snow again. David worked by instinct. They needed shelter, and for that, they needed to dig down. When their platform had at last been flattened, they spread out the tent and pushed the man inside as ballast against the wind. They staked out the corners and linked the poles and guyed two lines on each side before giving up and piling their packs and themselves into their thin nylon shelter.

The inside of the tent was a sopping mess. It had filled with snow when they loaded the man, and more came in on their packs and clothes. The tent was barely big enough for two—with three they couldn't move without hitting each other and knocking snow around. Every time they bumped the man, he screamed. David had lost most of the functionality in his hands, and he began to shake as his now-stationary body cooled further. He curled up against one end of the tent and tried to shiver himself warm. "What the hell do we do with him?" he yelled.

"Snap out of it. We've got to warm him up."

"But where did he come from?"

"Ask him. Fuck! Stop mumbling and answer the question." Ian kicked the man, and he screamed again. "Witch, stop blowing," Ian said. "Hell mouth."

The vapor in their exhalations froze immediately to the fabric walls, then fell in showers of ice whenever the wind shook the tent. Ian used his teeth to open one of their packs, and he spread the contents out over the top of the man, who thrashed weakly from side to side and moaned. David caught their squeeze bottle of oil—which they had carefully doled into their nightly soups—between his hands and sucked down half of it because he remembered a story of an Antarctic climber who drank olive oil to keep from freezing. He passed the bottle to Ian.

"Is he talking?" Ian asked.

"He looks Russian," David said.

"Speak up! What are you saying?"

"It sounds like Russian."

"You don't know any Russian."

They spread a sleeping bag—David's—out over the man and pulled off his harness and the frozen layers of his clothing until they had him down to long johns and gloves. David felt better, whether from the oil or because his body temperature had stabilized, he couldn't tell. He was sleepy and strongly tempted to lean back and catch a nap, but at least he knew that this was a bad sign, something to fight. He could squeeze between his thumb and forefinger now, which was useful when it came time to zip the sleeping bag up around the Russian. It was harder yet to get the stove lit, but he managed, and the blue flame had a hypnotic quality that seemed to pacify them all.

"We'll be dead from carbon monoxide," Ian said, "but at least we'll be warm and it won't hurt as much as freezing to death."

"I hear it actually feels pretty good by the time you're ready to die from the cold."

"He doesn't look like he's enjoying it."

The Russian moaned with every exhale. The ice had partly melted out of his beard, leaving him wet and matted. His eyelids were pinched into a shape that spoke of pain. When his eyes did occasionally flutter open, they were vacant. The pebble-sized blisters on his lips were filled with milky liquid. He would surely lose most of his nose. He took up one half of the tent. David sat at the back and minded the stove, while Ian sat at the other end, facing his partner. They had Ian's sleeping bag draped across them as a blanket. Out of the wind, with the three of them in the tent pressed against each other, David felt the python squeeze of the cold unclench.

"Ian, what's he doing here?"

"What do you think he's doing here?"

"He shouldn't be here," David said. "He doesn't belong here." David knew he wasn't really right in the head. The storm, his hypo-thermia, the stove gasses filling the tent—he knew his thoughts were insensible, nightmarish. They scuttled around the dark corners of his brain. He was not making clear sense out of the sudden appearance of this misshapen, pain-blistered face. It sickened him. He wanted to wish it away.

Ian shrugged. "Did you think you were the only one to ever hear of Yunshan? Hell, this is practically his backyard."

Ian fed the first pot of lukewarm water to the Russian. He dribbled it into his mouth with a spoon until half the pot was gone. Then he mixed one of their four remaining oatmeal packets into the pot and fed that to him as well. David said nothing, though he could not tear his eyes away from that oatmeal. *One packet. That's all right. We can afford it. We're not Ethiopian. Not yet.*

"But what's he doing *here*," David said. "Alone. You know what we've climbed through to get here."

"We haven't been able to see a damn thing all day. Maybe we traversed half the mountainside. Who knows where we are."

"Bullshit. We must be in the third eye. How did he get here?" David's voice sounded accusatory, even to his own ears, though he did not mean it to be. Maybe he did.

"Well, maybe he's got seven friends frozen out there in the snow," Ian said.

The next pot of water was hot, and Ian filled a bottle and placed it under the top of the sleeping bag and against the man's chest. Even though its grip had loosened, the cold still had David. A cupful of that hot water would be better than a Jacuzzi. He watched it disappear under the sleeping bag cover. The warmth liberated terrible odors: stale piss, flesh-rot. Occasionally, a spasm made the Russian's whole body clench. David could only imagine what could be happening in the man's extremities as his brain and nerves became reconnected. They hadn't seen his hands or feet—they'd left his gloves and boots on for fear of doing more damage than good.

Ian and David split the next pot of water to drink, and the plain warm water went down without touching David's thirst. On the outside, David felt damp and ice-crusted, but on the inside, he realized, he was stone dry. The next pot was for soup, and it seemed to take an age for the snow to melt, and fisheye, and boil. When the soup was finally ready, it tasted thin, bloodless, without the oil. David could tell he was fighting a losing battle against lethargy. He could feel himself sliding down.

A sharp, new odor reached David's flagging brain and brought him back to the surface. Ian nodded against the front corner of the tent.

"What's that smell?" David asked.

"What?"

"That smell, where's it coming from?" David reached out and unzipped his sleeping bag from around the Russian. The odor nearly made him gag. He pushed the Russian over on one side, ignoring the man's cries and Ian's commands to be gentle. Brown fluid seeped through the back of the man's long johns, the product of the relaxing of his rewarmed bowels.

"Goddamnit!" David yelled. The oatmeal, the nearly bursting tent, the longed-for rest now gone, his frozen fingers, the wasted stove gas, the snow still swirling inside their tent, and now this, his own sleeping bag beshitted. "Why are we keeping him? How are we going to go up if my sleeping bag is full of Russian shit!"

Ian stared, wide-eyed. "We're finished," he said. "Don't you know that? We're done. Tomorrow we're taking him down."

"He's already dead," David said. "Look at him. You think he's going to live through forty rappels? Out there? He's not even going to live through the night. We'll be lucky if we do."

"You want to just throw him out?"

"I want to keep going. We can leave him here in the tent. If he lives until we get back, we can talk about taking him down. Look at him. There's no reason to go down."

"If you want to keep going," Ian said, "you'll go on alone. Zip up his bag and get some sleep."

The night passed slowly. With the stove off and the three of them motionless, the tent grew cold and frozen. It was less comfortable, even, than their ledges of the previous nights, because David had nothing to lean against. Every time he shifted position, ice fell from the patchwork of rime layering the walls and ceiling of the tent. He listened to the Russian's labored breathing and realized, with no small amount of self-revulsion, that he hoped that those gasps would stop. One after another, he found himself rooting against the next wheeze and disappointed when it came. It was horrible, and fascinating, but he could not stop it, could not help wishing that the man would desist here and now and relieve them of the burden (and that he could be there, and aware, as it happened). He thought, too, of Ian's suggestion that he go on alone. The longer the night stretched out before and behind him, the more seriously he entertained the notion. *Why not?* he thought. *It can't be any worse than what we've put behind us. Without a rope, without stopping for belays, I would travel so fast. I would float.* He could go up until he'd run out of

mountain. But somewhere in his mind, he recognized the implausibil-
ity of this course. He was not that strong. He had too little left. He
wouldn't tackle Yunshan's crown alone.

When morning rolled around again, the Russian was still alive.

"Are you going up or coming down?" Ian asked.

"I'll follow you," David said. The disappointment was nauseating.

Outside, the storm had passed, leaving only a ceiling of scattered clouds in its wake. Ice-streaked cliffs towered over the men
and their tent. The rock kicked up out of the snow only fifty yards
back, though David had not even sensed the presence of all that stone
from within the storm. Above the cliffs, David could see sunlight
on Yunshan's last spires. *We'd be on top in the sunshine.* And for a
moment he considered heading in that direction, not saying anything,
just going. But he had already made words from his decision, and
his spirit was pointed downhill. They cleaned out the tent as best
they could, and Ian dressed the Russian in whatever could be salvaged from the man's clothes plus an extra layer from his own pack.
David's sleeping bag was foul, but he packed it anyway and tried not
to think about it. Disgusting or not, they would need it.

The Russian was barely mobile and had to be hoisted and dragged
by Ian, while David broke trail through the new snow left behind by
the storm. David felt dazed and numb. His body did not understand
their direction. For days (but really, for months), he had been clawing at this mountain. But now they were going down with mountain
still above them, and he didn't know why. His body had more to
give. The mountain hadn't exceeded him, not yet. Each step seemed
to tear out a length of his innards, which remained behind, stuck to

the ice-plastered stone. Above them, the final cliffs arched up out of the third eye. Below, the mountain curved and then dropped away.

Ian could barely move the Russian, and David had to give in and help after a while. After all, this was where David excelled, at lifting and hoisting dead weight. He clipped two lengths of webbing to the man's harness and put one over each of his shoulders, like backpack straps. Then he had Ian loop another piece under the man's armpits and around David's chest. With the Russian tied to him, David ended up bent halfway over, a hunchback with a body-sized tumor or a shadow made of flesh. But he could lurch along in Ian's tracks. Between thoughts—because he couldn't spare any air between breaths—David taunted himself. He could not think what else to do. *Your lists were off. You forgot to include one hundred and thirty pounds of dead Russian. You came to China to be an undertaker—no, a meat wagon.* But the Russian wasn't dead. That was the thing. Pressed against him, David could feel the bump-bump of the man's heart and the bellows-action of his lungs.

Before long (though David wasn't sure how much farther he could have lasted anyway), they ran out of walkable ground. Up ahead, the curve falling out of Yunshan's third eye steepened. A few steps more, and the ground slid away. David let himself fall backward into the snow and felt the Russian flinch and suck in air after they landed. Ian untied the strap around his chest, and David got back to his feet. Spasms ran up and down his legs and back, and he stumbled because he suddenly felt light and unanchored. Ian dribbled some water into the man's mouth and then squeezed in some GU, followed by more water. "I think his eyes are starting to focus better," Ian said.

They cut a bollard for their first anchor. They cleared the loose surface snow and then began to carve a turtleback shape in the hard snow below. The day was bright, and the sun was on them and the summit, too. "Ian," David said, still chopping the snow-ice with his axe. "You've got to help me. This hurts too much. Why are we doing this? What the hell am I supposed to be learning from this?"

"When we've got him down on the ground and he's walking around and laughing like a newborn, then it will make sense. You'll feel the higher purpose then. I guarantee it."

"How's he going to walk? His legs are frozen. They don't work." David reached over and lifted one of the Russian's boots, then let go. The leg boned into the boot flopped back into the snow. A sound came out of the Russian, something between a grunt and a yowl. "If we wanted to do good and save strays, we could have stayed in Oakland and wandered the docks at night."

Ian winced. "Buddy, you're hard. You know that? The bums on the docks aren't our people. They're not our business." Ian sat back and pointed his axe at the Russian, who remained flat where he had landed, face toward the sky. "He's one of us."

They finished the bollard, notched its uphill side, and threaded their ropes behind it. Ian would go first and find the next anchor, then David would follow with the Russian in tow. They did not have to discuss this; they knew their jobs. Ian backed down toward the edge and paused there.

"What do you think he's thinking?" Ian asked.

"Get going," David said. "If we're going to do this, we need to go. He thinks he's dead, and there are two ghosts hauling him to hell. Yeah. He's probably not far off. Maybe we're dead, too, and the three of us are being packed off together."

Ian disappeared, leaving David and the Russian alone together. The Russian's chest rose and fell, rose and fell, heaving air in and out. "Why are you doing that?" David said. "Don't you know you're already in hell?"

Ian's voice drifted up from down below. David threaded the ropes through his belay tube and clipped the Russian to a short loop attached to his harness. At first the Russian slid along in the snow like a sled, but as the ground cut away, more of his weight hung down off David's harness. David straddled the man to keep the weight centered and clipped a sling back under the Russian's armpits to keep his head clear of the wall. David could feel the strain of twice his usual weight in his brake hand.

When he arrived at the next anchor, he found Ian clipped to a single piton hammered sideways behind a cinder-block-sized rock. David made no comment. They had nine ice screws, fourteen cams, and eight—now seven—pitons. Each rappel would eat a fraction of the rack; they could not afford redundancy. They had played this game before. David found it best not to think about it, to simply trust Ian's gear implicitly. Of course, in the past, they had been two and had used stances to reduce the weight on each piece. Now they would have at least two bodies on every piece, every time. Ian clipped the Russian's harness sling to the piton, and David lowered himself until the pin took the Russian's weight. David watched the eye of the piton flex microscopically under its load, but the body of the pin held its crack without complaint. They pulled their ropes, which tumbled down in a cloud of snow, and rethreaded them on the one piton keeping them all attached to the mountain.

Now that they were back in the vertical, David took the downward lead, and Ian took charge of the Russian, a relief for David. It was easier to block out the present without the Russian gasping in his ear. David set off on rappel, sliding down their dangling cords, searching out the next link in their chain down the mountain.

The rappels were brutally slow. Maneuvering and resettling the Russian took hours of benumbed persistence. The sun passed over the summit and left them in shadow, though the cloud wisps scattered and the sky remained blue. David froze. The cold invaded his flesh and stroked his bones. He had nowhere to go and nothing to do to stay warm, so he hung from his harness and shivered and waited for Ian to arrive with the Russian slung below him. The anchors were horror shows. David had to clear away yards of snow and scrappy ice to search for solid placements. Even so, the anchor piece was usually jigged into disintegrating rock spider-lined with cracks and fractures. David tried not to look. Staring wouldn't hold the rock together. The mountain dropped away under their boots, long cliffs and curtains of ice tumbling down and down. David tried not to look there either. He could get lost in all that distance.

The Russian never fought but never helped. He hung limply from each anchor, a sack of flesh connected to a diaphragm that worked on and on like a metronome. His breathing remained a steady pained gasp. His inner workings—what was going on inside of him, if anything—remained a mystery. He babbled sometimes, though maybe it was only air bubbling up through his throat. For the first time, David began to think the man might live through the day. "You might be the luckiest stiff to ever end up in a snow bank," he told the Russian at one belay while Ian pulled their ropes. "How are you going to explain to your friends back home that two Americans dropped out of the sky to pull you off a mountain in south China?" Ian chortled, and the ropes whipped through the air. David readjusted the sling around the Russian's shoulders to keep his head from slumping into the snow. One of his lip blisters cracked, and clear fluid leaked out. David tried to blot it with the man's jacket collar but thought he might be doing more harm than good. "What is keeping you going?" David asked him. "I'd like to see your genes. The mountain can't stamp you out, the blizzard can't blow you away, the cold can't shut you down—though it's sure trying, isn't it?" But if he lived, then they would certainly not reach the ground today or tomorrow or even the day after that. By early afternoon, they had only completed five rappels.

Twilight dimmed into dusk, and there were no sitting-ledges in sight. David had spent the afternoon expecting this. He tried not to struggle against it or the darkness that was coming for them. They arranged slings to stand in and hung the stove to start melting snow for water. They draped the tent fly over themselves in the hopes of trapping some body heat and cutting the wind. They raced to secure some kind of foothold against the night, but already their hands and minds had lost their grip, so it was a slow, fumbling, maddening race. Under the fly, their headlamps seemed to cast more shadows than light. David mostly saw the black, crisscrossed lines hanging behind their rats' nest of slings and ropes and sleeping bags instead of the objects themselves. The Russian's blackened and blistered face floated at the center of the mess, where they had trussed him to the anchor. He seemed to sleep. His eyes were closed and his breathing even.

David withdrew. He gave up his feet and his hands. Dimly, he hoped he might have them back someday. He was too exhausted to force his blood out to those distant places. Sometimes he stood in the slings; sometimes he hung from his harness. Those were the poles of his existence. Moving caused the tent fly to crackle and slough ice on them all. The Russian gasped, and Ian shuffled through his own cycle of hanging and standing. Even though they were pressed together in a knot of flesh, David felt miles away from the other two men. He barely held onto his own consciousness. Imagining the consciousnesses of the other two flesh lumps to his left was not a feat his brain could perform in its state. He could feel all the leaks of night air through the sleeping bag wrapped around him—though he could do nothing about them.

The night tunneled on.

At times David caught a few minutes of feverish sleep slumped over in his harness, but then he would wake, trembling, suffocating either from the harness cutting through his middle or the tent fly on his face or the cold. His half-asleep and half-awake thoughts ran together in a maze of grotesque and insensible impressions. One small branch of his mind tried to calm him and gather him apart from what was happening to his body, but this faint voice was plowed under by a waterfall of brain noise.

Morning came all at once. The night faded fast. The day mind banished and tidied until all those half-made thoughts and dreams existed in a grey, twice-lost past. The sky turned blue and then pink, and then the sun opened its eye on the horizon. From their outpost on the east-facing wall, the light hit them right away, pale at first, but then brighter and stronger. David felt shaky and paper-thin. But glad. The sun brought him back. He could feel it in the loosening of his spine and shoulders and mind.

"Nights like that are the way to live to a hundred," Ian said. "I feel like it added five years to my life—that's how long it took."

They were all still alive. The Russian opened his eyes and took a long, startled-sounding breath.

"That sun is like a thousand-calorie breakfast," David said. "It's amazing. Imagine what it must feel like to be a plant in the arctic when the sun comes back after the winter."

The sun bathed them in light. David truly felt he could suck it down like cosmic juice. He imagined a million-mile straw with the sun, a giant orange, on one side and his lips on the other. He began to work on his hands. They were coming back, too. This gave him hope. If he had his hands, he could keep on. He had faith in his hands.

After the first reawakening, the fact that they were no longer frozen and benighted gradually became less extraordinary. The work of the day was the same; sunrise had neither brought the ground closer nor taken any weight out of the Russian. After a long hour of making water and untangling frozen ropes and feeling weak and spent despite the sun, David cast off again, groping for one more hundred-and-fifty-foot fraction of the distance down to the glacier.

The first new anchor of the day was a gift. A spike of rock jabbed out from the wall, and David draped a loop of webbing over it, clipped himself to it, and shouted up to Ian. It was good to have the first rappel over with so quickly. It began the day with a feeling of gathering momentum. If they could build up some pace, they could actually make progress. David extrapolated his way down the mountain, feeling optimistic, thinking about minutes instead of hours. They were going to be all right. They just needed to get the machinery of their system humming along. He imagined what Ian would be doing with the upper anchor and the Russian. First he'd take out the extra pieces they had used in the bivouac—maybe he had already done that. That would take a few minutes. He would put himself on rappel and clip the Russian short to his harness. Then he'd use a long sling running through a carabiner off the anchor to hoist the Russian up to give him the slack he needed to unclip the man from his direct umbilicus to the anchor. Give him five, okay ten, minutes for that. Then he'd lower the Russian back down until the weight settled on his harness and the long sling could be released and the rappel begun. Which meant that Ian with his dangling Russian should appear just about—now.

Nothing happened. Some morning updrafts swam past. David repeated the steps in his mind. He knew he was keyed up by the sunrise and the first rappel. He was probably sped up in his head, too, his thoughts moving faster than reality. If he ran the steps through once more to double his sense of the passing minutes, that should give Ian the time he needed.

Nothing happened. The sun floated up off the horizon toward midmorning. David felt his optimism deflate. He shifted back and forth in his harness. He was stuck again, watching the passing day and the glacier through a half mile of empty air. Being motionless was sucking the oxygen out of his brain. His instincts told him to run for his life—to be charging down the rappels, each moment choreographed for speed. But here he was instead, stuck, hanging, doing nothing. No progress. No action outside of his head.

Ian appeared a hundred feet overhead with the Russian slung between his legs.

"What happened?" David shouted up at him.

"What do you mean?" Ian said.

"Something get stuck?"

"No. What's gotten into you?"

"We're going too slow!" David said. "We need to get moving."

"Hey, man, calm down," Ian said. "You're not moving so fast yourself."

When Ian arrived at the anchor, David clipped the Russian to the sling around the horn. Ian lowered himself another foot until the man's weight passed to the anchor sling and Ian could unclip him from his own harness. Then he cranked himself back up to the anchor and clipped himself in. These steps happened automatically, the same each time. The Russian was always attached to Ian's harness, or the anchor, or both at once during the transition back and forth. Ian began pulling their ropes, while David resettled the Russian and adjusted his chest sling to keep the man's head upright and off the cliff wall.

"You two making friends?" Ian said.

Probably Ian meant this as a concession or peace offering, like the time David had said his soul was spotless. His tone was friendly, almost apologetic. David heard this, and knew it, and yet he was so strung out by their crawling escape from the mountain that he could not summon a bluff or brotherly answer to Ian or their situation. He dropped the sling he had been fiddling with, and the Russian listed toward Yunshan. "Ain't no friends up here," he said. He wanted to say more. *How much are you willing to give for him?* That was the question he wanted the answer to. *What's he worth?* But he did not feel sane enough for that discussion, and maybe he didn't want to know the answer. As far as he could tell, they were committed. Anyway, there wasn't time for talk. They needed to move.

Ian finished pulling the ropes, and they fell clear. They rethreaded them off the new anchor, and David put himself immediately on rappel. Finally, he was back in motion, though he felt stiff and clumsy from having hung in his harness for so long without moving. His mind raced ahead of his body. He tried to rein himself back in.

The new anchor would not come easy. He found brittle ice and fragile, warty rock that shattered into dust and gravel when he tested it. He scratched back and forth, knocking away snow and loose stones, looking for anything solid to hang themselves from. To his right he found a groove that took an angle piton. But when he bounced it, the rock shattered and the pin tore out, sending David spinning out over the ocean of air washing the mountain below him. Each effort—each piton he hammered and block he trundled—took minutes, and the minutes multiplied and scattered on the wind.

His mind ticked off the time. He swung back and forth, searching farther to the left and right, crampons scratching and catching. The ropes scraped snow and stones off from above, which rattled off his helmet. Forty feet to his left, a corner cut away and out of sight. He built up speed, practically running through the pendulum arc at the bottom of the ropes. He swung hard to the left and grabbed the edge of the corner, hoping for a miracle.

Tucked away inside the corner he found a half-inch crack filled with loose flakes. It wasn't a miracle, but it would do. He used the pick of his axe to scour its insides, hammered in a five-eighths pin to the eye, and clipped himself to it with relief that tasted strongly of panic. He looked back around the corner to where his ropes traveled a long slanted line up to Ian. Running back and forth with the Russian would never work. Even if Ian could make the horizontal distance, how would they maneuver the Russian around the corner to the anchor? David tensioned off the piton and leaned back around the corner to the main wall. He found a shallow pocket for a small cam. It was flared and overextended and David didn't trust it a bit, but it might work for a temporary anchor while they passed the Russian around to the good piton.

Ian began his rappel. He lowered himself and his cargo down while David pulled them over to the anchor with the trailing ends of the ropes. The two actions couldn't happen at once—Ian couldn't slide down the ropes while David pulled—so they worked out a pattern. Ian would drop five feet, and then David would pull him a short ways over, then Ian would drop again at the apex of David's pull, and then David would haul him in again before Ian began to swing back the other direction. The sequence came naturally. They didn't need to talk it through. They both knew what was needed. When Ian came level with David, he was only a few yards off from the anchor. David pulled in hard, and Ian clipped his ropes through the little cam in the pocket.

The cam held, but it was terrifying to see how it flexed and shifted. Rock turned to dust under the cam lobes, and it skated a millimeter closer to the surface. David tied Ian off short to the anchor so that if the piece broke free, Ian wouldn't fly back across the wall.

Ian leaned and strained and pressed himself and the Russian around the edge into the corner. David reached over and grabbed the Russian's harness with his right hand, helping to relieve Ian of the weight while hauling them both in. That was when the cam finally pulled. Ian lurched hard to the right, but David held the Russian and pulled them both back to the anchor. Ian reached across and clipped himself to the piton. Now they were both on the anchor, and all they needed to do was get the Russian attached as well. Ian helped David lift the man higher. One of them would need to let go in order to anchor the Russian, and Ian said he would if David could hold the man, and David agreed. So for a moment, David held the Russian, and the moment stretched on and on because Ian fumbled with the carabiners and the slings and unclipped the wrong one. So now the Russian was not attached to Ian's harness or to the anchor. David held the man with both hands on his harness. They were practically face-to-face because of the way David was twisted around to bear his weight. David watched the Russian's grey eyes, inches from his own, and since there was nothing there to see, he saw instead the three of them sleeping in slings, stalled out and unable to move, his stained sleeping bag draped across shivering shoulders, days and nights of this, and Yunshan's spired crown in the sun, and his own haggard, exhausted reflection. He had no faith in this, what they were doing with this man. He opened his left hand, and then his right hand, and the Russian's harness fell out of his fingers, and the man went tumbling through the air, bellowing into the wind.

Ian yelled, too, first a sound of fright, as if he wasn't sure who was falling, then a punctuated thunder-burst of rage. The Russian was still gaining speed, though he had narrowed in size. "Murderer!" Ian shouted. He sputtered broken syllables but then found traction again. "You can't hang onto anything."

David was tired and past caring. The Russian was gone now, and David's guts resettled from their first lurch when he had felt as if he were falling too. "Wake up. We were going to die. He's been trying to kill us since the moment he came out of the storm."

"No. We were going to make it. You were going to do something great. Now you're all alone. You don't believe in anything."

David thought this was insane. "What was there to believe in?" he said. "He never gave us a sign. He never lifted a finger to show us he was there."

David pulled the ropes from around the corner and threaded them through the new anchor. As soon as they were through, he was back on rappel. He had done what he needed to do to save them. He wasn't heartless. The falling man wrenched at him. That was enough, wasn't it? The remorse he felt seemed appropriate to what he thought he should feel. Couldn't he also admit to feeling unburdened? He could feel the sense of momentum again, or at least the potential for it. Now they could move. In his head, the Russian kept falling and falling. David did not dig into this vision, or attempt to stop it, so it continued to run. He didn't want to touch it, and he didn't have time. He had work to do. He wanted the ground.

The difference in speed was miraculous, as if they had been paralyzed and suddenly healed. At the next anchor, David shouted "off rappel," and he could feel Ian come shooting down the ropes just a few seconds later. Rappel followed rappel just like this. They reached the hollows under Yunshan's cheekbones, and the rock improved, and the anchors came faster and terrified them less.

Ian had cooled off, but David found his new voice more uncomfortable than his anger. He was quizzical and curious and completely calm. David imagined him poking at the broken-up bodies in Yosemite. It was not a pleasant thought now that he was on the receiving end of that scrutiny.

"I've never known a murderer before," Ian said at one anchor as he clipped himself in. "What does it feel like?"

"Cut it out," David said. "That wasn't murder."

"What would you call it?"

"He was already dead. He shouldn't have been with us in the first place." This was asinine. David knew it. He should just stick his lips together and let Ian talk to himself. But there was also something calming about hearing words outside his own head. Watching the Russian fall had wigged him out, no doubt about it. His feeling of lightness also made him feel unanchored, as if he could drift off their latest piece and fall himself. He felt suddenly insubstantial. He found he was double- and triple-checking his connection to the anchor.

"You wanted him dead?" Ian asked.

"I wanted him gone. Look—admit to me that he was going to kill us. Him being here meant we were going to die." Now, moving fast down the mountain, would David admit to himself that he wasn't completely sure this was true? Yes. Could he have lasted another night? Probably. A third night hanging? He was less sure about that. But why? What for? How many toes did he need to lose for the sake of Ian's fetish?

"You wanted to deny him?" Ian said. "You don't even believe he was alive, do you?"

David was losing Ian's track. "What the hell does that mean?" he said. "Keep pulling those ropes!" He had to keep them pressing forward.

"Buddy, just because you want something to not exist doesn't mean you get your way."

It went on like that. Ian was shamelessly persistent. The day sped by faster than them, but the ground kept coming closer. Night arrived, and they didn't stop. Neither of them even suggested it. They turned on their headlamps and carried on. The cold sank into them again, but David didn't feel it as much—maybe because they kept moving, maybe because he had run out of energy to shiver. He wrapped his sleeping bag around himself like a poncho and tied it there with an extra sling. They were alternating leads on the rappels now, leapfrogging each other down the mountain. The world disappeared once more, leaving only looming shadows outside the light-cones of their headlamps. David switched his light off at the anchor when he was waiting in order to conserve the batteries. Then the world disappeared altogether. The fragile spark in his own mind seemed to flutter and wink in all that blackness. He wondered where the moon had gone. Was it new already? He drifted off, only to jerk awake, blind in the dark, clutching for something to grab hold of until he found the mountain and his harness and remembered where he was. Ian had yelled him awake. The new anchor was set, and it was his turn to rappel. David switched his headlamp back on, and the world of his light-cone reappeared. From then on, they had to yell each other awake after every rappel.

When morning relit the mountain, they discovered they were only a few hundred feet above the glacier. David began their second-to-last rappel and reached the top of a broad ice sheet, a hard skin over the root-bulge of the mountain. He anchored them with a screw. A few feet to his right, a chunk had been broken out of the ice, and David saw streaks of red and black. His eyes wandered back there whenever he forgot to look elsewhere. Ian arrived, and when he saw the stain, he said, "I guess we did a good job of following the fall line, huh?"

Ian disappeared down the last rappel. When the ropes went slack, David followed him down to a short ramp of sixty-degree ice where the rope ends dangled. Ian was nowhere to be seen. David pulled the ropes, and they went skittering down to the glacier proper. He down-climbed the last few yards of ice, front-pointing carefully with wooden feet. He couldn't remember when he had felt his toes last. Yesterday? The day before? When he reached level ground, he felt unsteady. The earth had tilted ninety degrees, and he had no equilibrium for flatness. Behind him, the mountain wrenched up out of the snow, sheer and broad. The glacier magnified the sun and filled his eyes with white noise. The air seemed painfully saturated with light. Black crevasses cracked the top layer, playing tricks on him, making it difficult to tell between the sunspots crawling across his retinas and real gaps in the snow.

Ian appeared from around an old avalanche cone, his red suit fuzzing up out of the brightness and then sprouting arms and legs. He had something dark and battered in his hands. "This is all I found," Ian said. "It's all there is."

What was he carrying? Bloody fuck. The Russian's head. The man's nose and one eye socket had been crushed. Bone poked through the ragged collar of his neck.

"You're sick," David said. He felt like vomiting, but his stomach was a dried-up void.

"Don't you understand?" Ian said. "There's nothing else here. I've looked."

"The rest went down a crevasse," David said. He refused to acknowledge Ian's implication. He wanted no part of that. He had no intention of following Ian any further.

Ian pushed the head toward David. It was black, lopsided, bristly. Dried blood scabbed its ragged parts and crusted Ian's hands. "Don't turn away from this," Ian said. "Here's your chance to see below the surface. He's come back."

David was revolted. "Stop it. Throw it down a crevasse with the rest of the body. Give it some peace."

"He's yours," Ian said. He put the head down in the snow, faceup toward David and the mountain behind him. "Do what you like with him."

It looked foul in the snow. All David could think of was to get the head down a crevasse, out of sight, so the mountain could be clean and bare again. He took one step forward and punted the head toward the nearest crack. But the front points of his crampon stuck in the Russian's face, and the head stayed stuck to his boot—as if it were eating the front part of his foot—no matter how hard he kicked and swore. And Ian laughed and laughed at him, a sound like ice moving over rock.

PROUD LINE

I

THE CROIX VERTE hut was built on a flat step in the rock, level with the surface ice of the Gesner Glacier, during that brief time between the wars when the future could be imagined without alarm. The hut was designed so that the alpinist could step directly from the ice to the front porch, and with two steps more be inside and handed a cup of tea by the warden. But the glacier retreated and left the hut high above a newly born headwall. By 1987, the hut sat fifty feet above the glacier, with a sheer drop down to the ice.

Officially, the Croix Verte was abandoned, but rumor had it the hut was still used. Which is why Sam, having left his tent behind, found himself clambering hand over hand through the dregs of twilight up a knotted length of faded climbing rope someone had fixed to a porch beam long ago. Sam had left more than his tent. He'd left his home mountains, too. Back in Washington, he would have been climbing volcanoes on the Pacific Rim. Young mountains, those—cinder stacks, really, so recently piled they hadn't yet been dismantled and tossed into the sea by their glaciers, even though Sam could practically watch them crumble out from under his boots. Later in the summer, he'd move inland to where the granite peaks pushed up through the fleece of dark, wet pines. At night he'd read—he always brought a book because otherwise on a stormbound day the tent walls closed in and his watch ran slow and his head filled with restless lunatics. Sam escaped into stories about Terray and Messner and Rébuffat. He liked best the time of the beginning, when men and women quit lumbering around the mountains like the upright apes they were and began instead to climb, putting their monkey hands to good use. The orange nylon disappeared from around him, and he'd share nightmare bivies on the Eiger or follow Joe Brown up wet gritstone with nothing but a hemp rope, a wobbly piton, and their fingertips between them and gravity's hook.

From inside his tent under a volcano or a jag of Pacific granite, Sam made plans to go into the country of his books. Now that he'd arrived and was swimming up out of the twilight toward the hut, he saw everything doubled, the images off the page overlapping the real mountains around him. His hands yarded on the sun-bleached fixed rope, but there were other hands too, probably some he had read about, on the rope, on the rock. The shadows of the past roamed around him. Sam reached the porch, pulled himself over the edge, and had a seat. Perched there, he could have been a gargoyle on a battlement. His face was gaunt, all hollows and bones, a contradiction to his youth people found unsettling. He looked feverish. Sam tossed a few words down into the darkness to let his partner know it was his turn.

Five minutes later, Tyson surfaced and heaved himself up beside Sam. "Damn the Euros," he said. "That rope is thrashed."

Sam nodded. The sheath had disintegrated, and parts of the core were shot too. "Old-world standards," he muttered. "Everything's so old over here they probably don't see the problem."

"Lucky for them," Tyson said. "I'd rather they keep the raggy tapestries in their castles."

Sam didn't answer, his attention already taken back by the mountains. The moon was out, and the Gesner cut a silver stripe through black cliffs running up to jagged silhouettes. For a moment he saw the glacier as the tongue of a fabulous monster and the arc of mountains the teeth set in its lower jaw. *And we're the little sucker fish,* he thought. Was he ready for old-world mountains? All the tales he'd absorbed of bearded seekers with gorilla arms weren't just words anymore. The rock was real. So were the stories. Past climbers filled the night-mountains. Sam sensed them ghosting through the darkness. He'd walked into the realm of legend, and who was he? He'd read too damn much.

"We're not alone," Tyson said, jerking his head toward the front window of the hut, where a face and a candle appeared for a moment and then sank away behind the glass.

The lock on the door had been chiseled out, and what was left of the latch opened with a push of the thumb. Inside, a half dozen candles threw off more shadows than light. Unlit stubs and wax pools scabbed every surface, including the chairs and floor. Two men sat across from each other at the long table in the room's center, a wristwatch, a bottle of wine, and a candle between them. One of the two must have been up to look out the window, but now they seemed rooted. Maybe they'd hoped for someone other than a couple American wankers to wash up at the front door. The light barely found their faces, lighting the tips of their noses—one hooked, the other broad, broken, and flat—and the curls of their beards, but leaving the rest in shadow. "Oy," offered the one with the black beard and hooked nose.

"Room for two more?" Tyson asked.

"Depends," barked the redder, thinner beard, without looking up. "You two feeling protective towards your arse-holes?"

"Don't listen to 'im," the other said. "Bunks are on the other side. Check 'em for mouse turds."

Through the partition dividing the hut in half, they found the sleeping room, crammed floor to ceiling with wooden platforms and thin, mildewed mattresses. Sam and Tyson each chose a bunk and brushed away the rodent piles. Despite the thick blond timbers in the walls, the air inside was as cold as out, and the heat they'd made coming up the valley evaporated fast into the night. An old cast iron woodstove filled a corner in the other room, but it had looked rusty and stone-cold, and Sam figured that no one had bothered dragging fuel up here since the hut and glacier parted ways.

"It's like we're squatting in a museum," he said to Tyson. "I keep expecting faces to come out of the walls."

Back in the common room, the two Brits hadn't budged. Sam took a chair to the front window, where he could sit and look out at the moon and stars by shielding the glass with his hands. He felt unaccountably jittery. Despite the cold, his palms felt wet. Warnings, vague fears brushed by. He shook out his hands and poked around the corners of his mind, searching for the bad juju, then realized the atmosphere was so strained around the two at the table that he'd been infected from clear across the room.

"Looks like execution day," he said to the Brits.

"Ha! Close on it." That was the hook-nosed man again, who said his name was Nigel, his partner's James. His beard straggled off at his collarbone, and his eyebrows shagged down over his eyes, though it was hard to distinguish between shadow and the man's black wool. "Poor planning on our parts to wind up here with nothing to do apart from a bottle of wine. It's too much head time."

James slouched elaborately in his chair. Red fuzz covered his face, which was all sharp angles except for the nose, which looked like the aftermath of a half-hearted effort to smear a whole strawberry on a piece of toast. "Some beautiful riots been had under conditions like these," he said. "Shameful waste."

"Couldn't afford it," Nigel said. "Have to be in form tomorrow."

"Pah. Be worth it."

A honey-grained countertop ran along the backside of the hut and ended where a copper sink drained directly outside through a pipe cut down through the wall. Tyson levered himself up onto the counter and casually lotused his legs. "Don't make us guess," he said. "Got something famous planned?"

"It's the devil come to tempt us into the talking jinx," James said.

"Be strong, brother," Nigel answered.

"We'll have at the Center Route on the Aiguille de la Flèche," James said.

Nigel banged his hand down flat on the table. "Well done. You've avoided temptation. As always."

"I've never heard of it," Tyson said.

"The Yankees don't know their history."

"I've heard of it," Sam said. "That was Zapelli's retirement route."

"I was there," Nigel said, "when he came back from the climb. He'd been up there with a Frenchman. Everyone knew where they'd been. Zapelli walked into La Pierre d'Or, and the whole joint went silent the moment he opened the door. The first time in his life he looked old. He looked more than that. Absolutely spent. Vacant. Shuffling baby steps to a chair and table.

"I was seventeen, getting my bum handed to me by my first season in the Alps. I remember his face, like the life had been scooped out, naught left but the flesh. Marcel Tappes was there that day, celebrating his own tenth year of retirement. He walked over and put a hand on Zapelli's shoulder. He bent his head down to ask the question we all were waiting for the answer to. A young old man bent over an old young man, that's what it looked like. Zapelli just nodded his head.

"Tappes stood straight, and I wasn't sure whether he was going to salute or start passing out cigars. He shook Zapelli's hand and walked back to his table, kicking his feet like he'd vault the bar. We got noisy then. It's not every day you get to be there when one of the Last Greats hikes her skirts for a fellow. The barman himself got off his duff and took a glass of wine to Zapelli, and that was a big moment, as he had no love of Italians. We were all swilling and toasting. But I saw that few of us went over to talk to the man who was the cause of the celebrating. He'd gone beyond us. Who knows what he thought of himself, but we couldn't touch him just the same.

"He never said a thing about the route. But we could tell from his face what was up there. We could fill in the blanks. Pain and fear. Tattooed to his skin. That was his last big climb. He slid down into glory."

Nigel closed up, his mouth buried by his beard. The night had become turbulent outside. The sound of the wind rubbing against the rocks and the roof vibrated down through the walls, but the air inside remained still, the candle flames undisturbed.

"That was fifteen years back," James said. "And the beast ain't yet seen a second ascent. Fifteen fucking years. And not from lack of trying. Lowe went up there. And Harrison and Thule. And Dickey and Frémont. Not a single one of them made it to the top. They all abandoned the route. They came sleepwalking back with their tails between their legs, looking shattered, just like Zapelli, only tense and spooked instead of slack tired."

Sam looked back out through the window to see if the wind had brought any clouds, but it was still clear, the stars brilliant, almost caustic to his eyes. From inside the hut, the landscape looked unnatural—lunar, dangerous. He imagined the Italian, Zapelli, rafting out into that darkness, one warm spark between the mountains and the stars.

"You scared of it?" Tyson asked.

"Shitless," James said.

"To the point where I reckon I'll fall off the rope just coming down from the roost in the morning," Nigel said.

"No, we'll be better off then, when we can stop this sitting," James said.

"The morning's never going to come, brother," Nigel answered. "Look at the watch. You tired? I'm not. The night's never going to end."

▲

JUST BEFORE DAWN, Sam tossed off his sleeping bag. The Brits were long gone, already plunged into their war with history. Asleep, Sam had barely registered their departure in the middle of the night. He imagined them now, two bearded faces staring wide-eyed up into the unknown. He could feel their sweat freeze at the belays in the shadows on the immense north-facing wall. Sam found it uncomfortable to wake up rested and easy knowing that nearby, the two of them were working hard to stay alive. They had crossed over to a territory inhuman, and he was standing around inside a womb of milled wood. The air and floor were sharply cold, but Sam stayed barefoot and shirtless in defiance—of what, he couldn't say. He walked outside to piss off the porch into the stained snow below.

The mountain teeth in the first sunshine: big, sharp, erupting out of the earth and towering over the hut, tapering to points so slender Sam imagined balancing on their tops with one foot. Lower, closer mountains crowded forward and blocked his view of the Aiguille de la Flèche. A few cuts of steep, dark rock and curtains of ice hinted at the beast rising just there over the edge. Shivering, Sam retreated to the hut and told Tyson to get his carcass out of bed.

They climbed rock that day, following a zigzagging crack system for twelve hundred feet up the Tomas Spur. They climbed well; they climbed fast. It was a good day, the kind of day when gravity lets go and the rock reaches out and shakes your hand with a firm grip. The sun kept them warm, but the rock stayed crisp. Sam hand-traversed the final knife ridge to the summit, pasting his climbing shoes to bare friction, looking down past his feet through an immense well of air all the way to the glacier below. Following, Tyson stood up and took the edge on tiptoe, arms raised like a wire walker—because he could, because the stone was that good to them. The afternoon sun angled down and colored him gold, and Sam hooted and whistled from the summit like a spectator at the fair.

The top, a lightning-scarred anvil for the local thunderheads, allowed them just enough room to sit stuck together at the shoulder. They stared out at the surrounding peaks, which seemed built to shred the sky. Curling zephyrs and updrafts swam past, tugging the two climbers into space. On three sides, the ground fell away, stamped into flat two-dimensionality by the sheer distance down. On the fourth side, a notch connected them to the Azzu Massif, to which the Tomas Spur was really only a satellite. The Azzu dwarfed the Tomas to the west, but to the south, the Aiguille de la Flèche lifted its head high above them all.

The line was breathtaking—not like the Venus at the museum, breathtaking like being held underwater in the middle of a cold ocean. From east and west, two great planes of rock joined in the center, the prow of a stone ship cutting through the earth. From far back, the prow looked straight, monolithic. Spit from the summit on a dead-calm day, and you'd dampen the ground right where you'd started. But when Sam pried into the details, trying to piece together the climb in his head, he saw cut-stone roofs, cresting waves of rock, stacked icicles like stands of inverted white pines dangling down the wall. The mountain pushed him further and further into space with every move.

"Crazy," Tyson said. "Those Brits better not suck."

Sam looked for the Brits but saw no sign of them. This meant nothing. The mountain opened for him like a Chinese box each time he looked closer. The Brits could have been hidden in a hundred places. Still, Sam would have liked to have caught a glimpse of the two, to give the mountain some scale and put a chink in its armor.

"Come on," Tyson said. "We should go. Look at the sun."

Eleven rappels toward the shadows leaking from the base of the mountain took them back down to the Gesner. They slid down their ropes, letting gravity reclaim them, the work of the day undone in lengths of 150 feet. Then down the glacier and up the tatty rope and back into the hut, where they had food and goose down and protection from the twilight winds. Sam sat on the porch an extra few minutes, feet dangling over the glacier, watching the late sun drench the mountains in color. It had been a good day—a good day, but not a proud day, not the kind of day that added enough coal to the fire of satisfaction for it to be carried through the valleys and cities.

The last light leaked away slowly, and Sam spent some time cleaning the hut. He cleared the cobwebs and spider husks from the

corners. He wiped out the copper washbasin. He felt like an archae-
ologist. Restoring the hut's interior made it easier to see the climbers
who'd been there. Maybe the walls would tell him about Zapelli. The
night before, had the man been calm, jittery, wild? What had he done
to push himself over the Styx and off the map? With his pocketknife,
Sam pried candle wax off the walls and beams, uncovering the nail-less
joinery and the glow of the wood. Beautiful craftwork, clean, solid.

"It's not too late," Tyson said. "You could warden the hut. Hang
out your shingle, have hot dinner going, collect dimes or francs or
whatever. Become the old man of the mountain. Who'd bother chasing you away?"

"My cooking's lousy. I'd eat bark if it had calories."

"Good point. Nickels then."

Darkness settled, and the temperature dropped. Tyson brought out
his pack to find some warm clothes. He also produced a plastic bag
of reefer and rolling papers. He shrugged at Sam. "It's not wine, but
I bet the Brits will appreciate a little smoke. One way or the other."

"If they make it back tonight." Sam felt antsy when he thought
about the Brits facing the oncoming night. It was one thing to watch
darkness spread from behind wood and glass and another to be up
there, enveloped by the black cold, preparing for a night standing in
nylon slings, hoping the relentless drip-drip-drip of heat lost to the
void won't bleed your body dry.

"It's just enough to go around," Tyson said. "I'll save it."

With full dark in the hut, there wasn't much to do besides eat
and go to sleep, but Sam delayed both. The wind gusted past outside.
Twice Sam went out to check that the rope hadn't blown out of reach.

"This is a side of you I've never seen," Tyson said. "You're like a mother hen."

Sam dropped back into a chair. "I feel lazy sitting here. Those two are sticking out their necks, and I'm eating dinner off a table." He snapped his fingers in the air. "Garçon! Where's my baguette and claret?"

"Hey, man, I was stoked about today. Don't ruin it with your big ideas."

Toward midnight, the door banged open, and two men entered the hut, strangers at first, then barely recognizable. Both of them looked bewildered by the candlelight. They seemed to sag, all the elastic given out between muscle and skin. They dropped their packs and headlamps by the door without a downward glance. Nigel collapsed into the chair on Sam's left, and James took the one to his right.

"So?" Sam said, after a moment. He'd thought the answer would be obvious, but instead they just looked evacuated.

"So what?" Nigel snarled.

"Did you make it or not?" Tyson said.

"Of course not," Nigel said. "It's impossible."

"Impossible?" Sam asked, with visions of a shrunken little Italian man grinning and pounding on the bar for another round.

"Absolutely," James said. "Nearly dead twice, no progress made. Can't be done."

Sam watched the two of them uncoil in their chairs, the sap rising through their veins. They seemed to be reinflating, as if the walls and candles had summoned their souls back into their bodies. He marked the signs. Failed or not, they'd crossed the line, hadn't they?

Seen the dragon and returned. What would that do to a person? He watched their eyes relight. The blank inwardness they'd walked in with burned off like a fog.

"Did you two wait up for us?" James said. "Tell you what, that's better than my last girl."

Tyson ignored him and plopped his magic bag on the table.

"Now tell me, lad," Nigel said, "and don't be false. Is that her Royal Highness?"

"None other."

"Well," Nigel sighed. "I always was a believer in the monarchy." He reached for the bag, but too slow, and a pair of crooked hands from the opposite direction snatched it out from under his hooks. Nigel roared and leapt full length across the table, sending candles cartwheeling and flickering, his hands reaching for his partner's throat.

"Fuck, Nigel, are you crazy?" James hollered before his chair tipped back and Nigel landed on top of him on the floor. They rolled twice over with the bag lost somewhere between them, until Nigel leapt back to his feet with a tightly rolled joint clenched miraculously, like a magician's denouement, in his teeth. James remained on his back, making a honking noise through his misshapen nose that Sam identified as laughter.

Tyson handed Nigel a candle, and he lit up and took a puff. "Cheers, lads," he said. James, still lying flat and honking, built his own joint on his chest, and Nigel leaned over and lit his partner's smoke. "Quickly now, watch the wax, there you go." James propped his head up with one fist and took in three slow drags. Then he jumped to his feet and strutted over to the packs they had dropped by the door. He grabbed his two ice tools and one of Nigel's, and spun them in the air, spike over adze, his hands in constant motion, the end of his joint glowing orange with each inward breath.

"Better'n a juke-box, ain't he?" Nigel said. "Put in a penny, and he'll give you an hour's entertainment." The ice axes spun and flashed in the candlelight, and James spun underneath them, catching one behind his back, under his shoulder, between his legs. Nigel hummed a marching tune and clapped his hands in time to the beat of the twirling axes, while Tyson flapped his arms and shuffled out some sort of bent-legged dance, hopping up and down.

"Here," Tyson said, "throw one to me."

An axe flew toward his head, and he plucked it out of the air. In that curious way he had of transfiguring himself from loose-limbed awkwardness to graceful control, a moment Sam had witnessed every time they went climbing, Tyson took two measured steps toward the west end of the hut, then turned and threw the axe back across the room, over the empty chairs, and pick-first into the opposite wall, where it stuck with a knife-thrower's precision at eyelevel in a pine timber.

Maybe if he'd spoken up right away, Sam could have altered the course of the night, because he saw in that first moment of speechlessness not so much the destination as the shape of what was to come. But by the time he was ready to say *What the fuck, Tyson?* or to punch his partner in the arm, Nigel had already bellowed, "That was brilliant!" and grabbed the other two axes from James to try his hand. Looking back later, Sam wondered if that moment's pause had come because he himself had enjoyed too well the puncture of the axe through the hut wall, had found the flying splinters of old, gold wood too satisfying.

They were all terrible, except for Tyson, who could stick the same spot every time. But Nigel didn't seem to care. He hurled the axes against the wall over and over again, ignoring Tyson's suggestions as to how to make them stick. Eventually, he took a seat under the scarred wall and lit another joint. But he jumped back to his feet before the doobie was half gone and said, "James! Isn't it cold in here?"

"It's a bit arctic."

"Well, shake a leg, then, and fetch me my north-wall hammer."

The hammer was in a rucksack, and James took it out and handed it to Nigel, who stepped over to the wall that divided the hut in two and brought the hammer crashing down. For a moment, Sam thought the timbers might have the laugh and the hammer would bounce back into Nigel's face. Instead, the metal head burst through the panels, and Nigel bellowed, and white lines of spit stuck in his beard. Sam's blood was up, but the smoke was in his head, and rather than tackle Nigel and pin him to the floor, he manned the stove and stacked the shards inside it and used a candle to set the old wood ablaze, while James smashed chairs into kindling and Nigel and Tyson carved up the walls.

||

THE SUMMER SUN drifted south toward the horizon, and the air grew cold teeth that bit down into the mornings and evenings. Sam

and Tyson made big plans for big climbs but always ended up on
friendly routes instead. Tyson didn't seem to notice. After finishing a
climb early, he would go to town and drink wine dregs from abandoned glasses with the waiters behind the café, or go to the patisserie
where the baker's pretty daughter gave him day-olds, and a smile, for
free. When the ice froze blue and hard in the couloirs, Tyson headed
home to California.

Sam stayed. He'd come into the mountains of his dreams, and he
felt he hadn't reached them yet. Like in a dream, they were always
on the horizon. Even from a summit, he never felt he had found the
climb he was looking for, the line that needed so much from him that
it changed his words, his way of speaking about what had happened
between the bottom and top of the mountain. Alone, the woods and
wind were louder, and at first he chattered to himself to dampen the
noise, but gradually he learned to still his tongue and let the sounds
bury him. Sam's visa expired and still he stayed, and the winter covered the mountains in snow.

Sam felt his body turning to rails and stones, his skin stretching
tight, a months-long metamorphosis fueled by cold air, work, scant
food. He lived behind some trees in the prelude valley to the mountains, steep hills rising up on all sides, the sharp quills of the real
mountains spiking the air above. He had a pull-up bar hung from a
branch and a sheet of plastic lifted from a construction site that covered his little camp. For the first week, he worried he'd be rousted in
the dark by flashlights and dogs, but the gendarme never came, and
the expressions of the people he passed on the dirt trails and narrow
cobbled lanes remained impenetrable.

Each night as he put himself to sleep, he imagined the Aiguille de la Flèche and pulled cold air down into his lungs. But he never went up to look at the mountain because of the hut. He imagined the angry ghosts of old alpinists, there to visit the peaceful staging house of their glory climbs. He didn't feel ready to face them in person. The struggle against the climb was hard enough without confronting the shambles of his part in the mountain's history.

Town was a mile away from his camp, and some evenings he'd go there because nights were long in the middle of winter. He saw Zapelli once in La Pierre d'Or—he was smaller and slighter even than Sam had imagined—sitting on his own at a round table, hunched over a glass. His skin and hair were beginning to grey, but his forearms still looked powerful, and the veins stood out in the backs of his hands. Sam imagined walking up to the table and having a seat and asking a few questions, about the mountains, about the route, but he didn't. If he had been forced to explain, he might have said that he believed that when Zapelli opened his mouth, the words would come out in a foreign tongue, not Italian or French, but something else entirely.

Sam acquired a partner, a Frenchman who spoke a little English. Every few days, the man would show up at Sam's spot and say, "Tomorrow we climb Le Pilier" or "L'aiguille du Midi" or "Les Trois Dents," and Sam would say *oui*, and sometime in the night, they'd ski up out of the valley and by dawn would be climbing through strange shapes of wind-sculpted snow and ice glued to vertical walls of cold dark stone. Some of these climbs scared Sam badly: a pitch of unconsolidated rime on rock with a ledge below that would break him to pieces, an ice hose like a wineglass stem that vibrated when he swung his axes into it. Afterward, alone in the dark, he would swear off the mountains, or compromise and promise himself a good, black binge, though he had no money, so he knew this to be an empty offer. The day after would be hard because he'd feel shaky and thin, the wind off the mountains blowing right through him, but then the next day, he would force himself back up into the peaks to do something just as hard, usually alone. When his partner got scared the man unleashed monotonic rivers of profanity, mixing French and English, sometimes in the same word, hardly raising his voice beyond a low chant.

The sun returned and the snow melted and the lupine and edelweiss ruled the high valley meadows. Soon the nights were fleeting and the days long and the Aiguille de la Flèche grew tall on the horizon. Sam slept little. Each time he shut his eyes, he found himself lying on his back in the shadows, staring straight up at the mountain, which leaned back over him. His brain fought in vain to come up with some sense of scale, to piece together the route to the top. On one climb, Sam tried to crack a joke, something about falling off and tidying the gene pool, but his partner just stared back, and Sam thought maybe he'd reached the limit of the man's English. His fears—partly of dying, which he did not want, but also of not knowing enough, of not understanding what the mountains were telling him—lengthened his sleepless nights, and he raced around the mountains during the day through a somnambulant daze trying to outrun his scattered thoughts.

And then the rope hung down out of the darkness, and Sam pulled hard toward the hut. He was not looking forward to opening the door, but he did anyway and walked into the scarred and gutted interior. The precedent they'd set that night a year ago had not gone unnoticed. The stove looked sleek, fat, well fed, but the hut looked near collapse. The chairs were long gone, the dividing wall reduced to stub-ends of splintered boards, the mattresses stacked in one corner to give access to the bunk frames. Wind gusts blew through chinks in the walls. Sam's partner clucked his tongue and swore under his breath, but said nothing more. Sam had not spoken about that night, but he assumed the story had spread on the other side of the language barrier.

The ghosts of mountaineers past refused to materialize, leaving Sam alone with the wreckage and his partner. They sat against one wall with their backs to the wind and lit the paraffin stove to cook powdered soup for dinner. Sam consumed his share mechanically and was sorry when it was gone. The mountain was massive in his mind, a Chinese scroll a mile long. He went to the window but did not want to see what waited outside. He crossed the hut, over the ragged fringe of wall to the corner where the mattresses were stacked, but the smashup was total, there was nowhere to hide. He knew he was losing the head game. His mind produced two superimposed images of Zapelli: one of the quiet little man sitting alone at his table, the other a fun-house caricature with a skull-splitting grin, banging his fist against the bar for another drink. Here was the wrathful ghost he had expected after all.

Sam watched his partner as the man put away the stove and fuel bottle, then methodically packed his rucksack and leaned it against the wall by the door. Then he walked back across the hut, prodded Sam with his toe, and pointed at Sam's own pack, which sat empty on the floor. Sam got to his feet and organized his things for the morning, which would really still be the night. And he felt better, at least for a moment. But then he lay down in his sleeping bag on the floor of the hut, and the mountain reappeared, two miles tall now, while the corners of his mind felt black without offering sleep and his body felt heavy without being tired.

Sam had no memories of unconsciousness, but he couldn't remember the whole night either, so his mind must have left his body at some point before the alarm from his watch brought him to his feet. They turned on their headlamps, took up their packs, and were out on the glacier before reality and sleep came to full disconnection. The moon was on the other side of the earth, and the mountains were flat shapes etched against the stars.

The stone was still there. Soon enough, Sam could reach out and touch it. There at the base, half the sky was dark star-shadow as the mountain spread out above and before them. Their headlamps cast yellow cones up at the route, but the mountain swallowed the light without telling any secrets.

The first pitches followed a strip of ice the width of a plate glass window for five hundred feet up to where the mountain bulged out past vertical. They climbed into the darkness, needing to put the delicate glass below them before the sun lit the air and the ice began to melt. At the top of the ice, they hung in their harnesses from a hammered piton and holstered their axes. Sunrise filled in the mountain above and the land below. Sam had the next lead, but he stared up at the mountain, trying to make some sense of where the route would go through the overhangs and dangling icicles. He felt his partner's hand push down on his helmet, until Sam's eyes pointed straight ahead at the handholds five feet in front of him. Sam followed these features with his eyes, up a hundred feet, then another hundred and beyond, trying to piece it all together. His partner rapped Sam on the helmet with his knuckles.

This time, Sam kept his eyes forward and fastened his hands to the hold and pulled, and his body responded, surprising Sam so much he nearly let go. A hundred and fifty feet later, he stopped and brought his partner up to the belay. His partner climbed the next pitch, a wide, toothy crack that chewed the skin off their hands and forearms.

Sam's lead again. No cracks split the face, which meant no pins or cams for protection. The rope hung free below him, and a fall would already be a whistling dive into empty space. He held onto a crystal with his right hand, and he could see the next hold, but nothing above that. He called down, "It's blank up here," and his words were loud because the air was calm and they so rarely spoke to each other during a climb. His partner said nothing, but paid out more rope from the belay, as if to say, you may as well go up now, you'll fall the same distance either way. So Sam crimped the hold above the crystal, committed his weight to it, left the crystal behind. He reached up, and another hold appeared, a shallow, creased water track that took the ends of two fingers. The entire pitch unfolded like that, each new hold emerging from the stone only after Sam moved toward it, each move supported only by the conviction that he would make do with whatever the rock provided. When at last he found a crack for a piton, he stopped and hung and brought his partner up to join him.

Sam looked down and saw how far the rope hung out from the wall, with no pitons for protection, and he knew that a fall would have ripped out the lower anchor and that his partner had made a leap of faith as well.

After that pitch, the rope came alive between them. An electrical current seemed to hum along the nylon thread. They urged each other on through deep black chimneys locked in ice, up overhanging fingercracks, out through hanging forests of blue icicles that creaked and groaned. Reversing what they had climbed looked impossible— the ropes hung too far out into free air. They were utterly committed to the line. And though the summit never seemed any closer while the ground was wrenchingly far below, Sam didn't struggle against their position.

It was a surprise to reach the top. Sam hadn't even noticed its nearness, so focused had he become on the holds directly in front of his face and the flow of small moves linking one to the next. His surprise at running out of mountain to climb did not prevent a swelling joy, pure and sweet, from rushing through him and carrying his eyes over all the mountaintops in the uninhibited space on all sides. His partner smiled, a wide crack in the man's thin-boned, sun-browned face, something Sam realized he had never seen before. They shook hands, wrapped their arms around each other, then raced the setting sun down the far side of the mountain.

Back on the Gesner, the twilight winds were a noisy river above the ice, but Sam couldn't stop at the hut. It was too shameful, he did not want to think about what had happened there, so they put on speed and ran down the Gesner, working within the narrow beams of their headlamps. By the time they reached the valley below the mountains, it was deep into the night, but Sam didn't want to retire to his plastic hovel either. So they went down into town, which was dark and filled with sleep except for La Pierre d'Or. The bar was mostly empty, but even the few people there threw Sam's mind into confusion. He had not realized how far he'd retreated into his interior, that his body had been working mechanically through the night unguided. He stopped in the doorway and stared out through dazed eyes at the human shapes inside: arms, eyes, hands, mouths. His mind struggled to reconnect with the surface. He realized everyone was staring at him and his partner, waiting for the inevitable question to be asked and answered. It came from across the room. "Did you succeed? Is it done?"

Images, like startled birds from the alpine meadows, flew into Sam's mind. The route put down on paper and in magazines, passed from hand to hand. People there on weekdays and on weekends holding those pieces of paper up between their eyes and the mountain, chopping it to size, bleeding it dry. Zapelli coming to La Pierre d'Or to be slapped on the back and told tales about his route. The mountain of history behind the mountain of stone dynamited with a word.

"It's impossible," Sam said, and it sounded clear enough in his head, but distant and flat to his ears. "It can't be done."

His partner clapped him on the shoulder and took him to the bar and bought him a drink; the barman poured, saying, "Yes, yes, the mountains are better from here."

DOWN FROM THE COLD

IT HAPPENED IN the same place each time. Up near the top where the snow got a little steep and the air a little thin, where the mountain curved round them and squeezed out the lower world. That's where clients got scared. Where they started huffing and chuffing like mired horses and leaning into the ice, which was the worst thing they could do. Lisa felt for them, but it was no joke to catch a 250-pound galoot whose crampons had sheered out because he wanted to give the ice a hug, like the ice would hug him back. Catch him with no running belays, because they were *guides* and *guides* were freakin' omnipotent mountain demigods who hadn't needed running belays since the eighteen-whatevers in the Alps. Of course, those guides got pulled off and killed just the same as the current batch of pros, and if you did get pulled off, you might as well just let go and tumble yourself down into the bergschrund, because any guide who got yanked by a client must die of shame—it was written in the bylaws. Ice axe *seppuku*, right there in the snow.

So Lisa kept her clients on a short leash, treated them like a matador with a bull. Kept them close, but not *too* close. But really she felt like a midwife. Sometimes the labor was short, sometimes long and hard, but if all went well and they got through the heavy-breathing terror, then up on the summit out popped a little child, eyes freshly open to the world, hands clapping with delight. That was something to see.

The man this morning had had the shoulders of a cast iron stove and the potbelly to match. What did he say he did? Busy-ness of some kind, money farming for some corp. Red-raw cheeks that all but glowed. Lisa took right to him because he had a sense of humor about his fear. When he got scared, he *laughed*. Called himself a chickenshit. Seemed to think his own panicky cardio was the damnedest thing, like it was happening to someone else. Lisa could work with that. She kept him laughing, kept his feet moving, kept him upright until he was past the Gates, where the mountain eased climbers up to its summit ridge. On top, on trembling legs, he smiled like the sun and lurched around like a foal. *Whoa there, big fella, I got you.*

On the descent, with the upper mountain behind them, he did most of the talking, which suited Lisa fine because it was his afterglow and his day. She could happily stare south, across the thick green ocean of trees, to the next fire mountain, Jefferson, with its shapely sides, its glaciers knocking sunbeams around.

She left him at the lodge. He would go to the lunch bar, then his car, then the city. And she'd be here. In a day or two, his replacement would come to her, come up for air, and say, *Goddamn, that's the most beautiful thing I ever saw,* and she would say, *Yup.* As if it were some big surprise.

Lisa showered in the lodge's locker room, then put on flannel bottoms, a secondhand T, a baggy fleece, her regular after-work uniform. Outside, the parking lot was a quarter full, the weekend summer crowd of diehards skiing on slush and salt. There was heat in the sun and the radiating asphalt, but the air was too thin to hold it and too easily pushed around by the wind, so the warmth was mostly lost. Lisa slapped her way across the lot in flip-flops anyway, because her feet hated reentry into shoes after the hours spent in her plastic doubles.

Rust frosted the boxy corners of her van where the dark green paint had given up. The machine was seven years her junior, and she thought of it as something like a half-retarded brother with whom she cohabitated. In van-years it might be more like her grandfather, but that notion led to forebodings of senility, end-times, junkyards—and those were ideas she preferred not to entertain, as if her sisterly faith were all that kept the engine running. Her key no longer turned the door locks, so she carried a wire coat hanger for entry and left the ignition key under her seat.

A scrap of yellow paper fluttered under one windshield wiper. She pulled it loose and turned it over and found a familiar, neat hand.

Lisa! Recognized your van (of course). We've got a place down in town now. Come on by—you can meet my wife. We'll be there tonight. It's right where the pavement ends on Montgomery St. Love to see you.

—Greg

Inside she had hung wool curtains against the night, but she left one window uncovered so that the mountain would always be visible. That way she could talk to it, ask it questions when she had need. She draped her towel over the passenger seat and stretched out on her plywood bed in the back, propping her head so that she could stare at the view. Lanes of groomed snow snaked down toward the cars bunched together at the far end of the lot. Above, the solid sheets of glacier capped by cliffs and sulfurous vents and the summit etched against the sky. Her favorite time was cloudless early morning long before the sun, with so many stars the night seemed to be leaking away through a sieve and the mountain a pure outline. She felt fatigue tugging at the corners of her eyes. She elbowed herself upright before she drifted any further from the present.

Greg, goddamnit. Married. Ha! Settled down. Wonder if she knows what she's signed up for. Wonder if he knows. Nuts, the whole world.

She pulled a pair of jeans and a white shirt with buttons out of a cardboard box under the bed frame. She pulled a brush through her hair and slapped at her cheeks in an effort to perk up. She totaled the gas and thought of the looming brake job and imagined the starter dying down in town and decided to walk. The road switchbacked down off the mountain for twelve miles, but the trail was straight and steep and only three. Into old running shoes with her feet and a coat tied around her waist, she grabbed a clean yogurt tub and pushed off into the thin afternoon.

The trees were gaunt, straight, snow-shedding pines, green at the needle tips and grey in the woody center, packed thickly together but with room underfoot for the berry bushes. The purple dots shone dully under the leaves. Mountain huckleberries, these, small, tart, dispersed. An hour might yield up a quart. She pushed through the hip-high thickets, her hands disconnected from her forward progress, plucking carefully at the tiny circles.

Mount Robson. Ice. Cold. Brittle, nasty stuff, chunks falling all the time. Bruised all over, mine purple, his brown. Never saw him so strong. He felt it, too. In his shoulders. We could have climbed out of hell that day. No celebrating on top. No war whoop. All unnecessary.

A wife! Does she feel squishy under him? But maybe his bones are padded now, too. He has accumulated. Let the dragon get ahold of him, yup. House in the city, cabin on the mountain, cars for in-between. Art, cable, wine, teaspoons. Blankets in front of a fire and something hot and rain falling outside—nice, sure. Tags on little strings trailing off it all, printed with spinning numbers, interest compounding.

The yogurt tub was nearly full, the berries fading into the shadows under the leaves. Lisa moved toward the lights of the cabins on the outskirts of town. On Montgomery Street, where the pavement ends and the dirt begins, he had said. A little place. Wood shake roof, cobbled chimney, a cord or so of wood under the eaves. She lifted her fist and knocked the door.

The door swung forward, and Greg was there. "Lizzie," he said, and he crushed her in his arms like an affable bear. He was smoother around the edges, the old angles absorbed by new tissue. His cheeks were thicker. There would be jowls there some day. But right now he looked healthy and strong, a little pink, even. He wore a loose

Hawaiian shirt and faded canvas pants, the sour man-smell tamped down by soap. "I was hoping you'd come. Lizzie, this is Anne."

The clutter of inside sights struck the bottleneck in Lisa's brain left by the fading stillness of the woods. Ceramic dishes and framed pictures and tasteful little dangly ornaments. An extended hand with deft fingers connected to a thin, silver-bangled wrist. Four ivory tapers in clear glass sticks lighting a table in the corner by the windows. A wide, white smile, filled with little teeth. Wet blue eyes. An enclosed fire, not yet hot, a wooden bowl of peaches. A carefully piled mass of shiny blond ringlets.

"Greg says you'll have been up since midnight. You must be exhausted." Those light fingers on her shoulder, gentle pressure guiding her toward a stool by the woodstove, giving her the poker, telling her to do whatever she'd like with the fire.

"It's fine. I'm used to it, and I'm on my second wind. I brought some berries. They're fresh." The disconnected features merged and cohered. She was a cute, curvy woman wearing corduroys and a knit sweater. Lisa gripped the poker, something solid and metal to hang onto.

"That's kind. You've got so much more patience than me. I tried once, with the bushes around here, but I had to give it up because I got so frustrated and I didn't even have the bottom of my bowl covered."

Kiss him? Nope, don't feel it anymore. He used to look like hollowed-out death, and what does that say about me? "Your place is much smaller than I'd pictured. It's good." *She's staring.*

"It's an original." Greg's voice, from around the chimney corner. "From the thirties, back when the whole town was a government project. Some of the wood was cut right here."

Anne's eyes worked slowly down and then back up, taking their time, without concealment or any apparent sense of impropriety. Lisa, feeling slow and tongue-tied, gave up her attempt at unembarrassed calm and turned away, toward the *scree* of an oven door opening. The scent of pie drifted past. She looked back, and the eyes were back, where she knew they would be.

"Greg was there when it happened," Lisa said. "It's all right, I can hear fine."

"Can I touch it?"

Lisa pulled back her hair.

"It's so smooth. Scars fascinate me. I know that's weird."

Those soft fingers again! That light touch on the stub of her ear. They were like goddamn Vicodin. Did Greg's body hurt so much he needed that kind of treatment?

Greg returned from the kitchen, and the roasted fruit smell dissipated. "It was too warm on Tocllaraju," he said. "Like the mountain was shitting on us—the rocks wouldn't stay in place. Lizzie was leading, and she gave this little yelp, and I didn't think much of it until I got up to the next belay and half her ear was gone."

You never said down. I was proud of that, us. But it made me wonder, what's us—partners? lovers?—for the first time.

"Five more minutes," Greg said. He straightened the chairs by the table. "Peach and strawberry. How many times have you been up the mountain this season, Liz?"

"I don't know anymore. They've all blurred together. Twenty, anyway, so far."

"Any good ones?"

"The usual, pretty much." *Times of fear and joy and revelation that fall apart when you bring them downhill, fragile as dreams.* "Last week I had a triathlete. That was fun. He was set on seeing the sunrise, so we beat it up there pretty quick. Fairytale horizon out east, weird shadows and the sun making gold all over the desert. Nice day. Oh, in May I had a disaster. Wife promises to get in shape for her husband. Their anniversary and all. So awkward. The whole way up she kept talking, saying this meant no papers. Divorce papers, you know. Greg, last I heard of you was from Kit, and she said you were in Portland working tree removal. But that was—years now, I don't know, three or four."

Greg beamed. "Kindergarten. I'm a teacher. Little chaps with big eyes and new clothes their mothers have just bought. We've still got the same house I was in then, but it's better now, and we have a garden. Salad stuff now, blueberries ready in a week or so."

"Horseshit." *An act?* "Come on partner, don't snow me." *Tsk, no tact. Too tired. Please don't screw with me.*

Anne laughed, a sound like a lively wood fire. Greg's eyes shot up, and he rocked back in his chair, but then he bounced forward, guffawed, slapped at his knee. Lisa gave in and joined them, as if that had been her intention all along. How could she have known?

The pie came out of the oven, and Greg cut three rough wedges that Anne piled up with ice cream and huckleberries. All the blood went to Lisa's stomach. She could not remember when she'd eaten last. On the mountain? In the lodge? The heat turned the ice cream to slush that soaked through the dough. At the periphery, she registered Anne cutting little bites from the edges, Greg taking in big

forkfuls between satisfied pauses, Anne watching Lisa's own dwin-
dling plate.

"You're starving," Anne said.

Lisa swallowed, laughed, made herself pause. "Not really. I forget about food sometimes. Work on the mountain turns my head
around."

"Please, I like to watch you eat. I'll get you another slice, don't
get up."

Anne stood and turned through a swing of hip and breast that Greg
watched with a familiar hunger, though the expression was sleepier,
now, around the folds of his eyelids than what Lisa remembered. Anne's
curls bobbed up and down with the cutting, a heap of taffy springs.

"When were you married?" Lisa asked.

"Two years ago," Anne said. She lowered another two plates
of pie to the table. "At the Rose Garden. The smell was heavenly.
Greg's poor father, though, sneezed through the whole afternoon. He
was such a good sport."

"I never met your dad."

"We reconciled the year before. Now sometimes we go to a
hockey match."

Lisa abandoned herself again to the sugar and cream, the acid
in the huckleberries allowing for more of the rest to be eaten. The
accumulation seemed to press her spine back into the corner of her
chair, to tug her brain down against the bottom of her skull. She was
hardly conscious of when the humming began or when it turned to
music. It was sweet and low, a folk song, or a lullaby, about a boy
and a river, though the words hardly mattered. Greg leaned back in

his chair, hands behind his head, eyes even with the last inches of the candles. Nothing, in fact, existed beyond the circle of the candlelight filled by the sound coming from between Anne's lips.

The song ended, and Anne stood and stacked the plates. "All right, out, both of you. I'll do the dishes. You'll have plenty to talk about, go take a walk now." She snapped a dish towel at Greg and gave them both their jackets and pushed them toward the door.

Lisa still felt swaddled at the table even as her feet carried her out into the night. Their first steps were silent. The air was cold and flavored with pitch from the bordering pines. Her pupils relaxed in the dark. The stars were bright glittery dots, not quite so dense as higher on the mountain, but sharp and clear. The mountain itself was hidden by the trees, but the land all swelled up in that direction. The prickling air tightened the skin around her face and hands. She felt like she was being resuscitated.

"I had no idea this was what you wanted," Lisa said.

Greg arched his eyebrows, shook his head. "What? This isn't so strange."

"It is from the man who wore Gore-Tex to his sister's wedding because he didn't have anything else."

"Eh—sweetheart," he said, with nothing but affection, "you've lived too long in your van. The mountain's not your friend. You can't talk to it at night. That's just you talking to yourself."

Fuck—how'd he know about that? "Yeah? How many times did you tell me a roof over your head was one step from a coffin lid?" No, she didn't mean to needle him. She was supposed to be *above* that. "Greg, what you have, it seems really nice. You don't get bored?"

"No. Sometimes. I'm better now. You remember how relaxed I'd be after we did something really hard?"

"Of course."

"That's how I feel all the time, now."

That's it, then. Like the moment the classical station starts sounding good.

"How long did it take?" Lisa's night vision had begun to adjust. Ghostly shapes emerged in the woods on both sides. If only it were that easy with people.

"For what?"

"Skip it. I really don't want to know. You get enough from the mountain, now, just seeing it?"

"More, maybe. Could be it's hard to really enjoy its company when you're only ever thinking about climbing it."

"Yeah?" she said. "Now who's talking to the mountain?"

They ambled further up the old dirt track above town. The forest pressed in on them. For the first time all day, Lisa's muscles protested. The cabin and the fire called her inside. Her feet felt slow and heavy. Stars glowed through the chinks between the arms of the pines.

"I can't go back in there," she said, nodding back down the road.

"Okay." He grinned at her. "We're not infectious, you know."

"Yeah, well. You really garden?"

"It's great. Hands in the dirt, fresh salad on the porch."

She shook her head and put her hands up around Greg's neck and pulled down a little, to kiss his cheek. He kissed her back, behind her torn ear.

And she was off, back up the mountain, lengthening out her stride to build up speed. Her muscles turned hungry again, from the pace and from the promise of a destination, and rest. Upward steps brought colder air, but she took off her jacket anyway, to vent, and because the raw air felt good against her skin and stomach.

Eleven o'clock? Don't know. Lap myself before I'm done tonight. Sleep in maybe.

She topped a little rise where the forest thinned out, and there, cut into the sky, her mountain silhouette, as pure and cold as ever.

Looks the same. Maybe it won't ever change. Not yet, anyway.

After the forest, the empty lot looked flat and alien, unwalkable without texture. She stumbled across it, her muscles giving in, at last. Inside her van was as cold as outside, her sleeping bag holding an icy chill in its filling. Jeans and shirt were traded for long underwear, the first wave of goose bumps crawling by during the exchange. She curled in a fetal ball at the center of the bag to wait for her leftover heat to drive the bite away from its corners and fell asleep before she had the chance to stretch out.

OZDON

EO SALAZAAR UNDERSTOOD the mountains. You read a few phrases of his and thought, my god, rock became man and learned to talk and that's what's on the page. Graceful, weather-shaped words. Transcribed dreams of ice and stone.

Dane had known Leo since they were high school kids growing up in Salt Lake. If someone had told him then that his friend would become a post-Kerouac Emerson with a following of dewy-eyed, hairy-legged, granola-eating lit majors, Dane would have shrugged. Why not? Leo was a natural-born visionary. He was always seeing things on mountaintops Dane hadn't, or couldn't. But when Dane thought of Leo, he still pictured the brown kid with long bones and long hair disappearing up ahead through the trail dust. They'd banded together at first because they were misfits outside the iron embrace of the LDS church, and then they discovered they could both run mountain paths like hungry jackals. Before long they were eyeing the territory above the end of the trails, then egging each other on up dinosaur-back ridges and long drools of ice in the Wasatch Mountains.

Dane didn't see as much of Leo anymore. Their orbits had veered apart. Maybe Leo's had just expanded. Leo spent the year jetting between the Andes or Himalaya or Romsdalen—the old spiritual ranges—gathering material for his next project. Meanwhile, Dane had an Airstream trailer with a view of the Flat Irons on the ragged edge of Boulder, Colorado, where he worked as a contract welder for the physics and bio buildings at the university. Dane ministered to the usual gates and fences, but he also had a touch, and his number was posted on the corkboards of a dozen different labs as a last resort for when bad things happened to fussy, expensive equipment. So Dane wasn't exactly poor. As far as he knew, banks would happily have hitched him to a mortgage. But he liked knowing he could pull out of town on any given night, even though the light tipping down off the Rockies onto the plains each morning hit him like coffee and champagne, and he wasn't likely going anywhere.

The years of accumulated weathering were beginning to groove Dane's cheeks and arms. He looked like an animated bundle of rope, skin stretched a turn too tight over his inner cords. Most nights, he would drink a little Jimmy Beam and read a few pages from one of Leo's books, follow along with his old friend through mountains that bloomed at dawn and died at dusk. It wasn't just college kids who swooned for Leo. Dane had talked to young and old, greybeards and ropeguns, even a Kansan farmer who sold Dane an occasional beef quarter and had never seen the mountains. They'd all read Leo and turned all deep-eyed talking about beauty and elevation. It was impossible not to. When Dane read *Pine Mountain* with the moon and the mountains outside the portals of his trailer, he felt like Leo was sitting right there, taking the husk off the world and showing him the jewels. Which was what Dane needed, because lately, his own climbs had all been turning into knife fights. Thuggish rock, hairy ice, storms like Jack the Ripper in the sky. *Pine Mountain* took the edge off, made Dane feel less brutal.

Dane figured this was the other reason he and Leo saw less of each other. Their tastes had diverged, too. The last time they'd climbed together had been the previous winter, a wet winter turned hard and cold. Waterfall ice touched down in places it hadn't for years. Locals, Dane chief among them, climbed every day, freely letting small sectors of the Denver-Boulder metroplex grind to a halt, knowing that such an overflow of frozen wax slopped down their mountains would be gone in a month and might not return until the next ice age. But Dane saved something special for Leo, a hidden curtain named Kinky Undies that had been climbed just once fifteen years before and never seen again.

They might as well have tried climbing free-hanging window glass. The ice shivered and creaked, shorting-out Dane's nerves. Terrified of taking full swings with their tools, they hooked half-exploded air pockets, feeling tiny pops and fragmentations while searching out new placements that wouldn't unzip the whole curtain and fly them down onto the rocks below. Their screws gripped lenses of ice between empty gaps, and Dane was afraid to even hang on them. At one belay—a stubby screw that wiggled like a loose tooth and a hammered ice hook that looked about as useful as a lucky rabbit foot—Dane said: "Authors who die young always end up immortal, right?" He hadn't meant anything by it. They'd said that kind of thing to each other as teenagers. But Leo didn't reply, and Dane couldn't read him.

Afterward, flying high, Dane had suggested they go pick apples in celebration, which was the code they'd developed in high school for getting blind drunk on a warm summer night in the Wasatch foothills. Leo had answered that he needed to get a few pages down before he caught his flight to Chile. Dane wasn't offended. If his friend had acquired responsibilities to higher purposes of the brain, there was nothing wrong with that. In retrospect, if Dane had thought it through, he might have chosen a different route. Leo Salazaar, mountaintop prophet, wilderness poet for a whole new generation, might not have been psyched to risk dying on an obscure ice curtain named for see-through panties. And maybe Dane shouldn't have been either. But even though he read Leo and aspired to the places his friend described, he also liked piping red horror movies into his trailer: slasher flicks that spiked his adrenaline and popped his eyes, then made him bust up inappropriately when things got too gory.

Dane thought he'd learned from Kinky Undies. Leo planned to drop by Boulder again that summer, and Dane had a different stripe of climb picked out for them: a long ridge traverse into the high blue, on white, Coliseum granite with lakes on all sides. He showed up at the airport to meet Leo, feeling overeager. He'd come bearing gifts and wondered if Leo would notice his thoughtfulness.

Dane watched troops of passengers emerge from security and scatter. An hour after the flight from Yellowknife had arrived, it occurred to him that Leo was not in the building. Air Canada had a reservation but no record of Leo boarding their plane. Dane drove home, unconcerned. Sometimes a mountain took a liking to Leo and wouldn't let him go. It wouldn't be the first time a storm had held the man back a few days.

Five days passed with no word. Dane ran through a list of friends who either hadn't spoken to Leo or were away in the mountains themselves. He tried Leo's publisher in New York but got nowhere. Leo's publicist thought he was in Montana, but Dane realized that to the voice on the line, the distinctions between Montana, Canada, even Colorado, were local semantics mattering little. No one he talked to had actually spoken to Leo in months. What was Leo doing in the Northwest Territories? Dane didn't even know.

Eight days after Leo's missed flight, Dane bought himself a ticket to Yellowknife, one of the two names Leo had dropped in conversation, the other being Fort Clyde. A voice in Dane's head told him not to be an idiot. Did he think he could find Leo in the Canadian north? Canada wasn't small. Probably Leo was just off in the woods, communing with the wind. But Dane was the only one who seemed to know or care that Leo had gone missing, so Dane shoveled some gear in a duffel and flew over the border.

In an outbuilding at the Yellowknife airport, Dane found a silver-bearded pilot who agreed to fly him to Fort Clyde in his Twin Otter floatplane. Dane liked the man immediately because he looked like a real Santa Claus—hard around the face and in his consonants, able to fly out of the north in dead winter if he wanted. Dane imagined him airdropping shotgun shells and whisky to hard-bitten tundra homesteaders, yelling "Ho-Ho-Ho" out his cockpit window. They flung Dane's bag into the body of the plane, and Dane climbed into the copilot's seat. The pilot put them in the air and pointed to a switch on the headset hanging from a hook by Dane's knee.

"Never been out here before, heh?" the pilot said once Dane had the headset working.

"No."

"Hoping for gold? You don't look like a miner."

"No. Friend of mine, a mountain climber, was due out of Fort Clyde a week ago, and I haven't heard from him."

"Yeh? Brown man? Lanky? Know the fellow who took him in. Bout a month back."

"Leo Salazaar," Dane said. "That's his name." He felt better for getting his first sniff of Leo. He should have asked earlier. The pilots must know everything about who was moving around the north. Dane had studied the map. The other ways to Fort Clyde were a month-long overland expedition or a canoe ride down six hundred miles of the Mackenzie River. There weren't any roads. "Did he come back out?"

"Not so I've heard. Plenty pilots, though. Plenty planes."

The Twin Otter bumped and dropped. Black clouds metastasized across the sky. The pilot changed elevations. "Air out this way is always nasty," he said. "Even on clear days, it feels like hands on the bird."

"Do you know anything about the mountains?" Dane asked.

"Mountains?" The pilot looked over at Dane, then back out at the weather. "Around Fort Clyde, there's only one to speak of. Ugliest thing you'll ever see. I've heard miners from up that way say the sight of it makes it hard to believe in God. Burly men, you understand, with moose jackets they've made themselves and beards like mine."

"Must be something to see," Dane said. People overreacted to mountains. They pulled strange ideas out of thin air.

"Nasty sucker," the pilot continued. "Gives me the willies. You think your friend flew in to climb it?"

"I don't know," Dane said.

"Must be some kind of desperado. Man like that is tough on the friends. If he's gone missing in that country, you won't find him." The pilot spoke matter-of-factly, as if offering directions to the corner store. "Don't he have mountains closer by?"

"Leo's always climbing new mountains," Dane said. "He writes books about them."

"Oh, ho!" the pilot said. "You want to watch out for people who write things in books. They're a pack of liars. I don't care for mountains myself. Too much turbulence. Like old men farting. You can count on a steady stream of bad air. I like lakes. A place to land, and dinner under the skids. You ever eat arctic char fresh?"

Dane laughed. "No. I should probably ask you to take me to the best fishing lake around and then back to Yellowknife in a few days."

"You should," the pilot agreed. "We'd fry a couple for your friend, for sentiment and all. He'll get more out a that than a one-man ground search around Fort Clyde."

"You're a cynic," Dane said.

"Just practical."

Dane could laugh because he didn't know what he expected to find of Leo. The possibilities all seemed equally unlikely. *He's got an idea he can't let go of*, Dane thought. *He's in a tundra shack writing it out till his fingers bleed.* That was the image he returned to, the one he liked best. It fit Leo right, better than death or absent-mindedness. Dane would knock on the door, settle in, and they'd swap stories until Leo was done. Dane guessed his own flight north was a self-serving exercise. If something had happened to Leo, Dane didn't want to spend his life thinking that he'd twiddled his dick in Boulder, waiting. It didn't matter if he'd do as much good for Leo eating char with the pilot—the point was to do and have done, leaving no questions.

The clouds hardened into dark anvils, and the pilot began telling stories of friends who'd been lightning-struck in their planes. A ground layer of grey turned solid, and Dane could no longer see land, nothing but cloud below and piled black masses above. "We're close, now," the pilot said, and Dane wondered which seat sat the fool, but the pilot's grey seemed at least to signal a lucky fool. The plane fell out of the cloud layer, and Dane had only a few seconds to see an enormous elbow bend of river with tundra stretching away on both sides before the pilot splashed them down on the inside crook of the bend where the water was calm. A wooden dock stretched out from the land, and the plane pulled up alongside it.

"Better get out quick," the pilot said. "Things are worse'n I thought."

Dane jumped out on the dock and barely had his duffle by the handle when the plane pulled away. The water was grey-blue, the tundra grey-green, the sky grey-black. Dane felt grey himself, as if the clouds had gotten into his skin. He walked the dock to the land and a collection of cabins and shacks. The clouds were low overhead—dark, fast-moving shapes that dove down and expanded as he watched. There were no people in sight. *Where am I?* he thought. *Goddamn Arctic ghost town.* But it couldn't be a ghost town. He saw well-fed engines and machines parked under porches. The buildings were warped and faded, but none were collapsing. Dane walked north up what he took to be the main path through town.

The clouds on the near horizon parted, a two-second gap in the black swarm. The mountain leapt up over Dane and the shacks. Dane stopped and stared, paralyzed by its sudden nearness. The clouds closed again, and the world shrank. A hard burst of rain swept over him. What had he just seen? Something terrible. A claw ripping through the ground. He wanted to see it again and he didn't. It was obscene. A corpse on a stick. *Stop it,* he told himself. *It's nothing new. Rock. Snow.* But he felt dirty just for staring at the image in his mind. He waited for the clouds to open again. Now that he'd caught the mountain once, he'd have preferred it in plain sight, not lurking behind the storm.

The clouds thickened, and more rain hammered down. Dane realized it was cold, barely above freezing, and he was soaked. One shack had a light on in a window and a faded Budweiser poster on the door. Dane pushed the door, and it opened. Inside there were three tables with fold-out legs and a few chairs and a plywood sheet nailed between one wall and a counter. A flesh giant wearing sweatpants and a sweatshirt was hunched over the plywood, watching television. The television was small, and the man looked ready to put his face through the screen. Dane could hear a generator humming somewhere in back. He dropped his duffle by the door.

"What's that mountain called?" Dane asked.

The giant swiveled his head without moving his shoulders. "Mount Ozdon," he said. "Don't worry, you'll get used to it. I go days now without seeing it. Just keep my eyes on other things." He heaved himself upright, his flesh lagging behind his bones. "What'll you have? I carry cheap whisky, fancy whisky, and beer. The cheap whisky's cheapest on account of transport costs. But it's all money, so don't be surprised."

Dane looked out the window. It was unmistakably day, despite the storm. The hands on the clock on the bar's back wall were reaching for eleven. "Is that clock slow?" Dane asked.

"Nope, it's right."

"I've been traveling all day," Dane said. "It can't be morning."

The giant slapped his plywood bar and laughed. "Fellow, you're north. It's summer. Won't be night again till August." He hunched himself back over the plank, propped on forearms like pink balloons. "Hope you can sleep. I've seen 'em come up here and go crazy with the light. No sleep for days, you understand? Drifting around, awake and dreaming. It don't pay to be awake that long."

Dane lowered himself into a chair, cursing his wet clothes. He studied the barman. Twenty-four-hour light, high UV, and the man was pink and pale. He must never go outside. Another flight of rain hammered down. Like a hermit crab in his shell, only his shell was anchored to the tundra. Dane wondered if the man could leave. He might be too much for a Twin Otter to handle.

Dane asked, "Do you know of a guy, a climber, came through here about a month ago? Name was Leo Salazaar?"

"Ha! Now I know you," the man said. He opened two rows of sharp grey teeth. "Wondered what you were doing up here. You need to go talk to Asa about that business. You'll find him in the machine shop up the way. I'm closing now. The outside door doesn't lock. Leave whenever you want. Asa's usually up all hours." The man jacked himself up off his arms until he was upright, then lumbered out through a door behind the bar. It took Dane a moment to realize he wasn't coming back.

Dane staggered back out into the daylight and storm. The mountain did not reappear. On the line between tundra and cloud, the land seemed unfinished, still precipitating out of the primordial dawn. Dane suddenly missed Leo fiercely. A few words would do. He'd like to hear what his friend had to say about this place. He imagined clear days when the mountain would be squatted practically on top of Fort Clyde, requiring constant, eyes-averted penitence. How could a person live like that? Dane followed the mud track between pillboxes of plywood and sheet metal. None were marked, but the glow of a stick welder leaked from around the edges of a roll-down door set in the face of one of the last structures. Dane pounded on a side door until the light dimmed and he heard movement inside. A man— Asa, Dane told himself—wearing a leather apron and a flipped-up welder's hood, threw open the door.

"Fuck do you want?"

"Honestly?" Dane returned. "A bed and a bottle. Know anything about Leo Salazaar?"

Asa had a fleshless face, just skin and skull and a pair of blue-yellow eyes that seemed to want to incinerate Dane. Asa stood in the doorway a long moment, then disappeared back inside, leaving the door open. Dane followed into a crowded, meticulously ordered metalworking shop. Chains hung from the ceiling, tools covered the walls, lathes and drills stood idle on the concrete floor. Dark fog ran past the one window, and rain rattled down on the roof. Asa hung his hood on a peg.

"He's dead," Asa said. "Up there." He shrugged north, toward the mountain.

The moment the words were out, Dane felt the hole in his soul, right where he'd been covering it up. The image of Leo at work on some last great thought, or flying to the Andes, too rushed to make contact, shriveled back, obvious wishful thinking. Still, Dane couldn't make the reality true in his head either. Leo could die on a Himalayan icon, some monument to mountains and mountaineers. But not in a Canadian backwater on a mountain no one had ever heard of. *It's not the place*, Dane thought. *It's the mountain.* Leo couldn't die on something that ugly. Dane's glimpse of Ozdon was fading, but not the sick feeling it had left with him.

"How?" Dane asked.

"Badly," Asa said. "He was a fool. I told him so. Rainbow chaser to the very end."

"You poor fuck," Dane said. Grief flashed to anger. It was bad enough without some Podunk ragging on the dead. "Leo was no fool. You don't know who he was."

Asa blew air out his nose and gestured at one wall. Dane turned and saw a shelf of books. Leo's books.

"While y'all were kissing his ass," Asa said, "Leo was up here, with me. I know all about the Great Author."

Bright sunlight flashed outside the window. The back of the storm disappeared to the east. Dane fought the presumption of sunrise. It must have been near midnight. His brain felt snowed under. A thick separation distorted the outer world. Dane looked through the window and flinched back to find the mountain staring down at him. He looked again, trying to hold steady. Ozdon was huge, sheer. It seemed torn from the earth, a bone from below dripping with ice and crusted with jags of black rock. Dane heard or felt distant rumbling. *Thunder? No. Rockfall? Earthquake?*

"You know where Leo is?" Dane asked.

"Sure."

"You'd take me to him?" It was a nightmare: Leo's death, the mountain. Actually seeing Leo and tending his body seemed like the one thing Dane could do. Dane turned back around, taking a half-conscious step to the left so that his back was to the wall, not the window.

"I'll take you to the body if you'll climb the mountain with me," Asa said. He grinned, all teeth and jutting bones. "Partners out this way are kind of scarce."

"I'm not in the mood," Dane said.

"Do you need to consult your chi? Do a little yoga?" Asa took his hood back off its peg. "Go drink some tea or whatever. Then we'll talk."

"You're heartless, you know that? My buddy's dead up there."

"Yeah? Mine too. And I'm pissed about it. Been pissed off for two weeks. The mountain's been laughing in my head."

Is that what that sound is?

"You've been looking at it," Asa said. "I saw you. If you think Leo wants us to hug and light candles, you can run on back to your lower-forty-eight commune. Or we can do something great for him. Strip our souls. Have our own little exorcism. Just don't waste my time because I fucking hate indecision."

Could Dane come right out and admit he was already hooked, that he'd been wanting to climb the mountain since the pilot first invoked it? No. "Fine," he said. The roaring in his ears cranked up a notch.

Asa opened a cabinet in the corner of the shop. Dane looked over Asa's shoulder at a compact arsenal of alpine gear: ice tools, crampons, ropes. The picks of Asa's tools were beautifully resharpened— Dane suddenly saw Asa, the craftsman, hunched over his axes, grinding life back into his steel. Asa had sewn hard plastic scales to the outsides of the gloves hanging in the cabinet. Dane took one off its hook, put it on his hand, watched how the scales flexed and overlapped like a medieval gauntlet.

Asa grinned again, just teeth and no humor. "The inside armor's what matters," he said. "Put on what you've got."

"When do we go?" Dane asked.

"Sun's out," Asa said. He clapped Dane on the shoulder. "No time like now."

Dane wanted to say he hadn't slept, that he was a dead man walking, but he didn't care to weather more of Asa's scorn, and he couldn't see the point. He *was* dead on his feet, but he felt as remote from sleep as he did from reality. That bright sun! And the mountain was right *there*, even when he shut his eyes. And Leo was up there, somewhere, and Dane needed to find him, to ask Leo what the hell he was doing here.

Dane unpacked his gear from his duffle, and then they were out on the tundra with the brilliant midnight air running past them like a river and the mountain tearing into the sky. In his pack, Dane carried ice tools and crampons, one twin rope and half the rack, sleeping bag and pad, food for three hungry days. The closeness of the mountain was partly an illusion of its size. By the time the two men covered the miles from Fort Clyde, Ozdon had spread its wings, a black vulture nine thousand feet high.

On the tundra, Dane seemed to be following a wraith. Asa glided over the man-trapped ground, while Dane grunted and snorted twenty feet behind with the needle in the red. When he had enough breath, Dane caught hold of the questions swooping through his head.

"How did Leo find this place?"

"I found it," Asa said. "And then I found Leo. I read a book of his and thought, there's a rose-tinted douche bag who talks like an angel but thinks mountains are art or sun-children or some such bullshit. I sent him a picture of Ozdon and told him to come climb it with me and then call it beautiful. Called him out. He was a name on a book. I never thought he'd read what I wrote. I was pissed off, firing shots in the dark one night. Tired of people going out like they're collecting flowers and calling it climbing."

"But he came," Dane said. He could imagine the photograph worming into Leo's brain. Leo would have to see it himself, make it fit into his world. A mountain that shouldn't exist, but there it was.

"He came," Asa said. "Three years ago. Tall brown stick of a dude, up north to convert the infidel. Insufferable bastard. I wanted to strangle him."

The idea that Leo had traveled to Fort Clyde because of a photograph and some barbed words didn't surprise Dane. Leo had followed leads more slender into the mountains. Dane didn't understand why Leo had returned. Everything about the place—the concrete pillboxes, the mines, the fat pink hermit crab in the bar—ran foul of Leo's carefully tended Zen-garden inner world. And above all, the mountain, snarling and foaming at the mouth—Dane watched as an avalanche galloped off the mountain's shoulder, just to mark his thought. Who'd want to get bit by the same rabid dog twice?

"And he came back," Dane said.

"Half a dozen times since then. I told you he was here. It got to be I could sense him coming before I even heard the plane."

Dane didn't say it, but that was more times than he had seen Leo over the same period.

The land scarred up where the mountain burst out of the tundra, and Dane quit talking to save breath. He followed Asa through snowfields and over steep, broken ground. Above them, the mountain revealed new faces, an ugly, death-row lineup. Fresh snow bearded the rock. Icicles—they must have been big as trees—fell through space and shattered against buttresses, popping distant explosions on impact. Snaggle-toothed towers rooted in gums of dark old ice broke through the faces and ridgelines. Despite the sun, the cold licked at Dane like it was tasting to see if he was good to eat.

A second wave of tiredness swamped Dane. He felt mired in place, barely able to move. Asa agreed to nap until the sun crossed out of the east—the ice would be firmer if they climbed with the sun in the west. Dane unrolled his sleeping bag without a word and stretched himself out under the blank sky and leering mountain, but though he had been all but unconscious on his feet, he couldn't sleep. Now he thought of Leo, and Leo's absence stabbed him no matter which way he turned.

Dane felt inadequate to the job of mourning. He should be wearing black, brooding, walking in the rain while his fellow sufferers thought, ah, there's a man radioactive with loss. Instead he was climbing a mountain. Again. Which is what he did. The very mountain that had killed Leo. Did that make a difference? Leo's haunt would be up there. Which was terrifying—Dane felt his stomach drop at the thought of his hands on the last of Leo's holds—but so much better than an empty box and empty church. And the mountain, the slavering beast? He wanted to kill it! Ride up with gauntlets on his hands and put an axe in its neck. Leo would shake his head. What would he say, that Dane only wanted to kill the terror, the reflection inside? And did Leo have that much terror stockpiled that he needed to come back six times?

Dane had not realized how often Leo was in his head, had never told Leo, as far as he could remember, how much he looked forward to Leo's return. Leo was like a second moon, familiar and strange, visiting him from distant places. When Leo told him about the Karakorum, Dane felt like he'd been there, as if Leo had carried along a piece of him. Dead, Leo was a phantom limb Dane couldn't touch.

"At least he was doing something he loved," Dane said, half-heartedly, eyes closed.

"Wash your mouth," Asa said. "Best use lye."

"I know," Dane said, after a moment to study the platitude. "It's like people will sell out their friends for comfort, just to dilute the pain. Make themselves feel better." Then he fell asleep.

When Dane woke, the sky was a hairy underbelly of grey and black clouds. "So much for our weather window," he said.

Asa was awake. Dane wondered if the man had slept, if he ever did sleep. Maybe Asa was one of the ones who'd gone crazy with the light.

"They never stick," Asa said. "The next storm is always coming."

The clouds pressed down, and the mountain disappeared, standing just behind the curtain, at the edge of perception. Each time Dane blinked, he thought he could see it, but when he opened his eyes, he saw nothing but grey. The two men packed their things, and Dane followed Asa deeper under the mountain's shadow. Naked waves of stone heaved out of the clouds. They clipped on their crampons and climbed steep slashes of snow poxed with stones spat from the cliffs above. Hail hissed against the stone and swarmed around their boots.

Dane no longer felt like a zombie, but the wide-awake world was an uneasy place. He was sprinting toward a killer peak with a stranger, some kind of northern goblin who lived on the tundra with his rock and his tools, luring climbers to his mountain. The mountain had gotten into Leo's head, the man who understood more about high places than anyone Dane knew. It had called Leo back, when Leo could have been climbing anywhere in the world. And then it kept him for good.

"What do you do in between?" Dane asked Asa. "Just wait for other climbers to fall out of the sky?"

"They come," Asa said. "Can't help themselves."

Vertical steps of ice pushed through the snow. Asa took out both tools, made no mention of the rope. The hail slowed, but clouds squeezed in and blinded Dane. Asa was a dark shadow above and right, knocking loose a contrail of falling ice. Dane could see nothing but angry grey air below his feet. He had the impression the clouds were deep. The ice they kicked free seemed to accelerate unnaturally, as if sucked away into the storm.

Asa led them up a narrow ribbon of rime, ice, and snow, all Frankensteined together. The man was clearly a lunatic. Dane followed, internal alarms jangling his brainpan and tinting his vision. The snow was unreformed powder—it could barely support its own weight, let alone Dane's. Dane reached high and snapped off a big swing, trying to cut through the outer layer and find a solid stick somewhere below. His tool rebounded off rock. His second axe, the only thing keeping Dane from spinning off into the clouds, crunched lower in sugar-crystal ice. Dane felt sick, shaky. He locked off again, cleared away the rotten powder, dry-tooled the cracked black stone below it. Intrusions of rotten ice wormed into the rock. It had happened again: he was hacking and scraping at a mountain for his life. *You should quit climbing*, Dane told himself. *Go into grave digging.*

Dane caught up with Asa on top of a broken buttress slashed with ledges. Hail spiraled around them. Rock cased in a withered old skin of ice leaned out over their heads and disappeared up through the weather.

"Rope!" Dane yelled into the wind.

Asa hooted. "You—you're a psycho, man. I started thinking you'd never call it. I thought you were going to get us both killed."

For one brief instant between slaps of wind, Dane imagined throwing Asa off the buttress. He could do it now, before the rope bound them together, then retreat. Just hook the hood of Asa's shell and yank hard. Dane would dagger something evil out of the world, the man if not the mountain—and Leo would be avenged, an eye for an eye, ancient scales creaking into balance.

This small fantasy, sweet in its moment, dispersed fast. Dane didn't feel murderous. Instead, he was flying unexpectedly high. Asa was a snake, but the truth was, Dane liked the way the man hissed and showed his teeth. Already, the sick desperation of the pitch below was fading, replaced by a rising sureness that *this* was the way to climb a killer mountain: mad, scared, running for your life. No margin for error, since that was just illusion anyway. Stripped of all pretenses, he and Asa could spur each other along mercilessly.

Asa already had on his harness, their absurd miniskirt of gear racked around his waist. Four screws, five pitons, a few nuts, a two-thirds set of cams. The pieces had been Asa's choices, since he knew the mountain. Dane reached out, unclipped one of the pitons from Asa's harness, made sure Asa was watching him, and flipped it over his shoulder.

"Seemed like the rack was heavy," Dane said.

Asa watched the pin fall. Then Asa unclipped a second piton from his harness, held it out, and let it loose.

Dane savored, for a wind-blasted moment, just how goddamned stupid this was, each dropped piton slicing through tendons of rationality. Dane shrugged and reached for a third.

Asa clapped one hand to his waist, blocking Dane's. He drilled Dane with a searchlight glare, then his face broke open, split by the first real pleasure Dane had seen on the man. "Crazy fuck!" Asa barked. "Where'd you come from? You win. Your lead."

Dane took the gear from Asa and tied the ends of the ropes through his harness. He'd gotten what he'd wanted. He'd put a crack in Asa's shell and cut himself loose of reason. Dane climbed off the ledge into the falling hail. The wind flapped past him. He felt like some huge dark bird sailing the storm. Hail popcorned off the wall, hitting his hood, the rock, his face. He pounded one of their remaining pins behind a loose tombstone, glued to the mountain by ice or vampire bat shit or god knows what, then torqued the picks of his axes into the joints of the stone, feeling the rock creak and grind. Dane growled at it, and the stone growled back.

Asa dropped away below. The hail turned to snow that flocked and wheeled midair. Dane followed a smear of thin, hard ice that he chipped and hooked. He was balanced on the tips of his monopoints, two steel toenails holding his meat to the mountain. He imagined falling and his body blatting out air like a popped balloon. Dane chipped out another quarter-inch edge and gained a foot at the cost of one more ounce of sanity. Over-gripping his tools, he squeezed and squeezed, as if holding on tighter would enlarge the scum of ice keeping him from winging off. Acid smoked out of his muscles. He was dissolving in his own juices.

Asa disappeared under the snowfall. A spike of rock stabbed out of the wall over Dane's head. Dane half lunged, half fell, hooking one tool around it, then the second. He swung his feet up onto a stance. Something gave way inside him, more collapse than relief. Dane wrapped a sling around the finger of rock, clipped himself in, and yelled down into the blizzard telling Asa to climb.

Dane had hoped the trick he'd played with the pins would make the climbing easy. Believing in his own invincibility, he'd turn the mountain to butter and cut his way up it like a hero. Instead, fear slithered through him like dysentery, and he wondered if the heroes of old also felt a constant pressure to crap their psycho-spiritual armor and that part just didn't make it into the songs.

Asa emerged below Dane, looking like a gargoyle crusted over with snow. His face, Dane realized, would have been the last Leo saw. Leo, who should rightfully have been ushered out by friends and disciples, had instead been with a troll who matched his mountain the way some people echo their pets. Dane kept trying to put Leo into this place, but Leo wouldn't come, staying in the sun, on an arête of porcelain snow, baring a gleaming sliver of teeth below mirrored glacier glasses. Feeling shaggy as a goat, Dane tried to shake the ice out of his beard.

Asa passed through Dane's stance and scratched his way up more brittle rock and cellophane ice. Twenty feet out, he'd still found no gear, and Dane willed Asa not to fall and spit himself on the spike at the belay, where he'd bleed out in Dane's lap, an image that somehow seemed more real than the reality of Asa holding on and slowly dematerializing into the snow. A hundred feet ago, Dane had watched his own hand throw Asa off the mountain, but now the knots had been tied, and Dane silently urged Asa higher.

The climbing was like living on the edge of an exploding bomb. Shrapnel came on the wind; ice and snow flew through the air. They swung leads, and Dane felt shattered after every pitch. At one belay, a powder avalanche swept over Dane, dragging along a hundred little fists of rock. Dane remembered the hard scales Asa had sewn to his gloves. It was all dirty tricks, a mountain made for poisoned minds.

One verse of the perpetual storm ended, and blue sky yawned open. The mountain stretched out in both directions, while Dane dangled from a sling attached to a peeling scab of rock and waited for Asa to finish getting mauled by an off-width crack greased with ice. Dane had expected to be relieved if the wind ever stopped blowing out his eardrums and rattling chunks of the mountain off his helmet. Instead he half missed the way the storm wrapped around him, kept him from seeing into the abyss. Looking up was worse because the mountain stared back. Under the suddenly eyes-wide sky, Dane felt like a rat out in the open with nowhere to hide from Ozdon's beak and talons.

Dane followed Asa's lead. The next anchor was a bottoming nut and tied-off knife blade, equalized in grooves inside the crack Asa had climbed. Asa was half wedged himself, trying to keep his weight off the gear.

"You should have told me not to fall," Dane said.

"Might as well tell someone not to think about an elephant," Asa muttered, not looking at Dane.

Dane dry-tooled up next to Asa, feeling suddenly overcautious, painfully aware that a slip would probably strip them both off. Asa was right: it was better not to know they had two bad pieces and a body wedge holding them to the mountain. Asa seemed grey and grave. Reticent. Like he'd put on years.

"You look like you've seen a ghost," Dane said, hanging from his tools, forcing a laugh.

"Get on with it," Asa grumbled, shifting his knee lock inside the crack. "Sick bastard. Climbing with you is like a ticket to the creep show."

Coming from Asa, that seemed farfetched, but Dane preferred being under the man's skin to in his crosshairs, so he didn't bother saying *right back at you*. Dane took their hardware one-handed. The crack above widened to a bottomless groove slicing into the mountain, and the angle dropped down off vertical. The rock whispered and flexed under Dane's crampon points. A millimeter of ice glazed the hollow stone. Outside the groove, giant stone teeth twisted up out of a pair of jawbone ridges. They looked grotesquely unstable, with no earthly reason Dane could see for them to stay upright.

Twenty feet. Fifty feet. No gear. The rope trailed below Dane uninterrupted. Dane scraped and pressed against the shifty rock, bridging the groove, one foot on either side. Each hold was a time bomb. Dane's blood ticked off the seconds. Eighty feet. Dane nodded his head to the beat of his pulse. A hundred feet. It didn't matter. He knew the rock better than himself, knew just which holds to use and how to use them. He couldn't be shook loose.

A stone thrummed through the air outside the groove, crashed off a snaggled horn, then gathered momentum again. Dane passed a nylon sling, barely held by a vein of rotted ice. Asa had been here. Dane gave the sling a controlled yank, and it ripped free. How much ice had there been? The mountain was shedding its skin. Everything he saw was temporary.

A hundred and fifty feet. No matter how unkillable Dane felt, he'd have to stop and belay, and he'd seen nothing so far but papery rock in overlapping leaves and scales. No cracks, nothing to anchor two human bodies in even the most illusory way. Dane looked around, looked up. Higher, he saw a mushroom blob wedged into the groove. A chockstone? A deeper lode of ice? Dane padded up toward it, the rock creaking, his crampons squeaking, reaching it just at the end of the rope.

Not ice. Not a wedged stone. Leo.

Wedged head down in the groove. Come to rest with his legs bent and splayed. Iced over and locked in. Rope ends trailed down into the groove. Dane levered experimentally on one of Leo's stiff frozen legs. No movement, no shifting. In all of that frail rock and shattery ice, Leo was stuck fast, fixed to the mountain for however long it would hold him. Dane unclipped the anchor cord from his harness, wrapped it around Leo's thighs, clipped himself in, leaned back, and yelled down to Asa to climb.

"Thanks, buddy," Dane whispered, after a long moment. How much should he say to Leo's body? Dane shifted his stance but saw how the cord bit into Leo and kept himself still. Brother? Miss you? Damn you? For falling up here and leaving us all more alone? It was so fucking futile, seeing how the mountain had smashed and half eaten him. On our earthly hell, the dirt eats us, one and all. Maybe you get a cross (or a leg) sticking out for a time to comfort your friends. Asa must have known Leo would be here. No wonder he looked drawn. And Dane yukking about ghosts. He *was* the goddamn creep show.

Asa came up from below. Dane leaned aside to let him see. Asa locked his crampons across the groove, stopped, shut his eyes, opened them, canted his head.

"You cocky son of a bitch," Asa said to Dane, with a kind of soft wonderment. "You are going to get me in trouble." Asa reached up with one axe and poked Leo in the hip.

Dane hadn't intended any disrespect, turning Leo into a bollard. It had just happened. In fact, Dane sensed a rightness in being held to the mountain by Leo, though an upside-down Leo made the rightness grim. The world was grim, covered two miles deep in geologic piles of dead critters. Leo's sum of pretty words didn't change the nature of the dirt.

So to Asa, Dane said, "I wouldn't worry. You're nowhere near as dark as the universe." The only protest Dane saw—the one thing that didn't follow the deterministic biological imperatives to get fat and multiply, to spread more little deaths far and wide—was to go right at the darkness, find its scariest earthly representatives, and attack them. The futility itself, the rank illogic, was its own escape.

Asa took back his axe and said, "I'm cheerful fucking company compared to the universe." Dane had to lean in to hear, Asa spoke so low: "It had been a good, fast day. We were in a lull, like now, the sun was out." *He's had no one to tell this to*, Dane realized, and he thought of a confessional, a sick thought, with no one to hear it but himself and Ozdon. "He was sixty feet up, and he yelled down he wanted to go look at that rock up there." Asa pointed to a gigantic corkscrew tusk of mottled stone. That was Leo, wandering off to see things. He must have been desperate—the spire was cock-ugly, Satan with syphilis, and the traverse out of the groove climbed detached shingles that looked hung by force of habit only. "I told him not to go up there. I told him not to fall. Then the rock clapped, and the rope went slack, and I thought we were both dead for sure. He went in headfirst. Like the coyote, like a fucking cartoon. I cut the ropes and rapped off a sling in the ice." Asa looked at Dane as if he'd just remembered Dane was there. "We need to move. It's haunted here. And you're no help."

Asa took the gear, put a hand on Leo and whispered something Dane couldn't catch, then he climbed past and was gone.

Dane didn't mind having another moment alone with Leo. He caught Leo up on small things. After all the winter snow, the flax and columbine had been outrageous in the spring. There was a woman he had a thing for back at one of the labs, a runner, and with her lab coat and corn silk ponytail, he thought Leo would approve. Driving through thunderstorms in the desert on a full-moon night, he'd seen a midnight rainbow like an oil slick in the sky. A lot stores up in a man over half a year. Dane noticed that one of Leo's legs bent the wrong way. The force of the fall, or maybe debris flushing through the groove. And Dane thought: what's more horrifying than the mind's ability to adapt itself to horror? Asa's voice fell down to him out of the hard blue sky. The rope went tight, and Dane climbed, leaving Leo below.

Dane's thoughts wandered back to the Wasatch, where it all began so casually. No plans, no purpose, just two kids and the mountains. On Ozdon, he hooked the wrong flake and popped off a plaque like a saw blade, which smoked through empty air while Dane caught himself on one tool. Mountain and mind were each full of traps. The groove disappeared under a stack of overhangs. Asa led out through cracks bleeding clear ice. Dane dry-tooled a vertical wall of quarter-inch edges, working to keep his brain in a narrow tube, only one direction to see. A flight of hail rattled by. Wind gusts pounced.

The weather closed back in. Heavy clouds dumped snow into a banshee wind. Perched side by side on a crumbling shelf of rock, Dane and Asa each wrapped an arm around the other's shoulder and huddled their heads.

"Can't climb," Asa shouted. "Might as well sleep."

"Hope we wake up," Dane said.

"Just listen for the yelling," Asa said. "I never sleep long. Too much can go wrong."

Dane wrapped himself in his bivy sack and sleeping bag, allowing about a bushel of snowflakes to press in before he sealed out the world. He curled up on the ledge, a tight umbilical connecting him to the anchor. Through his nylon skin, Dane felt the wind all around him, the snow outside and in. Gravity fingered the parts of him that hung over the edge. Asa, in his own cocoon, wedged against Dane to share the fattest part of the ledge. Leo leaned against him on the other side. Dane closed his eyes anyway and fell down a dark shaft of sleep.

Dane woke with a pillow pressed over his face. No. Snowfall. He pushed away the fabric of his bivy sack and felt a pile of snow slough off. The cold had invaded. His feet were frozen blocks. The wind had dropped to a background pulse. And Asa was screaming. Dane could only make out a word in three, but he caught the gist. Asa was cursing Ozdon, taunting it.

For the first time, Dane considered what it would do to a man to climb only this one mountain, where there was nothing to love, no break from the rituals of combat. Nothing pretty to make the eyes glad. And if he feared sleep? Could Asa sleep in winter, when it was night only, and the rest of northern humanity hibernated like bears? Or did he stay awake then too, in his shop, knowing the mountain was out there waiting for him in the dark?

Dane unzipped the hood of his bivy sack. Windblown ice scraped by him, but the worst of the storm was past. Asa was sitting upright on the ledge, wrapped in his sleeping gear, still yelling. "Asa," Dane said, "don't you ever leave Fort Clyde?"

Asa quit his tirade. The cowl of his sleeping bag turned Dane's way. "You're awake. I was starting to wonder. Been years. I know my place."

"You don't have to marry her. You can climb other mountains."

"Fuck you. I'm trying to kill it, not marry it."

Leo bubbled back up in Dane's head: "Leo would think you're just trying to kill off something inside yourself."

"He and I agreed on that."

"And that's fine with you? Most people enjoy climbing."

"Thrill seekers and hypocrites. They want a little taste of death, just enough to get their juices flowing. Then they run back home and puff up around their friends. A little spoonful of death right in the vein for fun on the weekend. Soulless motherfuckers make me want to puke."

"Leo was trying to help you, wasn't he?" Dane said to Asa. He was still trying to justify Leo's presence on the mountain in his own mind. "He thought he could make you see different." Dane looked around for an example, a piece of the mountain Leo would point to and make one of his poeticisms. Something better than a twisted devil dick. No luck. Dane felt like a fly staring up at a spider.

Asa laughed and squeezed Dane's shoulder with one gloved hand, giving it a shake. "Our boy Leo had horns and fangs. And he didn't know what to do with 'em. Didn't fit his image at all." Asa unzipped his sleeping gear, tightened himself to the anchor, emptied his pee bottle. "I'm doing the world a favor. I could be bombing people's countries or shooting their sons. People been doing that for all time, trying to kill off their own demons. I've got my corner of the world, and I stay put. Fight for the territory inside. I'm goddamn civilized."

Dane tried and failed to grow horns on Leo. They wouldn't take. All he could see were two legs sticking out of the rock—Leo kept slipping away until Dane couldn't even trust that image of him grinning in the sun and porcelain snow. Was it from a mountain they'd shared? A book jacket? Dane flexed blood into his toes and slapped the rock with his hands because they felt like plastic and it was his lead.

Powder snow on black ice, hard as concrete. Guillotine flakes of rock, shifting and creaking. Dane watched a hundred-pound scab slough loose and chop the rope, the anchor, Asa, then had to wake himself to the reality that he was still holding the flake's edge, feeling the rock grind. The wind razored past the mountain, and when it hailed, Dane felt the ice shiv into his brain.

Delusions and terrors crowded Dane's mind. He kept seeing what the mountain could do to them. The images were so close to the surface he stopped trying to defuse them. He hunkered down away from his imagination, from the future, from any thoughts past stabbing the mountain and pulling his corpse higher.

At the belays, they traded gear in silence, a pair of hooded monks executing rituals that already felt old as the mountain. They'd stopped needing words with each other. The rope swap happened automatically. When Asa was climbing, Dane could all but see out of Asa's eyes. And when the rope was stretched out between them at the end of a pitch, they couldn't have dented the wind with megaphones, so they spoke through the movement of the cord that bound them.

At first Dane had resisted the connection to Asa because Asa was such a malignant motherfucker and Dane wanted no comingling of their minds. But the truth was, Dane knew what was going through Asa's head just by the way the rope twitched. Pretending otherwise was pointless.

The storm shredded them. Dane could hardly believe there was anything left of the mountain, that it hadn't been worn to a stub by the weather. The wind was alive, bloodthirsty. It jumped down Dane's throat, tried to turn him inside out.

Dane lost his grip on where they were or what they were doing. There was one direction: up. One way to pull, one way to fall. Time quit moving forward—it only cycled between the ebb and flow of the storm.

The mountain stopped. Dane didn't know what to do. He almost fell over. The summit was an island of vertigo in the wind, nothing but dirty air circling a spike-head of stone. They spent all of ten seconds on top, the time it took Asa to rig their first rappel.

They slid down their ropes, undoing what they'd done. Down and down. Falling snow turned day into twilight, the wind still smacked them around, but gravity had come round in their favor. They downclimbed anything they could solo and rappelled the rest. Asa knew the route down so well there was nothing for Dane to do but string along and let his mind out to wander. They followed snow couloirs, perfect avalanche hatcheries. Dane could hear the layers squeak under his boots. But they bombed down them anyway because it was fast, and they were heroes returning, invincible.

Consciousness—of the larger worlds outside and in—refilled Dane as he descended. The lower he dropped, the less ghostly he felt, the more full of life. Tired, sure, stumbling and dragging, making bad decisions and grousing jokes about dying like putzes on the descent. But also keen, farseeing. By the time they reached the ground and lay down on flat earth out of reach of the mountain, where Ozdon couldn't kill them, Dane felt fully awake for the first time since setting foot in Fort Clyde.

Dane stared up at grey clouds, his legs twitching and cramping, his arms like wet clay. He had gone to the mountain to tend Leo's body, and Leo remained there without so much as a cairn to mark him. Dane was pretty sure he hadn't even adequately cared for Leo in his own mind. Leo would have claimed he never wanted to mark any mountain, but Dane didn't know if he believed the man's claims, and anyway, it was bad for his own state of mind to leave Leo festering up there.

He and Asa hauled themselves upright and began the long tundra slog to Fort Clyde. The only hurry was to end the physical misery of their bodies. Food. Drink. Chairs. Behind them, the mountain shrouded itself in clouds and a pyrotechnic lightning storm. Rain slashed down over the tundra.

"Just be glad we didn't get caught in that," Asa said, after a thunderclap that rattled Dane's eyes.

"We should do something for Leo," Dane said, rain streaming off his Gore-Tex. "Go back up and make him a monument or something."

"Sure," Asa said, looking bemused, "we should go back up there."

When they staggered into town, they went straight to Baxter's, the name of the flesh giant tending bar. They ate elk sausage. They lined up shots of the cheap whisky. Rain rattled the roof. Two other men griped back and forth with Baxter and watched the climbers.

"Like we're zoo monkeys," Dane muttered.

"They know about Leo," Asa said.

Dane and Asa clinked glasses, drank. Dane gave the mountain the finger—there weren't any windows at Baxter's, but he and Asa both knew which direction the mountain stood, and Asa chortled. Dane cocked his arm round until his finger was jabbed at the men at the bar. They were square-fisted, red-faced hulks, insulated against the north with their own meat, and Dane saw in their eyes the calculation each made—that punching Dane would be like popping some skinny, strung-out addict, not worth a busted knuckle or a blood disease, and they turned back to Baxter. In his own outstretched hand, Dane saw the twisted claw of Ozdon, and he put it back down on the table. He and Asa hunched over their drinks, touched glasses again.

"To Leo," Dane said.

"To Leo."

"He should have stayed away," Dane said. "I wish he had. He had no business up there."

"He should have left it for sick fucks like you and me," Asa said.

"But he didn't. He came back."

"That's right. I told you, climbers come here. Can't help themselves. Like flies to meat." Asa threw his last glass against the wall keeping Ozdon out of the room, and Baxter threw them out into the rain.

COWARDS RUN

ERE'S WHAT A seventeen-year-old will do: he'll come into class one day with a leather jacket or a moustache or the key to a '78 Power Wagon on its second engine and act like he's scratching the world's balls. For Skim, it was the day after he acquired his uncle's boat, a nineteen-foot sloop named *Coward's Run*. "First thing I did," Skim drawled out from a tipped-back chair in zero period, an octave lower and twice as slow as I'd ever heard him talk before, "was paint out that damned apostrophe." I'd never heard him concern himself with punctuation. What next? I braced for poetry. He had a dangerous look to him.

Now, "sloop" might sound handsome to you. It did to me, until I hunted up *Simpson's Nautical* in the Gustavus public library and found out that a hog trough with a single mast through its middle and two sails would qualify, and that's about what it looked like Skim's uncle had given him. But Skim was ready to navigate the high seas. He wanted to smuggle in bales of weed from British Columbia or invade North Korea and bring justice to the commies. He bragged about the boat's—*his* boat's—shallow draft and lift-up centerboard. He could land it on a beach in the middle of the night and no one would be a gnat's fart wiser.

Wasn't I seventeen, too? I listened to him rhapsodize about beach landings while we hunted and pecked through keyboard drills, then interrupted to ask the question which had been burning my mind for at least ten minutes: "Yo, Skim, why don't we sail north, land your cockleshell in Lituya Bay, and climb Mount Fairweather from tidewater?" I watched his wheels spin like a four-wheeler in mud month— then he got traction, and we talked about nothing else till summer.

We grew up four houses apart on the old Strawberry Point, at the mouth of Glacier Bay. Skim's dad taught him fishing and sea ballads; my parents gave me geology and Homer. We got on well with each other and our place in the world. Two hundred years ago, the present-day glaciers were all tributaries, and the Bay was the trunk of a honkin' ice river. Strawberry Point was nothing more than the outflow plain of sand and gravel where the big glacier crapped out all the crushed-up mountain it had digested. When the big glacier absconded to join the mastodons and brontosaurs, the ocean filled in, and Strawberry Point became beachfront. To the south, we had waves and whales and cruise ships, the latter sliding by like alien rockets with no time for the natives. To the north was rain, snow, and mountains. Skim and I, we headed north when we could. We'd just walk out of town with our backpacks on, step into the woods, go uphill till we hit snow and ridgelines and summits.

The school and library were sidelong to the airstrip, and in summers, guys with carefully packed North Face duffels would land, hire ski-planes, and fly off to Fairweather or Mount Crillon. So we knew that there were bigger mountains around us, the kind that people from other states and countries would travel around the world to climb. But buying time in a ski-plane was a luxury beyond us. Money slipped by on the cruise ships, like seeing Los Angeles on TV. Folks in town went out to work the water, catching fish or tourist dollars as they could, but we were a stagnant little eddy outside the global currents. Besides, as I said to Skim one day on a practice run in the Icy Strait while we were disentangling the mainsheet in a rain squall that was about one degree too warm to be a blizzard, a ski-plane is a damned inelegant thing. Once you flew a plane to a mountain, what kept you from landing higher? Why not land a hundred feet below the summit? But a boat! No boat would float you higher than sea level.

All through the spring—a local euphemism for unending grey dampness—Mount Fairweather occupied the northern horizon of our minds. Child of earthquakes, mother of snow. Glaciers crawled down its shoulders like dreadlocked snakes on a Medusa. From the summit, you could see deep Pacific waves strike the edge of North America, and the black-white wilderness of the Canadian interior, and maybe even your own soul.

The first day of summer freedom, we had a little party on the public dock. We'd loaded *Cowards Run* to the gunwales with beans and rice and our tatty third-hand mountaineering gear. Skim had found a bucket hat and a straight-stemmed mahogany pipe at the church thrift. He was cousin to a stork, pale-faced and gangly, with a blue vinyl storm suit draped on him like a coat on a hat rack. He kept the brim of his new lid a half inch off his nose and worked that unlit pipe around his mouth like a stick of fossil chewing gum, grinning and muttering the refrain of "Farewell to Nova Scotia" under his breath. Skim's dad, twice as broad as his son, a hairy ape of a crab pot fisherman, played Hawaiian airs on a slack-key guitar, looking like a spider strangling a fly. My parents sat hand in hand dockside, on a plank bench, with complicated expressions on their faces that I tried not to interpret too closely for fear of losing my outgoing tide.

Eventually, Captain Skim swung up onto the bow and said: "Never fear, we'll keep between the sea and the sky. And come home men." Skim's dad popped a loud raspberry through his fingers, and Skim added: "Thanks, Dad. I guess when men go to sea, they come back boys." Then his dad broke a bottle of homebrew against the boat's prow and cut his thumb, which both he and Skim interpreted as a fabulous sign. They raced back and forth along *Cowards Run*, pressing bloody thumbprints up and down her hull to give her a proper baptism.

While they ritualized onboard, and our friends stood around drinking from unbroken bottles and discussing the fine points of sea-going superstition, my mom gave me a paperback copy of Captain Cook's expedition journals. The world, my little corner of it, anyway, suddenly looked clearer. It dawned on me that my parents had been seventeen, too. I saw my dad's proud, thunderhead beard, my mom's long black hair twitching in the wind with the grey sea and restless Alaskan sky behind her—and I thought, maybe they still are. The book had a two-dollar bill for a bookmark. The money wouldn't do me any good where I was going, but I understood: two-dollar bills were what they used to pay sailors when they returned home.

I traded places with Skim's dad and undid the dock lines. We lacked a motor, so Skim's dad grabbed our prow and heaved us backward. Our departure was voluntary, but it looked to me like the ocean god tossing Odysseus out to sea. Skim raised the main, and I cleated the starboard jib sheet, and the south wind—fair, sweet wind we called the peach—brought us around and filled the sails. We had two months' of food and could travel as far as the wind and our sail canvas would take us. Sure as I was that I would return, I barely looked back. We bobbed out past the mouth of Glacier Bay over two-foot waves, light as a cork.

Rain swept across us. In June in southeast Alaska, rain is about as common as daylight. You may not be able to see the sun, but you can always see the rain. The boat slapped the Icy Strait. The rain hissed against the sea. Fat liquid berries filled the air and splattered the deck. Points of land disappeared around us until everything dissolved into water. The only sure sign we weren't sinking was that we could still breathe.

"Feels like weather for a skeleton ship," I said.

It didn't take much to part the primeval mists around a worm-holed bowsprit, tattered sails, long-bearded phantasms groaning in Russian or Old Spanish. It occurred to me that if we blundered by some tourist's yacht, we'd be the ghost ship. *Cowards Run* had been orange once upon a time, but its fiberglass had yellowed sometime in a prior decade. In the rain, it looked like a driftwood bone.

"It's like we've gone back in time," Skim said.

He had his hand on the tiller, his back pressed against the side deck of his boat. The rain sheeted off his slicker. He looked up at the wind cock swinging round on the masthead, looked at the floating compass above the cabin hatch. He looked cheerful. And I thought, sure, you could do it. Booky fools talk wistfully of other times, but Skim could shake off decades like a dog climbing out of a lake. He could also learn. His dad, happy sea god though he might be, had enough vision to want a future for his boy beyond the death struggle with the crabs. Too few crabs left, and each year, too many fishermen gone down to feed the survivors. Skim studied. He'd even taken up Chinese lately—though he liked to be clear: he only wanted to eavesdrop on the enemy. He had smart genes, simple needs. The kind of kid who could skin a moose while mangling a sonnet. I'd heard him do it: "Time feeds on the rarities of nature—and ain't I the hand of time?" With red up to his triceps.

I looked up and down the boat as it wallowed and creaked through the deluge. "You still think we could sail this tub to Asia?" I asked.

"Why not? The Tlingits came over in canoes, didn't they?"

I was pretty sure they hadn't, but that didn't seem to be Skim's point. The wind blew steady from the southeast, and the boat, presumably, jerked forward. I couldn't see a single solid point to mark our progress. Experience suggested we weren't moving fast.

"Skim? What do we do if we can't see land?" I asked.

"What do you mean?"

"What if we can't see Lemesurier Island? Or the North Passage?"

"It can't rain this way forever."

That was true, but it deluged like a river in the sky for two solid days, which, under the circumstances, felt like an appreciable fraction of forever. The wind cock swung round till it pointed due east, the raven wind, right back to Gustavus. We tacked and groped through whitecaps and ropy snot rockets of cold saltwater spray. Wet, black cliffs thumped by massive waves faded in and out of view. Anytime we sighted land, we had to fall all over ourselves bringing the boat around because the rocks already stood so close. We gave up trying to recognize landmarks. Keeping the boat from getting chewed apart was about all we could manage.

Within hours, our mental map of the Icy Strait disappeared out from under us. Our world was water and rocks, not place names, soundings, or lines of latitude. We could tell ourselves that Quartz Point, Lemesurier Island, and Point Adolphus kept us hemmed into the same pocket of water, but for all we knew with any certainty, we'd been flicked into the Bering Sea.

We worked four-hour shifts at the tiller. When we weren't about to run aground, one of us could handle *Cowards Run* on his own. In theory, the other one could sleep in a crawl space we'd left atop our tarp-wrapped provisions in the tiny forward cabin. This proved about as easy as napping on a roller coaster in an earthquake, with the added possibility that the ride might at any moment derail and sink. After the first day, the cabin, which had never been the most weather-tight space, began to flood. So while Skim sailed us back and forth, trying to keep in the open and hold our ground against the wind, I bailed shin-deep water out of the boat with a cracked one-gallon bucket I found under a seat hatch. Wading between the hemorrhaging cabin and the storm, trying to fight an ocean and the rain with a pail, panic started to squeeze in. Any little knob of me that had stayed dry up till then got drowned. I began to doubt that I ever had slept, that sleep was something humans really did.

Near shift change, with only an inch of water left in the bilge, I took a seat next to Skim on the side deck bench. We gravitated toward each other when we could—for companionship, and also because if we pressed shoulder to shoulder, we left that much less surface area exposed to the storm. Between the wind and the waves and the boiling sound of the rain, we had to shout into each other's faces to be heard.

"You cold?" Skim asked.

"No," I said. "I'm shivering for fun. So are you."

"You scared?"

"What? Of this little hurricane?"

"I think I should be more terrified," Skim said. "What would you do if we flipped?"

"I don't know. Swim for shore."

"See?" he said. "I don't think it would be that easy. I think there might be something wrong with us."

It was one of the things I most liked about Skim: We had to be an inch away from hypothermia, shipwreck, and drowning before he began to wonder if we were in fact a pair of goddamn fools.

If we had one stroke of luck, it was that *Cowards Run* was a miracle boat. For all our care, we got ourselves buggered behind a picket fence of rocks—I mean trapped with no way out—and she popped through like a watermelon seed, like she had a nose for the space where she would fit. Huge broadside waves rushed us out of nowhere, and I thought for sure we'd be testing my swimming hypothesis. But with her wide beam and flat bottom, she just bucked up and over, a kind of jujitsu roll I never would have imagined possible for her. I noticed Skim at the tiller patting the boat with his free hand like a cowboy stroking the neck of his horse. *Good girl. You're a rockstar. You're hell on a hull.* And I started doing the same. I suppose that meant there was a corner of my mind dry enough to appreciate that we were two kids in a creaky wonder ship surviving the full kitchen-sink treatment from an Alaskan gale.

When the rain stopped, the clouds blinked away all at once, and the sun dazzled us. What we saw when our eyes recovered was the Gustavus dock not a quarter mile away. We'd been treading water in hailing distance from where we'd started.

For a long moment, neither of us said anything. *Cowards Run* drifted. In ten minutes, we could land, dry off, get hot meals in our own kitchens. There was some powerful gravity at work.

Skim spoke first: "No, no, no. The sun's out. North Passage is that way."

"If we land, we'll never leave," I said.

Ceremoniously, we set our backs to the dock and put the wind to work.

"You know," Skim said. "I've never even seen Fairweather."

"We looked at pictures together in the book."

"I've seen pictures of Saturn and liver cells and Brooklyn Decker's bare butt," Skim said. "That doesn't mean I'd sail a boat over the horizon expecting to find any of them waiting for me."

"So why go?"

"Good question. Don't know." He'd kept his pipe through the storm. He gave it a chew, passed it from one side of his beak to the other. "Must be a pilgrimage. You don't go on pilgrimage expecting to meet Buddha at the end. You look for Buddha on the way."

"You're Buddhist now?"

"Buddha, Jesus, Fairweather—just names."

"Faces of a coin?"

"Sides of a dice."

We sailed through the afternoon, in the sun, in a steaming torpor, unwilling to sleep until we'd made progress. We passed through North Passage and anchored in a cove in the Inian Islands. The tide lifted us up and down. Arctic terns gloried in the sun they'd chased round the world. Sea lions barked. We slept deep as two corpses.

When we'd stockpiled enough blackness to feel human, the sky had changed again. Ramparts of fog drifted past. One moment we could see creeping grey walls and castles, and the next we could barely see the top of the mast. We lifted the anchor and raised sail anyway—because it wasn't raining and we had visibility at least half the time, which suddenly seemed like fine weather.

The channels and coves in the Inian Islands were narrow, and the storm seemed to have stirred up the sea bottom and shore. We nosed *Cowards Run* through driftwood and kelp. A massive round cedar trunk poked through a wall of fog and floated by.

"Perfect canoe log," Skim said, pointing. "There's your ghost ship. I see your mom's great-grandfathers paddling away from home."

"Lacking Gore-Tex, they hunted bear instead of mountain," I said. Then: "Lacking sense, they flipped and swam for the rocks." We both cackled.

"At least they could cook their bear," Skim said. "You ever eat bear? It's candy."

Emerging from the islands, we broad-reached southwest out through Cross Sound. The fog parted, and bolts of sun stabbed through low grey clouds. The western horizon slid over the curve of the earth. Breakers that had walked across the Pacific rolled under us. "The hungry ocean gained advantage on the kingdom of the shore," Skim muttered. He looked wary, a bird hunched on a branch with a cat below. We swung north around the lighthouse on Cape Spencer and tacked up the coast.

I was born and bred in the inside passage. Skim, too. Saltwater was a moody beast, but it was caged by interlocking islands to the west. Now the cage was off, and the ocean seemed wide and dark as space. We were out in the world. We could point the bow and go anywhere.

"We could disappear out here, man," Skim said.

"Gone," I said. "No trace."

While Skim held the tiller, I paged through Captain Cook's sea journals. The man had sailed three times round the world when the map was still covered in dragons. His second voyage took three years. He and his crew went out of sight of land for months. They'd been below the Antarctic Circle and up to Tahiti and had rebuilt whole sections of their boat clawed into by storms and reefs. He'd made no breath-held plunge. He'd *lived* out there, suspended over the deep.

We sailed past Graves Harbor, Murk Bay, Torch Bay, long fingers of water cut into the mountains by departed glaciers. We edged along the ocean, never far from land.

We napped between shifts but slept little. As I recall, we didn't need to sleep. There was too much to see, and the presence of the ocean was too disturbing. Asian waves crashed against the feet of the mountains—and we were right there, at the meeting of ocean and continent, water and snow. Skim spent hours seesawing with the ocean up on the bow, one hand wrapped around the jib yard, watching the world come to him. Besides, we had wind and weather that weren't trying to kill us. We felt compelled to drop miles under our keel. Fairweather called us from the north. We'd come this way for a reason, for the frozen Buddha sitting pretty as a blade up in the ice and thin air. We strained for a glimpse, but the land and clouds never aligned, and the mountain remained in our heads. Skim cobbled together a ditty he tried out to different tunes, from Schooner Fare to Pink Floyd:

South wind baby, west wind boy
North wind for ice, fair wind for joy
Hammer me between the mountain and mast
Sleep me below in the cradle

Past Icy Point, an immense glacier broke through the mountains and lowered itself into the waves. Ice blocks tumbled off its front, and seals flopped on and off the bergs. The wind spun round to the east and doubled, then doubled again. *Cowards Run* heeled over, and we braced our legs across the side decks to keep from pitching into the water. Moving around the boat felt like climbing across a jungle gym. We luffed *Cowards Run*, took in the jib, and reefed the sail until we ran out of reefs and had a napkin of sail cloth left, and still it felt like the wind would bury us in the sea. *Cowards Run* strained along, close hauled. Its sinews creaked and popped, shudders running down the length of the tiller and up through the fiberglass.

The wind fueled the waves. First they were up to the boom, then half as tall as our mast, then the troughs went so deep our sail would go slack at the bottom and *Cowards Run* would begin to right herself, until we climbed up the next wave and the wind knocked us flat. We were afloat on a toy, a leaf—but we were afloat. *Cowards Run* kept the ocean below her hull, and I stroked the sunburned fiberglass with one hand and kept a death grip on the tiller with the other. The friction of the atmosphere against the boat and the waves and our own selves buried us beneath a roar that came down hard as hail. A blizzard of foam filled the air and our ship. The top of each wave crest was nothing but boiling bubbles. The diaper of sailcloth stretched between the mast and boom screamed and warped.

The ocean became a mountain range, ten thousand white-topped peaks. We climbed their faces and skied down their backsides. On top of one gigantic wave, I realized that the wind had scattered the clouds. The sun was low and heavy over the pole. The wind and foam blew right through me. Cresting the next wave, I saw Fairweather. A snow giant, portentous as a comet. Fairweather stood above the sea-peaks, the glaciers, the other ice-mountains around it, and the last exploded clouds.

I'd have looked and looked, but the moment the mountain froze me was long enough that I drifted at the tiller and the next wave

nearly swamped us. I couldn't stare. I had to keep *Cowards Run*
lined up with the wind and weather. I had to concentrate! And probably it was just as well I had my task—it doesn't do to make moon
eyes with Medusa for too long, beautiful as she might be with her
snakes and porcelain face. Turning to stone wasn't out of the question, and I was too far away and surrounded by a good deal too
much water. The mountain was there, fantastic but no figment, and
that had to be enough. It would be there tomorrow. But for the com-
ings and goings of the glaciers, Fairweather was the same as the day
Captain Cook had named it on his third voyage, leaving a kind of
colossal cartographic joke scribbled on the Alaska panhandle. Still, I
kept sneaking peeks, like a snake-charmed rat.

The mouth of Lituya Bay bored through the shoreline. At first
it looked like a crack, not an inlet. Inside, the bay was supposed to
be still water and easy living. But the tide running either direction
through the hourglass neck between the rocks had killed men and
sunk ships. Cenotaph Island, a mile-wide rock in the middle of the
bay, was named for twenty-one drowned Frenchmen. We sailed by,
and the inlet looked like a river pouring through a canyon as the
ocean slopped west on an outgoing tide.

We turned back south and changed skippers. For a kid who
claimed to know nothing beyond the next turn of the earth, Skim
piloted the boat like he could see the next ten seconds clear as now,
like he knew what the wind was going to do before it did it. Wind
gusts punched hard, but Skim had already pushed back with the tiller
before they arrived, so that *Cowards Run* never even quivered. He
did all of that while asking me how Captain Cook kept his men from

becoming rotting bags of scurvy (sauerkraut) and what the crew did between shifts (I wasn't sure, but I imagined it had something to do with the three thousand gallons of wine and the drummer Cook took onboard at his last European port). Skim seemed to be adding my answers to his mental file, another few pages between how to raise a barn and what to eat on the tundra. His talents were wasted on the present. He should have been off discovering new islands in a square-rigged log raft.

There was nothing for it but to wait until the wind and slack tide lined up right for us to slip into Lituya Bay. We paced back and forth outside the entrance through waves like movable mountains and the gale, which kept trying to plow us under. The earth finished another quarter turn under the moon, and we had our first chance at the passage through the neck, but we were out of position, and by the time we had *Cowards Run*'s nose pointed down the hourglass, the water poured against the rocks, raising white caps and recirculation holes bigger than our boat. So we went back to pacing, waiting for the heavenly clockwork to align. We'd gotten so numb to the wind we barely heard it or anything else anymore. Our ears shut down, and we talked through signs. The wind pinned *Cowards Run* at a permanent slant. We forgot about flat ground. It was a blue-sky storm, everything sparking and flashing in the lowering sun.

High tide returned after our daily dose of twilight, and we nailed the slack water perfectly. We passed Scylla on the left, Charybdis on the right. Skim had the tiller, and he was masterful, bending our little arrow of fiberglass through the rocks, *Cowards Run* zipping happily between the wet teeth all around her. Skim hooted and slapped

Coward Run's side. "I've got the wind in a bag!" he said. And I believed he did—that right there, he could have put his finger in the air and pirouetted *Cowards Run* with a twirl of the rudder. We squirted through the opening, and that's when the crosswind jumped out from behind the rocks and hit us sideways across the mouth of the bay, flicking us over into the stone teeth on the other side.

The first rock we hit tore the bottom out of the boat. Spun around with its tail to the wind, *Cowards Run*'s boom thrashed back and forth, the sail convulsed, the main sheets cracked against their blocks. The boat was dying under me, and then I was in the water and crushed by the cold. I couldn't move, couldn't breathe. Frozen brine went in my eyes and up my nose and down my veins. I wrestled out of my jacket and boots and kicked for the rocks. At least I must have, because when my thinking self rebooted, I was in sweater and socks and water up to my ears, clutching a peninsula of stone with my forearms because my fingers were solid wax. Upright shelves lifted out of the water above me, but they slid out of my grip. I had no grip. The wind drove the water over my head. Saltwater pushed down my throat. I thought: *numb hands gonna kill me.* I made my elbows do the work instead, hooking and arching and spluttering and kicking. I hung my middle over a spine of rock and puked out saltwater till I could breathe.

I crawled along the spine to a solid ledge eight feet above the waves. The point of *Cowards Run*'s bow jutted out of the water a hundred feet from my rocks. The mast veered off vertical and rocked side to side. Water and stone, mountains and forest, plus that splinter of broken boat—that's what I could see. A monster stab of loneliness pinned me there. No boat, no partner, not even my hands, which were still blocks. I was outcast, exiled. I got up to look for Skim because I realized I'd even take the company of his corpse. I found him half in the water and half out where he'd lodged himself head-first in a sheltered angle in the rock. He was breathing and shivering and barely knew I was there.

I hooked my wrists under his armpits and hauled him up out of the water. We leaned against each other, and he shook his head side to side. We stumbled across ribs of rock together, over to where the arm of land that separated the bay from the ocean became a wide spit with sand and trees to the east and rock on the west. Skim's legs didn't work so well. I forced him to take steps while half dragging him. I found a wind-sheltered patch of sun and peeled off our saturated clothes, then marched us back and forth until Skim could stand on his own.

"Slavedriver," was the first thing Skim said to me. "Whips and chains."

"Welcome back," I said.

"I'd given up," Skim said. "I thought I never would, but I did."

"Everyone gives up eventually," I said. "Unless you get shot or die in your sleep."

"Cheerful thought. I feel like I died twice. Once in the water, and again doing whatever you did to bring me back."

"See anything interesting along the way?"

"Big nothing and deep sleep," Skim said. "Real peaceful. Little dream flickers up above. Then a demon with a pitchfork came and lit me on fire."

"You're welcome."

We were far from warm and not moving very well, but we hobbled up to the divide and sat down where we could see *Cowards Run*. The front quarter of the boat broke the water, settled at a steep angle. We guessed the tide was about half out, which meant three hours had gone since we wrecked. Three minutes or three years seemed more right.

Set there above the waves, cold but not dying from it, watching *Cowards Run* broken on the rocks, I felt deeply mellow. Nothing pushed me forward. I was in a nice, still-water eddy. We were going to need to find water and food and sort out how to stay alive. But right there at that moment, I had no boat to steer, no ambitions. Fairweather was a luminous cone on the near horizon, and I barely noticed. It was just scenery.

"I hear some people fantasize about prison," I said. "Nothing to do. Nowhere to go. Stop the world and get off."

"We could start a business," Skim said. "Chartered catastrophes. We'd crash boats and planes onto uninhabited islands for folks who need a break. No soap on a rope. Way better views."

"The insurance would kill us."

"It'd be a fly-by-night sort of thing. Cash and balaclavas."

The water ran out through the mouth of the bay. Inch by inch, *Cowards Run* surfaced. "A few high tides will break her," Skim said. I said nothing. He was intruding on my serenity. A hundred more monster teeth poked through as the water flowed toward Asia. Skim continued: "She's not broken up yet." I refused to go with him. He said, "We'll raid the cabin at low tide."

"I'm not going back out there." My calm had shrunk to a life ring, but I gripped it tight.

"Sure you are," Skim said. "But we might as well get warm first." He stood and chucked my life ring into the water. My blissful complacency popped. I was hungry. I was thirsty. There were clouds in the west and, if we were lucky, a tent in *Cowards Run*. And Skim, who'd been four-fifths dead, was getting ready to do wind sprints.

We organized the Castaways Beach Olympiad. We threw rocks and caber-tossed drift logs. We steeplechased boulders. We were seventeen. We lost track of being shipwrecked. Skim found a spot where he could do a running gainer off a cliff into the sand. I found an overhanging prow of rock and did pull-ups till my head swam. We couldn't start a fire, so we burned our own bodies for heat. My stomach cursed me so long and loud I was actually looking forward to the swim to *Cowards Run*.

We sat on the divide in our underwear. As I recall, the land seemed as raw and restless as we were. The mountains and glaciers and woods and tides were all unfinished, on the move. We watched the water. The outgoing river slowed. As soon as the white caps around the rock turned to ripples, we charged. We gained the first fifty feet by rock hopping and wading. Then Skim slugged my shoulder, yelled, "Feed no fish!" and we kicked off and swam. The water was black and as heavy-cold as before. It wanted to paralyze me and pull me down like a stone. But we were revved up, instead of sitting fat and foolish, flushed with success, and we hit *Cowards Run* side by side and heaved ourselves onto the tilted deck.

We took two minutes to unclench ourselves. My hands were half gone again. Skim tried jumping jacks but nearly fell back overboard. *Cowards Run* shifted and ground against the rocks under our feet. I felt the fiberglass cracking. "One tide will do it," I said. "The ocean's coming back." The clockwork was ticking. We got to work.

All our things were in bags and duffels in the cabin, a nine-foot-long shoebox that was damp and smelled like brown piss even on dry days. The storms and the wreck had stirred it up with a dressing of bilge water, but at least the hole in the stern end of the hull had levered the cabin above the low-tide waterline. Skim dove full length into the reeking crawl space atop the gear, squirming back out minutes later with our two butterfly coils of rope. I flaked the ropes while Skim hauled out sodden gear bags and stacked them in the crook of the slanted deck. When I was done, Skim tied the rope ends around his waist. He beat his chest, and I threw him into the water, which is what he'd told me to do back on our perch on the rocks. While he swam for shore, I pulled more bags out of the cabin.

We didn't have time to unpack and inventory the things we wanted most. Water was already flowing through the bottleneck into our end of the hourglass. We'd decided to grab as much as we could and make do with whatever we got. When Skim reached the rocks, he scrambled up onto the spine of rock where we'd sat, yelling and shaking off water, rat-a-tatting hellfire and damnation till it was verse. He looped the ends of the ropes around a three-ton boulder and tied them off. I ran the middle of one strand around *Coward Run*'s starboard windlass and cranked the rope tight, trying not to listen as *Cowards Run* creaked and popped. When the rope was tensioned between the boat and Skim's rock, I put a knot in the middle of the second rope and clipped it and a duffel bag to the taut line.

Skim pulled on his end, and the duffel rafted across the water, half submerged and half suspended.

The bag stuck against a rock and we worked it free, pulling back and forth on the haul line. It stuck again, and we wiggled it loose. It took long minutes to deliver the bag to the shore. I could feel the moon circling closer, pulling water into the bay. We worked like maniacs, the water climbed higher, and *Cowards Run* groaned and rocked against the waves.

We'd ferried half a dozen bags to shore when *Cowards Run* lurched hard to its starboard side. I turned, released the windlass, watched the rope run free, then dove off the port gunwale as the boat rolled out from under my feet. Just before I hit the water, I heard a big, wet, burping crunch. When I surfaced, our boat was sinking in pieces. I swam back for the last time, feeling leaky and pretty near sinking myself. Skim fished me out of the water and hauled me up to the rock spine with the ropes and gear.

Like bears grubbing under logs, we tore open the bags, hunting food. Two pounds of dried salmon disappeared behind bared teeth and greasy fingers. We chased the salmon with a jug of honey we'd planned to make last a month, swapping hits off the bottle, downing it easy as Gatorade.

Everything was rank and sea-slimed—our food bags, our gear bags, our soul bags, too—and the clouds in the west had piled into mile-high masses. We upended our duffels, spreading our salvage on the rocks, trying to dry the gear before the next storm. Our tent and two tarps had made it to shore, so we constructed a little shanty in a sandy cove well above the tide line, tensioning the corners to cracks in the rock with our ice axes and odds and ends from the climbing kit. Then we split a brick of cheddar and built a driftwood bonfire that would have been visible on Mars.

We slept through the brief night and through much of the next day. When we were awake, we ate and moved gear around, trying to get it all dry and kept out of the rain squalls that swooped down on our camp every few hours. I'd been so occupied with not drowning or freezing or starving, I hadn't gotten much time to think. When I did start thinking, it occurred to me I'd been expecting calamity of one sort or another since I was old enough to notice the winds changing with the seasons. I was three-quarters Russo-Alaskan and a quarter Indie, and apocalyptic blood drained down both sets of veins. There were earthquakes, blizzards, bears the size of jeeps, white invasions, brown rebellions, and a goddamn lot of guns and spears and anarcho-libertarian fervor. Badness was all around, and I checked my fingers and toes half expecting to find I'd lost one while I was preoccupied. Besides, I'd read the books: *Treasure Island*, *Robinson Crusoe*, *The Odyssey*. If you didn't get marooned somewhere wild by the time you were out of your teens, you weren't really trying.

So it was only natural that I spent some time stamping around the fire, yelling at the ocean and the sky. I let the gods know I was wise to their ways. Meantime, Skim was down at the waterline practicing Chinese calligraphy in the sand with a pointed driftwood stick. A wave would roll out, he'd step down into the wet sand, trace out a single character, then jump away when the water reached back to claim it. "I read that monks do this in summer with a waterbrush on asphalt," he said. "You get a few seconds to make your mark, then a few seconds to see what you've done, then it's gone." I asked him to translate. "Wheel," he said, jumping back from the water. "Wind." "Wave." "Wheel."

There was time for disappointment, too. Whenever the clouds weren't spitting their guts all over us, Fairweather stood right there, fifteen miles away and three full miles high. It had never been so close and never looked so far away. The base of the mountain might as well have been in Siberia for all the good proximity did us.

The second night turned to dusk, but we weren't tired, having slept so much of the day. When we built up the fire, it glowed against the low clouds draped over our camp, making strange ghosts in the sky.

"How long do you think we'll be here before a boat comes by?" I asked. Fishermen used Lituya Bay. It could be a week, it could be a month, but someone was bound to show up.

"Cowards run," Skim said.

I realized we hadn't talked about Skim's boat yet, and I felt bad for avoiding the subject. "Hey, man," I said, "I know she was your baby."

"Cowards run."

I wasn't sure what to say. Skim was hardly the sentimental type, but that boat had been an extension of him. I'd been thinking about losing digits, but maybe Skim had already lost a whole arm. "I've got some savings," I said. "Not much, but I'd go in with you on a new boat when we get back."

"Listen to me," Skim said, "cowards *run*."

It occurred to me that I'd been the one adding capital letters, not Skim. Then I understood what he was suggesting. I looked around our camp. We had ropes, climbing gear, tent, sleeping bags. We had food. We hadn't planned on sailing overland to basecamp anyway. "We're not waiting here for a rescue, are we?" I said.

"Nope."

"We can wait for a rescue next month just as well as we can this month."

"Yup."

The prison bars melted. The mountain was, in fact, as close as it looked. And just as stepping out of prison is supposed to be as bad as stepping in, our night world seemed suddenly perched on the edge of a cliff. The mountain had been much less terrifying when it stood in Siberia.

We started packing. Once the decision was made, we couldn't sit still. The ocean slapped the sand, heavy fog wrapped its wet arms around our camp, and we kept the fire high and took inventory of the things we'd carry to the mountain. We had two sleeping bags and one sleeping pad. We'd lost the pickets but had all our ice screws. One of the snowshoes had snapped. The twenty-pound bag of dry beans we'd planned on eating trekking to and from the mountain was gone. "Just think how much easier the approach will be without all that stuff," Skim said. That hadn't been my dominant thought, but it was true enough.

The sun drifted up above the fog—so we surmised, at least, when the darkness trickled away, leaving behind a cold, white blindness. By midmorning, we'd finished dividing our gear into four loads we'd relay to the base of the mountain. Fairweather, when we could see it, looked almost close enough to shoot, but the fifteen straight-line miles between us were a 3D Escher maze of mountains, glaciers, and rivers filled in with hectares of slide alder and raw boulders. Others had passed the labyrinth—it just wasn't at all clear how. We sat on our packs, not quite willing to begin, stalling over a ration of dry fish we couldn't really afford to eat.

"I guess this is why people hire the ski plane," I said.

"When Cook landed somewhere, did he climb the mountains?" Skim asked.

"White guys didn't start climbing mountains till they'd finished with the oceans and jungles."

"Sure, that makes sense," Skim said. "First Ma Ocean, then the subconscious, the steamy thickets, then up into snow-white soul-land. Trying to escape to the heights but always falling back to their earthbound selves. Tragic."

Skim would go ballad hunting like a dog chasing the wind in the trees. But I was rooted in practicalities. "Bag hauling," I said. "I bet it was their luggage. On the ocean, you've got a boat. In the jungle, you chain a bunch of locals together and make them carry the bullets for the rifle you're pointing at them. But in the mountains—even Sherpas would only go so far. Those Brits would do anything to keep from being their own mules." Skim brayed like a donkey, put his pack on his back, and we started walking.

Days passed in a blur of downpours, sand, and boulders, repeated in varying combinations. We muled our gear north along the narrow terra firma between waves and rainforest. The only dents in the wilderness were rusted machines from long-abandoned mines pushing out through the fog and woods. In all that time, we never once saw the mountain. We barely even saw the local spruce-tops. It didn't matter. The mountain had become an article of faith. We'd made our choice between two doors ahead of us. Through one, the summit looked like empty real estate after you've survived shipwreck and drowning. Through the other, the top was the one place on earth worth risking shipwreck, drowning, avalanche, icefall, frostbite. The reward behind door number two would grow in proportion to what it took to get there, and that was the door for us, a pair of fanatics doubling down with each step toward the mountain. Or as Skim put it, as we sat huddled against a boulder that offered minor psychological protection from a particularly nasty squall: "You'd have to pay me six figures to do this as a job. But for free, I'll bulldog the mountain to the end."

"That's probably why you barely scraped a pass out of econ," I said.

"That's probably why I'll be hungry and poor."

"I never hear you talk about the future."

"Man, that's the present."

In fact, we gave up on time. We'd already borrowed heavily against the bank, so it didn't seem to matter how slow or fast we went. The local clocks—the sun, the tides, the rain—spun through their own broad circles, and we kept to ours. We slept, we walked, we ate, doing each when it seemed right. On a long tidal flat, I chased down a nine-inch crab that had been pushed up on the beach by a freak wave, so we stopped and stuffed ourselves on Dungeness around a wet, smoking fire. In a deep creek splitting out through bent old spruces, Skim found a scrum of Dolly Varden and spent an afternoon patiently thinning their ranks with a net made from a stuff sack webbed onto a long stick. When *Cowards Run* sank, our umbilicus snapped. We drifted forward, a life raft of two in the wilderness. Everything beyond the mountain faded off the map. Overhead, the strangled throat-clearing of migrating sandhill cranes fell down through low grey clouds. The salmon, the birds, the grizzlies mining streamsides for protein, they all had a direction, and so did we, fulfilling some part of our lifecycle sure as a Chinook swimming upstream.

At the outflow of the first of the snake's nest of creeks draining the Fairweather Glacier, we turned inland—into a wall of slide alder and devil's club. We bulled forward, snorting and grunting like moose. The harder we pushed, the stronger the brush pushed back. Branches hooked all our crotches: groin, neck, knees, pits. Leaves filled our eyes and mouths. Our packs suddenly weighed twice what they had on the beach. Each step came with a price, like getting whipped repeatedly by a jujitsu master. I'd never seen Skim enraged. He cursed the alder right down the evolutionary tree, all the way back to the first chlorophyll, but it was him who degenerated into howls and moans. We retreated, which cost us every bit of what we'd spent pushing forward, but at least we could see daylight to the rear.

We regrouped in a fringe of meadow by the creek, lying down with our heads on our packs, picking devil's club spines out of our hands and necks. The water banged down its streambed. It was fast and loaded with silt. It looked almost silver.

"What do you figure?" Skim said. "Snow gets dumped on the mountain, gets buried by more snow, turns to ice, walks down inside the glacier. And it takes, what, a hundred, a thousand years for it to reach the end of the glacier and melt out into this creek?"

"Could be. The snow Cook saw on the mountain is maybe going past us now."

"That's patience."

We put our packs back on and sniffed around the wall of alder, trying not to get sucked in, looking for cracks and leads. We found a bear track clodded up with fresh huckleberry shits. An old streambed. A talus pile the brush hadn't fully colonized. Skim cut a short stiff center branch from the last patch of alders to lash to the frame of our broken snowshoe, so it wouldn't be completely worthless. Actually, he cut half a dozen, muttering to himself each time that the one he'd just cut wasn't *quite* right—until I realized what he was about and hustled him onward. Before long, we were up on moraines the size of mountains and old ice covered in crushed rock where nothing grew at all.

The next day, the clouds lifted and vanished. The world stood revealed, all bright, white light: crystal underfoot, crystal overhead, and the incandescent radiance of Fairweather blasting through us like cosmic rays. Veins of meltwater roared past us and poured down boreholes in the ice. We couldn't look directly at the mountain. It hurt our eyes and set our ears ringing. We kept our eyes down and scrabbled up the old ice where the glacier died and bled to the sea.

The ocean disappeared over the edge of the ice. The air turned thin and dry. When we reached fresh snow, we roped up. The piggish lips of crevasses were just beginning to open from their winter hibernation. I threaded the buckle of my harness and found I had to pull it an extra two inches past the webbing's accustomed spot. We were both fading away, hungry all the time. Food became a game. We accused each other of ever-more-elaborate thefts. Skim spent an hour explaining how I'd used our repair needle to boost the filling out of his morning Snickers before sealing the seam in the wrapper with toothpaste.

The crevasses terrified us. They were the unknown, the crack in reality, the plunge into darkness. We shied away from the faintest line in the snow. "You know," Skim said, throwing ice chunks down one deep crack and waiting for echoes to surface, "reading up on Z-pulley diagrams and klemheist knots in the library with you made me feel like a pro. But actually pulling one of us back out from down there seems kind of far-fetched."

"Great," I said. "Glad to hear it. Maybe you should go first."

"Hell," Skim said, "what do we have to go back to? Books and fishes? Out here, we're heroes. Watching you dive off *Cowards Run* a second before it sank, I thought I was at the movies. You won't get to do that back home. I don't think you can get back home from here."

With pitfalls all around us, was it any wonder our conversations turned morbid? We were boys with muscles—the threads tying us to our place and our people hadn't fully developed yet. There in the mountain's lap, we had the rope between us, and beyond that, we barely seemed tied to anything at all. We could fantasize about glory on the mountain like it truly mattered.

Still, fear throbbed up through the glacial skin. I felt like a cat trying to cross a lake, unwilling to weight my feet for fear of the next step. Skim broke through the ceiling of one crevasse and landed on a bridge five feet down. He pulled himself back out, panting and heaving. "It's unreal," he said. "It goes down forever, and the walls glow blue." Then he puked in the snow.

When the snow turned soft in the afternoon, we balked and pitched the tent. We probed the immediate area as best we could, but I still couldn't shake the image of us sitting on a skin of snow over a tent-eating monster. We belayed each other just to step fifteen feet away to take a dump. Inside, we stretched out on our backs on our sleeping bags, trying to unwind the tension from our minds. The tent filled with groans and tick-clicks as the snow settled and flexed in the sun. We could crawl under the nylon and hide, but we couldn't get away from the underworld of voids and trapdoors.

"We're not supposed to be here, are we?" Skim said. "I had no idea how much I'd feel like an interloper."

In the morning, Fairweather was still there. A cold white light two miles high. It burned our brains right through our glacier glasses. We couldn't resist it. The mountain was dense as a star, that's how much gravity it had.

"I'm coming, I'm coming," Skim grumbled as he laced up his boots. "I feel like a damn moth next to a candle."

We'd gained four thousand feet over the ocean, and any time the sun wasn't direct, the cold peeled back our layers. Those little jobs, tying boots, priming the stove, collapsing the tent, turned our fingers numb and dumb. I was inside out with hunger. I wanted to bathe in food, to roll around in a tub of spaghetti till the stuff went through my skin and right into my blood.

Rather than head down to the elevation of Dolly Varden and wayward crabs, I jacked my pack up onto my shoulders and pointed myself uphill. I'd drawn the front, and Skim was waiting for me. And Skim was right. I didn't have anywhere else to go. Cracks had opened up behind me even bigger than the Fairweather crevasses. I looked back at Gustavus, and it seemed more terra incognita than the mountain.

The crevasses multiplied as the ground levered up. The glacier tumbled off the mountain. Four days prior, it had been a shriveled geriatric, dying into the Pacific. Now it was young and fast, frozen mid-rapid. We spent the morning tiptoeing around, scaring the snot out of ourselves on snow bridges straight out of a cracked architect's nightmare while shuttling our gear up to the base of an icefall that Skim dubbed God's Class VI Kayak Run. To me, it leaned like a house of cards, only the cards were hundred-foot slices of glacial ice.

We climbed down into pinched-off crevasses and chimneyed up between their blue walls. Neither of us had climbed vertical ice before, so we were too green to be scared. I swung my tools, and they stuck in the ice, and I did a lot of pull-ups. At least the bottom wasn't going to drop out from under me. From an anchor of two ice screws below a twenty-foot gargoyle that looked like Dali's take on *Winged Victory*, I hauled our bags and belayed Skim. He led out a ramp of sun-rotted snow, then into another crevasse chimney. Up above, the glacier leveled off, and we planned to set a fixed basecamp where we'd leave our snowshoes and a reserve of food while we climbed off the glacier and onto the mountain. Skim spelunked deeper into the slot he'd entered, drumming away with his axes and calling out the things he was looking forward to once we'd stopped in the placid

snow above the icefall. "An unroped piss!" he yelled, deep inside the
ice. "A pizza and a beer!"

Did I mention we were the only green things in the whole temple
of blue and white light? We were slow as winter. We heckled each
other mercilessly, yelling back and forth, the words warping off the
ice. The sun came round and caught us, and the ice began to drip. But
we were actually enjoying ourselves, because this kind of climbing we
could do with our arms, and the top of the icefall was close. I had one
short headwall to finish, which felt as good and simple as chopping
wood. I hauled the bags and belayed Skim up to join me. When he
arrived, I just shook my head.

We weren't safe. We were buggered. It had all been a trick—
we'd filled the unknown with our wishes like Greeks filling the
night sky with gods. A shattered glass of crevasses spiderwebbed
out from the top of the icefall. Towers of pressed snow stood above
the crevasses, a gang of evil-looking jack-in-the-boxes ejected from
below by pressures that made my testes want to climb my spine.
The towers were three and four stories high, small enough that we
hadn't seen them from below, big enough to thumb us flat and
bury our pancaked bodies so deep the blood wouldn't even stain
the glacier. And the sun was on them, and I could see them melting
and teetering. Fresh debris from yesterday's collapses was piled all
around us. An avalanche swept down off the southwest ridge of the
mountain.

Skim took four steps away from the belay to get a better look and
fell into a crevasse to his waist. He kicked his feet, trying to stick his
crampons into something solid, but the snow was so soft, he couldn't

tell whether he had snow or air under him. He swam back to me like a drowning man while I kept the rope tight.

We were paralyzed. Minutes passed, and I could feel the sun lowering, locking onto us like a death ray. Icicles and snow mushrooms sloughed into the crevasses. The towers were drooling, ready to pounce.

"We can't stay here," Skim said.

"We go down," I said.

"Through the icefall? It'll be a rattrap. The whole thing could collapse."

"No. Down there." I pointed into the last crevasse he'd tunneled through. He looked and took my meaning—and he shrugged. We were that desperate.

We sank four screws into the hardest ice we could find, and buried one of the packs deep in the glop as a gigantic deadman anchor. Then we fixed both our ropes in case one got cut, and I rappelled back over the final headwall, which was already coming apart in chunks. When I reached the slot Skim had climbed, I swung inside of it.

The crevasse angled into the pack. I bridged my feet, spiking the parallel walls of blue ice with my crampons, filling the three feet of space between with my body. I burrowed into darkness, the walls turning from blue to black and the temperature dropping as I scraped and tensioned deeper. All I wanted was an alcove or a ledge that could keep two idiots alive for a half turn of the earth. My standards were low and falling fast. I could hear Skim hollering at me.

Under a shallow curve, I found two sloping dishes good for about a butt cheek each. The rest of the crevasse seemed cut by a cleaver.

I spiraled in two screws above the lower dish, clipped them, then bellowed up to Skim that I was off rappel. The crevasse pinched off overhead. A well of blackness dropped away below. Thirty feet to my right, a slice of white-hot light, the outside world, blinded me if I turned that way. I sank our last two screws above the second dish for Skim. We wouldn't sleep and we might freeze, but nothing looked ready to crush us, short of the whole uphill chunk of the glacier slipping forward a yard—which would happen, but probably not in the next twelve hours.

Skim arrived, sliding down the ropes and shouldering himself in from the outside. He looked around, taking in the screws and the stances, one of which was occupied by my foot. "Four stars," he said. He clipped himself and his pack to the anchor I'd placed for him. "This is going to leave scars. But we'll probably live." We got to work.

Full swings with an axe would have turned that narrow space into a blender, so we chipped away, feeling like two chained prisoners trying to crack concrete. We enlarged our "settin' porches"—as Skim called them—one sliver at a time. When my ledge had grown roomy enough for both cheeks, I pronounced it home and got the stove running in my lap to begin melting ice chips for water.

"We're in the guts," Skim said. He gestured down into the darkness below our feet. "Just imagine if you fell down there. You'd be ground up, and some day your juices would come out in the creeks at the other end."

"The glacier won't eat us. Too skinny—no meat left."

"Was it Jonah who got swallowed by a whale?" Skim asked. "What'd he do to deserve that?"

I had a kind of greatest-hits knowledge of the Christian book: Sampson, Daniel, Jonah, Lazarus. "You'll like it," I said. "God started talking to him, and he tried to run away."

"Ah-ha! I *knew* running was a bad idea. Though we're not doing much better."

"Yeah, but when Jonah got puked up on the beach, he still had to go to Nineveh. So running just made his trip longer."

Skim kept hacking away at his seat in the ice, feeding me the chips for the pot of water. I couldn't move because the stove was precarious and I could only hold it perched on our shovel blade with gloves on my hands. Half my weight was on my ledge, the other half hanging through my harness off the anchor, and I'd added a length of sling as a foot stirrup to keep myself from sliding, so I was well and truly trussed. I'd insulated my butt and back with my sleeping pad, but now that I'd stopped chopping ice, I could feel my blood slowing down and the cold creeping in. It wasn't good to stare into the black chasm below us, but it was hard not to look. Outside, a few tons of ice smashed past. Our ropes, fixed to the anchor we'd left above, swayed back and forth. Skim paused to listen.

"Things must have been pretty gnarly up there," he said. "I'm not near as freaked out by this bivy as I think I should be."

"Maybe you're getting comfortable with the mountain."

"No way, man. We're in outer space."

I felt it then, the alienness of the ice. Black longing for kitchen-talk and the four walls of my parents' house reached up and snagged me. I felt suddenly used up.

"I thought you said we couldn't go back home," I said.

"We can go back," Skim said. "It just might not be home when we get there." He returned to cutting ice. "Like the sailors with Cook. Spend three years sailing the dragon side of the planet. And the whole way, even when times are good and they're getting fed breadfruit by island girls, they dream of home: red-cheeked dairymaids and pasties and the moors or whatever. Then when they get back home, they turn around and sign up for another voyage."

There it was. Skim wasn't the type for fake cheeriness, and I suppose if I wanted that, I wouldn't be camped out on an ice wall in the guts of a glacier.

The stove hissed in my lap. Outside, the light looked dense, yellow, a fourth wall of our meat-locker sanctuary. Skim gave up trying to expand his porch and wedged his butt onto the ledge he'd made. We traded off with the stove so that I could wrap my sleeping bag around me. Something big collapsed above, shaking the crevasse. Blocks tumbled down outside, dark shadows flying past. Our ropes jerked and twanged. A second collapse followed the first. The afternoon sun had reached some kind of critical point. Skim shut his eyes and worked through the lines of Frost's poem about the world ending in fire or ice. For half an hour, explosions rippled the airspace above us and walked down the ice wall at our backs. I started hollering back, and Skim joined me, because, goddamnit, why not? If we were going to die, we might as well go down yelling, and if not, it felt good to join in and make some noise. We yelled till the mountain went quiet and our echoes sounded like howls in an empty church. Our bomb shelter had held. The world hadn't ended.

Silence and cold dropped over us. We'd emptied ourselves out. The wall of yellow light outside the crevasse paled and turned blue. We fixed ourselves on the stove. Each pan took a geologic age to melt and bubble. And you'd think that somewhere between the eras, I could catch some rest. But each time I nodded, my sleep-self began to slide down into the blackness below us, and I snapped awake. We took turns with the stove, torching our throats with water fresh off a boil, trying to get some heat into our bodies.

Blue faded to black. Time stretched. Our headlamps showed the other wall of the crevasse, three feet from our faces. Numbness crawled down my legs. I had two inches to move left or right on my ledge. Half conscious, I began to think we'd missed a day and been down the crevasse for thirty hours instead of ten.

Somewhere in the middle of the dark hours, at maybe one or two in the morning, with the cold deep in our bones, Skim said, "I'm done," and I said, "Let's go." We were robots with rusty hinges. It took an hour just to pack the stove and sleeping bags. Our two ropes still ran up out of the crevasse and into the night despite the abuse they'd taken—though one or both of them might be hanging by a nylon thread for all we knew. Skim didn't hesitate or ritualize or go eenie-meanie to hang responsibility on fate. He just grabbed the blue strand and wrapped his prusiks around it, eyes wide open like a cold-blooded stoic. Or maybe he was just cold and beyond caring. He caterpillared up the rope on his prusik cords and disappeared into the night. Thirty minutes later, his voice filtered down through the heavy blackness, telling me to come up.

I reached the anchor as dawn began to open the sky. The place looked bombed. We whispered, not wanting to wake the dead. Jags of ice and compressed snow fanned out where towers and avalanches had fallen. The four ice screws we'd placed dangled uselessly from the ropes—they'd heated up, melted the ice, and fallen out. The pack we'd buried as a deadman had taken a direct hit and been re-buried by five extra feet of debris, which had frozen hard as concrete overnight. Without a word, we cut the ropes where they emerged, leaving the ends and the pack embedded. Then we roped ourselves together and fled for the ridgeline at the glacier's edge.

Maybe the world had ended after all. Sunrise was bleak. Bands of grey clouds rubbed up against the mountain. We saw nothing but white and grey. Shattered ice creaked and popped under our crampons. I felt ghostly, intrusive, nosing my way around the underworld or Valhalla—some place where the powers had duked it out. It wasn't clear to me if anyone had survived, ourselves included. We followed the debris tracks, telling ourselves those would be the thickest layer. Everything was so frozen we probably could have trusted an eggshell over a crevasse. We moved fast, racing the turning earth and the sun, feeling as if a Valkyrie might come winging past any moment to mark us for the bloody-corpse-in-the-ice treatment.

At the edge of the glacier, we paused to divvy a candy bar—breakfast. We couldn't stop long. A thousand feet up the flat face of the ridge, a hanging wall of seracs and fresh pack looked dangerous as the future, about a photon away from avalanching down on our heads. We angled west toward the ridgeline and were damn slow because the snow was steep and our consolidated packs were heavy and we'd each had about a thimbleful of food and sleep. I drifted through waking nightmares in which the snow suspended above us began to fall, like horsemen in a cavalry charge, and I cartwheeled down under the white hooves, and then I'd return to my body and take another step and slip away when the snow fell again.

We reached the ridgeline and relative safety. The avalanches would come, but they'd fall left and right. Skim stamped out a little platform and sat on his pack with his head in his hands. Wind rasped along the ridge, scraping off snow and ice, blowing it in our faces. We'd put the glacier far below. Above, the mountain disappeared in clouds, which had fattened, looking about ready to split and drop their feathers all over the place. Between the layers out west, I caught sight of an immense grey surface speckled white. The sea. I'd forgotten it was there. It looked imaginary. We hadn't come that way. Might as well talk about beanstalks or Middle Earth.

The clouds closed, and the wind cut me open. Skim hadn't gotten back up since he sat down, and I was afraid the same thing would happen to me. I started digging into the hardpack under the surface of the ridge, using my ice axe to chop and my helmet to scoop, until Skim grabbed my shoulder and stopped me.

"What are you doing?" He had to shout to punch through the wind.

"Digging!" I said. He waved his hands at me to say, *no shit, I see the hole.* "Snow cave!" I yelled.

"What for?"

I blinked back at him for a moment, then realized he was serious. "The tent's in the pack on the glacier!" I yelled.

Skim froze hard. Another time and place, I'd have taken some satisfaction from that. It wasn't often the boy let surprise show. Under the circumstances, I might've enjoyed some brotherly bullshit better. I stuck my head back in the pit I'd dug, feeling like a strung-out badger going to ground.

It was a one-man job until I'd excavated enough space to get us both inside. As soon as he could, Skim joined me, and we chopped up snow with our hands and kicked it out with our feet, lying horizontally, side by side, two worms in a frozen apple.

"You ever dug a snow cave before?" Skim asked.

"I read about it in a book."

That was all Skim needed to hear, that I had only a rudimentary idea of what I was doing. Meaning he had freedom to work out the details himself. He took over. I was the blunt tool you used to break ground and test the shape of a plan. Skim was the craftsman who turned schemes into substance. By the time he was done, the hole I'd dug had become a tiny cabin with elevated bunks and a platform for the stove, all carved from the snow. We had room to sit up and lie down flat. He engineered an overlap at the entrance that kept blown snow out without suffocating us. It would have been halfway comfortable, a safe house from the blade of the wind and the avalanches. But I could only think of going to sleep.

I woke from deep blackness. Something had hold of me. Was yanking at me. I peeled an eye open. *Skim* had hold of me. "What?" I managed, about as articulate as a side of beef.

"We need to go," he said. "Or we're fucked. We're already fucked. We need to *go*."

I got my second eye open. A checklist flashed inside my skull: Avalanche. Blizzard. Valkyrie. I listened a moment, heard nothing, concluded that none of those pertained.

"What?" I said again.

Skim was sitting on his snow bunk with his feet in his plastic doubles down in the narrow well between the two of us. He had some food between his feet. A few candy bars, a few packets of soup, an end of cheese, a handful of peanuts bagged in plastic.

"This is all of our food," Skim said.

Ah. Correction. He had *all* our food between his feet.

"I couldn't sleep," Skim said. "I haven't slept at all. All I could think about was eating. I'd eat toothpaste. I'd eat sand." He waved at our pathetic little pile. "I could eat this all in two minutes with the wrappers. Or I could wake you up."

I realized he'd been sitting there, with the food between his feet, for I didn't know how long. Outside the cave, light seemed to be seeping back through the Arctic twilight. I'd been asleep for maybe five hours. An avalanche snapped free, shaking the pack, breaking bones from the sound of it. We waited and watched each other's reactions to confirm the massiveness of the slide. The noise and tremors died off.

"That was early," I said.

"Yesterday, that would have been us," Skim said.

I nodded.

The roof of our snow cave collapsed.

The wind was on us before I'd even drawn breath. It got in my nose, eyes, and sleeping bag, carrying a load of ice with it. Hard pieces of the cave roof had slammed down all around me, and one side of my face was mashed numb, while the other side was frozen numb—two different sensations, as it turned out. I balled up inside my sleeping bag. I'd left my outer layers in the footwell of my bag overnight in order to keep them warm. I zippered them on, wriggling around inside my cocoon, thinking of Houdini in a straight jacket.

When I emerged, fully armored, the wind had already drifted six inches of loose snow into the now-open bowl of our cave. Skim was on his hands and knees, fishing around in the powder, howling about the food. I dug for my boot-shells, emptied them out, shoved my feet in with snow flying all around. I found my backpack and began trawling the floor, stuffing in anything I found—stove, Snickers, helmet, rope coil. Skim and I put our heads together and yelled out an inventory. Then we dove back in for the missing pieces.

The cold took me to the edge of paralysis. I signaled to Skim that I needed to get moving. He nodded, we threw on our packs, and we rolled ourselves out of the cave and onto the ridgeline, into the full blast of the wind.

When we were upright, I turned back to Skim and waggled my head once up the mountain and once back down. *Up still?* Skim cocked his head uphill and shrugged. *Yep, up. Don't ask why.* I suppose our gestures could have had a dozen interpretations. At the time, I knew what Skim was saying, strong as telepathy.

It took twenty minutes of shivering and step-kicking to drive the cold into remission—it never left, but it wasn't eating my bones. For fifteen hundred feet below us, the snow ridge knifed down toward the glacier. Up above, it disappeared into shelves of clouds. Snow

fell, and the wind whipped it around us. I caught glimpses of the surrounding mountains, arrows and piles of snow flashing up out of the
weather and then blinking out of existence.

We climbed through a hive-swarm of noise. Pistol shots whined
through the wind. Curtains of ice-flak rasped past. Avalanches followed each other like train cars. Skim and I were silent—we'd have
needed megaphones to reach each other, and it was getting hard
enough just to breathe.

My stomach gnawed and squirmed, coveting my blood, my flesh,
the fatty tissue behind my eyes. I felt hollow, shadowy. But my legs
moved my boots higher, and my ice axe spiked the snow. When I
pushed my nose down into my jacket to warm my face, I smelled the
ammoniac reek of my muscles breaking down, my body burning its
own walls for fuel.

The snow ridge pushed up through the clouds, up through the
wind. It seemed geometric. A continuum without beginning or end.
I saw snatches of the future—on the mountain, beyond the mountain—but the images flicked out of sight like the mountains in the
storm. I had trouble placing myself, linking past and present. How
had we come to be here? Time seemed broken off.

In a half-sheltered crotch in the snow, we stopped and ate a candy
bar, a pro forma exercise. It made no difference—we were taking a
piss in the sea.

Wind-chiseled gargoyles of ice forced us off onto the faces of the
ridge, and the faces cut away below my crampons. I looked straight
down onto clouds. Just looking, I could feel myself dropping, falling, though I wasn't. I wanted the rope, but I didn't want to stop

and wrangle it out of the pack while I was hung out over space. And climbing up would be no worse than climbing back.

The clouds thickened. Snow poured down. It sloughed off the ridge to either side, and there was no good reason to stop, so we kept climbing. The dimensions of our reality had been stripped bare. We moved in a monochromatic bubble, a few hundred square feet of whites and darks, carrying less than we needed on our backs. The only direction was up. The only time was now.

The snow slowed and stopped. The clouds unraveled then blew apart. Fairweather looked down on us through a well of blue sky a mile deep. The mountain! A splinter of star, a whiff of infinite space still smoking off its razor sides. Any shield I might once have had to protect myself from Fairweather's direct stare, I'd lost somewhere on the way. I was pierced. You couldn't have yanked the mountain out of my chest without killing me.

Clouds rolled back in, and the storm-eye closed. My axe pricked the skin of the snow. The ridgeline plunged below my heels. I'd been standing still, in a pair of kicked steps, for how long? Skim was beside me. The wind had dropped in the calm. I felt it breathing back to life.

"That was it," Skim said. "The moment the mountain speaks. Tongues in trees and sermons in stone."

"What did it say to you?" I asked.

"What else? Don't run."

"Yeah? Did it offer you *I am the light and the life* or anything?"

"The opposite, actually. Seemed possessive about eternity. Unlikely to share."

A belch of wind nearly toppled me out of my steps. "We better go," I said.

"We better."

We ascended through storm and snow for hours more, until the sun seemed to be low over the mountain's shoulder—not that we'd really seen the sun since it tried to explode the icefall on our heads down on the glacier. We stopped at a dip in the ridgeline where we could stand in the snow flat-footed. Skim promised he had worked out the kinks in his design, chose a wall of snow like pressed Styrofoam, and began to dig. Three hours later, in twilight, we finished chopping out the last corners of a new cave.

I had the stove going for water. I unrolled my sleeping pad and bag. There wasn't much else to do. We went through our simple tasks of preparation. By silent agreement, we stacked our food into a little shrine between us. Five candy bars, three packets of soup, and the peanuts.

"Tomorrow, the top," I said, and I dumped the soup and the peanuts into the pot. "I'd rather be hungry tomorrow night than tomorrow." I didn't bother saying that we had one shot at the summit, and after that, no matter the outcome, we'd be eating snow.

"No panic, right?" Skim said, watching the soup dissolve with a look like a heron stalking a frog. "It's only food. We'll have to get through tomorrow in order to face the day after, anyway."

I ate slowly, ritualistically, fighting the emptiness at the bottom of my bowl. It was the last dinner we'd see for—well, I had no idea. And my teenage metabolism found that prospect scary as death. So even though the soup was more water than gruel, we gave it its due respect and licked our bowls shiny. Then there really was nothing to do, other than shush our half-roused, mostly-empty bellies and go to sleep.

Deep blackness wouldn't come for me. My head filled with sea waves, long silver rollers. I tried to suck water, to bury myself below the waves, but kept bobbing up to the surface.

The sun made its brief swing over the pole. We hauled ourselves upright about the time it came flying back toward Alaska, though we had ice, mountain, and clouds between us, so our cave was a little tank of night. We took two candy bars each for ourselves and left one in the cave. Skim put the last wizened Snickers inside my sleeping bag and then rolled up my sleeping bag inside of his, muttering: "Little fucker might grow legs. It's a million to one, but better to be safe."

Outside, we could see, but the line between snow and cloud was muddy as the line between night and day. Thick, gristly vapors wrapped the mountain like fat on meat. We had to all but scrape them aside to find the snow. Hunger and sleep clouded up my internal sky. My eyes connected world and brain like two long tubes, and they got longer and narrower the higher I climbed.

The connections between moments got real slack. I'd snap into the present and find myself leading sixty-degree ice, the rope running down below my boots, two screws already clipped, and me hacking away, clearing an inch of crust to get to the good ice below. And I had to assume everything was okay—knots tied, Skim belaying, some kind of anchor down there in the grey where the ropes disappeared.

We were roped together but not belaying. The ridge was broad and flat on top. The sides dropped into the abyss, but we couldn't see that. Wind poured over us. Exploded clouds and loose snow flew by. I hauled in two breaths, stepped forward, hauled in another two, stepped forward. At least I hoped that forward was the same direction the rope was running.

Skim belayed me from above. The ice was wind-scoured concrete. My tools bounced. My calves shook. My front points skated. At the belay, where snowflakes spiraled around us like moths, we began to crack.

"We won't find our way down through this," Skim said, swatting at the blizzard with his hands.

"I don't know if I can keep bouncing back," I said. "Muscle's all gone. I'm eating brain."

"What's the mountain worth?"

"Nothing," I said.

"Nothing," he repeated.

We nodded at each other. We'd made up our minds. Skim handed me the leftover ice screws from his lead. I racked them. And I began climbing—up—while Skim settled back into the belay.

How this happened is hard to explain. We'd decided to go down; I intended to go down. I expected to see—remember, I was watching through some long, skinny plumbing—my hands go to work setting up a rappel so we could retreat. When the opposite happened, my mind in its skull castle threw a fit. I'd felt panic before, and I braced, expecting my hands to shake, my breath to come drowning-man fast. Instead, I reached my left arm up, flicked a clot of snow off the surface of the ice with the pick of my axe, reached back, and drilled the exact spot I wanted, easy as a dart in the bull's eye. Could be it was sheer dumb, unturnable momentum that moved me. Words only cut so deep, and we'd been plowing ahead toward Fairweather since approximately the dawn of man. That ship might not be the kind to reverse itself on a dime. In any case, my inner-I concluded it wasn't alone and didn't control the body near as tightly as it thought. There was another agency up there, in the flesh, or maybe something called up between Skim and me, a third person on the mountain that was neither one of us but no one else either. Meanwhile, Skim said nothing to contradict me as I scratched up the next pitch of ice, and I presumed he'd ceded his own internal ground just as I had.

The snow whirled around me. My crampons nicked the ice. My muscles jumped around inside my skin, reminding me of a dead frog in an electric current. I had time to think about dead frogs. My mind had taken a backseat.

We traded leads where the ridge narrowed. Skim climbed the back of a white dinosaur, around plates and horns of ice. I hunkered down in a notch, eyes closed, feeding out rope, listening to the wind.

A wall of green ice disappeared up into the weather. It couldn't have, but it glowed, turning the clouds that wreathed it a nuclear shade. The ice was stone, kryptonite. It slagged my forearms. The green light infected me. My fingers melted; my stomach-rat turned flips. The wind moaned and raged. Maybe it was me moaning and raging. It hardly mattered.

Above the green wall, the ridge tunneled through the wind and flying snow. We waded through new powder, a zombie pair, the alpine undead driven higher by a pressure as elemental as a hurricane. We stayed roped, ten feet apart, for no reason other than to feel bound together. I babbled wordlessly to myself, to the mountain, to the third climber tied between us. Skim dropped and puked because of the altitude and his starvation, then got up and said, "Good. I was feeling heavy. Now I'll float."

The earth spun below us. I don't remember it getting dark, but I couldn't swear to the day, and I wasn't sure sub-Arctic night at fifteen thousand feet would be much different from the twilight of the storm.

When the snow fell away on all sides of us, nothing overhead but weather, elation didn't take me. I don't think I had enough calories left in my tissues for that. We planted ourselves shoulder to shoulder, backs to the wind. Two moons, desire and circumstance, converged in their orbits, and all the contrary tides below ran smooth. Despite the naked, howling air and freezing cold, it was the most peaceful place. I could see beyond the mountain for the first time. The future knit itself to the past. A thin, sickly looking thing, my immediate future, but there it was.

ACKNOWLEDGMENTS

I FEEL VERY FORTUNATE to be associated with Counterpoint Press, particularly since they seem content to let me play around in my own little corner of the literary world. My thanks go to my agent, Felicia Eth, my editor at Counterpoint, Dan Smetanka, and the entire Counterpoint staff for their thoughtful approach to books and attention to detail. I am also lucky to be from a family of talented writers and sharp readers. My two frontline readers, my wife, Ashley Laird, and my mom, Stephanie Arnold, are insightful and hard to please, qualities I value beyond measure. Finally, my thanks go to two decades' worth of climbing partners—the good, the bad, and the ugly. I've been all three myself over the years.